Winter Wishes
in the
Scottish Highlands

BOOKS BY DONNA ASHCROFT

The Little Christmas Teashop of Second Chances
The Christmas Countdown
If Every Day Was Christmas

CHRISTMAS VILLAGE SERIES
Christmas in the Scottish Highlands
Snowflakes and Secrets in the Scottish Highlands
Christmas Secrets in the Scottish Highlands

Summer at the Castle Cafe
The Little Guesthouse of New Beginnings
The Little Village of New Starts
Summer in the Scottish Highlands
The Little Cornish House
Summer at the Cornish Beach Cafe

Donna Ashcroft

Winter Wishes
in the
Scottish Highlands

bookouture

Published by Bookouture in 2024

An imprint of Storyfire Ltd.
Carmelite House
50 Victoria Embankment
London EC4Y 0DZ

www.bookouture.com

ISBN: 978-1-83790-755-7
eBook ISBN: 978-1-83790-754-0

Alison Phillips
Thank you for all your amazing support – one day I promise to write about sea lions!

1

IVY

Ivy Heart admired the snow-covered Scottish mountains that framed Hawthorn Castle as she drew close to the end of her short walk to work. She glanced up at the stunning old building with its pointy turrets and white stone facade, before taking in the heavy oak portcullis draped with lush green holly that the gardeners had hung the day before.

Ivy pushed the door open and stepped inside the striking hallway. She stopped again to appreciate the high ceilings and sumptuous fir trees that lined the walls, which had been decorated in an abundance of tasteful baubles that matched the red, blue and gold of the Ballentine coat of arms. Then she heard her boss – Miriam Ballentine – shriek something from the office and Ivy tried to remain calm.

Just a normal day at work, Ivy soothed herself, breathing in the heady menthol fragrance from the Christmas trees. Then she lifted her chin and made her way along the hallway, rhythmically tapping on the tiles in her shiny red boots.

The small room that Ivy used as her workspace was situated outside of Miriam's office. It was empty when Ivy entered and she pulled off her new green coat and hung it on a hook, before placing her bag on the ground. Then she flinched as Miriam's door suddenly swung open and Simon Ballentine – Miriam's grandson – immediately charged out.

'If you leave now, you'll never be Laird of Hawthorn Castle!' Miriam shouted after him with fury in her voice.

'I don't care. You'll have to get yourself a new puppet. I can't do this on my own – I was never the only person for this job. I'm leaving today and I'm not coming back!' Simon roared as, looking more than a touch unhappy, he practically sprinted past Ivy.

She started to turn to go after him. 'Ivy, I need you!' Miriam yelled through the open doorway and Ivy almost slid on the oak floorboards in her haste to obey. She'd been covering Miriam's PA's maternity leave for five months now and knew her boss would be annoyed if she had to wait.

Stay calm, she's Mum's oldest friend from university – and you have to impress her. Remember Mum's mantra, 'the best views come after the hardest climb', Ivy reminded herself as she took a moment to smell the blooming African Violet on her desk, feeling the knot in her stomach ease.

Ivy grabbed a notepad and pen and scrambled into Miriam's office at speed. The room was impressive. Three walls were lined with floor-to-ceiling bookshelves, each crammed with antique, leather-bound journals and novels Ivy suspected hadn't been so much as dusted in years. The floor was covered in a sumptuous red woollen rug and Ivy made her way across it towards the imposing six-foot desk her boss was currently hunched behind.

'Sit!' Miriam ordered abruptly in her rough Scottish lilt, nodding at the low wooden chair Ivy knew had been earmarked for uninvited guests, her grandson and staff. No doubt in an attempt to intimidate them.

Ivy carefully sank onto the seat, trying to look professional as her knees rose until they were angled a few inches above her thighs. She fidgeted, trying to get comfortable, and poised the pen over the pad ready to take notes.

'Is everything okay with Simon?' she asked quietly. 'Do you want me to see if he's okay?'

Miriam took a moment to study Ivy, her blue eyes critical. She wore her usual immaculate outfit which included a grey woollen suit, crisp white shirt and pearls.

'My grandson has made an appalling decision and you can't help with that,' she snapped. 'However, I have a plan to put things right and I need you to do something important for me.' She pursed her lips.

'What do you need?' Ivy straightened her shoulders and determinedly met Miriam's eyes.

'I need you to track down my youngest grandson and bring him back to Hawthorn Castle. If Simon's really determined to' – Miriam twisted a hand in the air as she searched for the correct word – '*abandon* his position here, then I need a new heir to take on his responsibilities. Unless of course Simon changes his mind.' She sniffed, her cool eyes calculating. 'In the meantime, it's essential I find an alternative,' she said carefully.

'I thought Simon was an only child!' Ivy blurted, immediately regretting the remark when her boss's expression clouded. She knew the older woman wasn't keen on sharing confidences so usually kept her questions to herself.

'I have two grandsons, but Ross and I have been... estranged for years,' Miriam said, looking annoyed.

Ivy wanted to ask why they were estranged but wasn't sure how the older woman would react. 'Will he come back if I ask?' she said instead.

Miriam reached up and began to fiddle with the string of pearls around her neck. 'Ross understands duty,' she murmured, although Ivy detected a hint of something odd in her tone. 'He's... not been around for a while, but he was raised to appreciate that he might be required to step up one day. Despite everything, I've no doubt he will if the correct pressure is applied.' Her eyes bored into Ivy as she waited for her to agree. The corners of Miriam's mouth lifted when Ivy nodded.

'How will I find him?' Ivy asked, feeling unsure. When she'd taken on the role of Miriam's PA, she hadn't been expecting assignments like these.

'My grandson is in one of those pictures over there. Take it so you'll be able to recognise him.' Miriam waved a hand at the numerous frames on the long sideboard situated under the window. 'Not that one,' she snapped as Ivy searched through the photos – most of which featured Simon, his deceased parents, their extended family, or Miriam – before she finally settled on a simple wooden frame at the back. It was of a tall man with a beard standing beside a large, blooming flowerbed in front of the servants' entrance to Hawthorn Castle. He was holding a spade and there was mud on one of his cheeks. 'That's him. It's a few years old so he might not look exactly the same now,' Miriam said, waiting while Ivy studied the man's face.

He looked a little like Simon, although his features were more rugged than refined and the dark whiskers on his cheeks and chin made him look sexy and a little wild. His jaw was square and he had a full mouth and brown eyes that in a wistful moment Ivy might describe as sad. His brown hair was ruffled, and Ivy guessed it was because he'd just been working outside. The khaki cargo trousers and black T-shirt hugged his frame, giving enough away for Ivy to suspect the body underneath was muscular. An unwelcome frisson of attraction shot through her and she placed a palm over the photo, then rested the frame face down on her knees as she sat.

'What happened to him?' Ivy asked hoarsely.

'Nothing,' Miriam snapped, before letting out a long breath.

'I suppose you might need some background though.' She looked bored. 'When my son and his wife died in a sailing accident almost sixteen years ago Simon became first in line to inherit Hawthorn Castle, the land and Laird title when he turns thirty – which is just a month from now. I've been preparing him to take on the responsibility since he was fourteen.' Miriam's voice was emotionless.

'And Ross?' Ivy asked, intrigued.

'Ross is two years younger than his brother so had the option to live a more ordinary life.' Miriam's voice was clipped. 'Since Simon is...' She hesitated. 'Intent on abandoning his position, I'm afraid Ross no longer has that luxury. It's imperative that he return and pick up the reins.' Her icy blue eyes were serious.

'Okay,' Ivy agreed, wondering how easy it would be to convince Ross of that.

'There's a lot to learn, so I require him back at the castle by Christmas Eve at the latest – we have plenty of time.' Miriam raised her chin, her expression determined.

Ivy knew from experience there was no point in arguing with her boss when she was in this mood: everyone was expected to fall into line.

'Since it's the second of December tomorrow, that gives him a full twenty-two days to organise himself. I intend for him to attend the party you've been organising. It's very important everyone hears about Simon leaving and that I've got a replacement lined up.' She looked towards the door and her eyes glittered.

Ivy nodded. The plans for the Christmas Eve soiree at the castle were already in place, and for a few months the gathering had consumed every second of her working day.

'It'll be the perfect opportunity for me to reintroduce my youngest grandson back into society and to announce that he'll be the new successor to the family title and wealth.' For the first time since Ivy had sat down, Miriam looked satisfied.

'Do you have a number for Ross so I can warn him I'm coming?' Ivy asked, repositioning the pen as she balanced the pad on top of the picture frame.

'Ross doesn't believe in phones,' Miriam barked. 'He doesn't believe in letters or emails either because he's not responded to any of the communications my last three assistants have sent.' She jerked her chin, looking irritated. 'Until today I was quite happy to leave him to live his own life.'

'Right.' Ivy nodded. The whole family had obviously had a serious falling out. But why – and could she help to fix it? Hopefully she'd find that out from the man himself. She turned the picture over again and studied Ross's handsome face. 'So how do I contact him?'

'You're going to have to speak to him face-to-face,' the older woman explained. 'That way you can inform him what's happened with Simon and tell him exactly what I need him to do.'

'Okay...' Ivy murmured, feeling a niggle in the pit of her stomach. Ross obviously hadn't been to Hawthorn Castle in years and had ignored any opportunity to reconnect, totally cutting himself off from his family. Not that his family seemed to have made much effort with him. This was the first time she'd ever heard of the younger grandson in the five months she'd worked here. Would Ross be as willing to return as his grandmother suspected? Then again, did he really have a choice? 'That sounds simple enough...' Ivy said slowly, ignoring the niggle, which had quickly started to nag.

'That's exactly what I wanted to hear,' Miriam replied, smiling.

'Where is Ross now?' Ivy asked, still staring at the photo, feeling strangely drawn to his desolate face.

'I believe he's employed by Christmas Resort as some kind of groundsman and adventure guide,' Miriam said, her tone offhand. 'The place is situated about a mile outside of Christmas Village. You'll find the exact location on Google Maps. It's less than a thirty-minute drive from here.' Miriam tapped a pen on her desk. 'It won't take long to get there; I suggest you depart tomorrow.'

Ivy nodded thoughtfully. 'If I leave first thing I could be back by late afternoon.'

Miriam began to fiddle with her pearls again. 'It's possible Ross might need to be convinced.' She cleared her throat. 'My youngest grandson can be... stubborn.' She shrugged her bony shoulders. 'I'm sure once you meet him, you'll be able to work out exactly what he needs to hear. But you should probably pack a bag just in case he needs time to come to the correct decision. Once he does, I look forward to seeing you here with good news. And Ivy...' Miriam smiled her tiger's smile. 'If you succeed in this task, I'll ensure you get a place on the Trainee Financial Trader Programme your mother is so keen for you to join when your contract finishes at the end of the month. You know it's almost impossible to get onto without the right contacts.'

Ivy stilled as her pulse fluttered. This was what she'd been waiting for. A place on a coveted training and induction course at one of London's top investment houses which would provide a springboard to a highly lucrative career. A glowing endorsement from Miriam Ballentine into the right person's ear would spell the start of her new vocation. It was way past time her mother stopped fretting about her future, and Ivy knew she had a responsibility to finally fulfil her potential.

'Goodbye, Ivy.' Miriam clicked her fingers, nodded at the door and turned her attention back to her laptop.

Ivy slowly rose from chair, clutching the photo frame, wondering what exactly had made Ross Ballentine leave the castle and his family – and whether it would really be as easy as Miriam hoped to persuade him to return.

Ivy knew she had to do everything in her power to convince him that he should. Her future – and her mother's – depended on her success.

2

IVY

Ivy pulled her car to a stop and squinted at the trail of red tail lights ahead of her. The journey had taken over two hours so far, due to various weather-related delays, and it was clear her electric Mini had found the journey taxing because the battery was almost flat. But if the satnav was correct, she'd be at her destination soon.

'Finally!' She let out a long sigh of relief as she spotted the pretty red and green sign directing her to Christmas Resort.

She followed the arrow and took the next right, joining a long wide driveway lined with trees decorated with various baubles, pom-poms and multicoloured fairy lights. The main track had been cleared of snow and Ivy spotted more lights in the far distance scattered across the roof of a large wooden building where she hoped she'd find the resort's reception area and then Ross. She momentarily paused the car halfway up the driveway so she could admire the scatter of quaint wooden cabins positioned between the trees. Then, on impulse, she wound down the window of her Mini and took in a deep breath, immediately picking up the earthy fragrance of the blue spruces and smiling before she realised what she was doing.

She frowned, grumbling at herself as she pressed a foot to the accelerator and shot forwards. *Stop wasting time and focus on why you're here. Find Ross Ballentine and your new career awaits.*

As soon as Ivy parked in front of the building, the front door swung open and 'We Wish You a Merry Christmas' began to play loudly outside. Then a curvaceous woman dressed in a red velvet Santa suit skipped across the festive decking and down the steps.

'Greetings,' the woman boomed as Ivy opened the driver's door. 'I'm Bonnibell Baker. My husband Connell and I are part-owners of Christmas Resort. I think we spoke on the phone yesterday evening. Are you Ivy Heart?'

'Yes, I'm so sorry I'm late. The traffic was a lot heavier than I expected,' Ivy explained as she got out, almost slipping on the icy pathway in her shiny red boots. They were a mistake, but when she'd dressed this morning, she'd been thinking more about impressing Ross Ballentine than practical footwear. Besides, since working for Miriam, she'd been fancying up her wardrobe, swopping old favourites for more glamorous clothes in the hope it might persuade her boss that she'd be perfect for the Trainee Financial Trader Programme. But as she was hit by a sudden gust of cold air, goosebumps erupted across her skin and Ivy pulled her new silky green coat tighter around her chest.

'Why don't you come inside, hen?' Bonnibell suggested, linking her arm through Ivy's and leading her up the wide wooden steps onto decking that had been decorated with every imaginable size and shape of Christmas decoration. 'We haven't got any guests staying at the moment, but I've made some hot chocolate and a fresh batch of mince pies, so you can rest and refresh in the kitchen after your drive.'

'Is Ross here already?' Ivy asked hopefully.

Bonnibell's forehead pinched and for the first time since

they'd met her smile dimmed. 'He was supposed to join us half an hour ago. We told him exactly when you were due. I'm afraid he didn't turn up so Connell's gone to see if he can find him. Don't fret, I'm sure they won't be long.' She smiled reassuringly as she guided Ivy into a large hallway swathed in fresh garlands of holly and mistletoe interspersed with multicoloured lights that twinkled through the greenery.

'This is beautiful, you've really brought the outdoors inside,' Ivy murmured, taking in a deep restorative breath as she took in the scene. 'You've done an amazing job of keeping those berries looking so plump, that couldn't have been easy.' She moved closer to the display and stroked an absent hand over the fruit and leaves, revelling in the different textures.

'Ach, that's Connell again. He rotates it and waters everything regularly to keep it fresh,' Bonnibell explained, beaming. 'How lovely of you to notice, lass.'

Ivy shrugged, annoyed that she'd let herself get off track. 'I read that you offer the full Christmas experience from January to December here, is that correct?'

'Aye. Book a break and you can have your Christmas anytime of the year.'

Ivy smiled. 'Sounds wonderful.'

'That's the idea! Our guests stay in festive cabins with all the greenery and sparkles that we can find.' At Ivy's nod she continued. 'During their break they can help to dress the tree, build snowmen, dance, sing carols, take sleigh rides and bake mince pies.' Her pink cheeks glowed. 'Our visitors can do all the traditional things together that they might not normally have the opportunity to do because the festive period is always so busy.'

Ivy felt a pang in her chest as she tried to recall the last time that she'd had a family Christmas or done any of the things Bonnibell had just mentioned, but couldn't. Hopefully next year she'd be enjoying the fruits of her new career, perhaps if she was lucky, she'd be working too?

Bonnibell swept an arm towards two huge Christmas trees that stood on either side of a staircase situated at the far end of the space before grabbing Ivy's elbow again and sweeping them both straight past. 'The kitchen is just through here,' she explained, leading Ivy into a big room which probably took up most of the back of the lodge.

It had high ceilings which had been decorated with sumptuous garlands of poinsettia leaves, shimmering lights and tinsel. Ivy had to control her awe. There was barely a surface that wasn't twinkling or sparkling, and it was obvious no expense had been spared. The kitchen cabinets that lined the walls were a charming forest-green colour and there was a large stainless-steel counter in the centre of the room, which Ivy guessed would provide plenty of space for food preparation. Novelty cutting boards in the shape of snowmen and matching place mats had been strewn across every available flat surface, adding splashes of colour and yet more festive fun.

Bonnibell grabbed a couple of Santa-shaped mugs from one of the green cupboards and poured them both hot chocolate, layering the drinks with marshmallows and sprinkles. Then she indicated to Ivy that she should sit on one of the wooden barstools closest to the counter. She gave Ivy her drink before offering her a plate piled high with mince pies.

'Do you think your husband will track Mr Ballentine down soon?' Ivy asked, picking up a mince pie and biting into it – humming because it was so delicious.

'I couldn't say, hen. Ross has a habit of disappearing,' Bonnibell confided as she sipped from her steaming mug. 'He loves the outdoors and often loses track of time. He doesn't carry a mobile phone so it's not always easy to contact him.'

Ivy recalled what Miriam had said about her grandson. 'Isn't that a problem?' she asked.

Bonnibell shook her head. 'He has a walkie-talkie in his cabin for emergencies. Connell spoke to him after our call yesterday evening and he said he'd come to the lodge to meet you today. When he didn't show up my husband decided to go looking for him. I'm sure he's just lost track of time.' The crease in the older woman's forehead suggested she wasn't so sure.

'Couldn't I visit him in his cabin?' Ivy asked, glancing out the window. Snow was falling again, and she didn't fancy her chances of getting back to Hawthorn Castle tonight if she didn't speak to the man soon. She needed time to explain what had happened with Simon and to thrash out arrangements for him coming back. It was bound to take a couple of hours.

'Ach, lass, his house is out in the wilderness and the chances are he won't be there. The lad goes on walkabouts with his pets more often than not and he's really fond of camping too, even in temperatures like these. He regularly runs trips for our guests in this weather.' She shuddered. 'He can be elusive when he wants to be, which is most of the time.' She screwed up her nose.

Ivy nodded. Perhaps Ross's reluctance to stay in touch with his family was more about his desire to keep himself to himself than anything else. 'In that case, I should probably find a place to charge my car, and if your husband doesn't find Mr Ballentine soon, I might need to organise some overnight accommodation.' Her mouth twisted. 'I should have booked something before I came.' Miriam had hinted that she might need to and Ivy should have listened. Ivy's stomach tightened. 'Are there any hotels in Christmas Village you can recommend?'

Bonnibell pulled a face. 'No lass. A hotel's being built just outside of the village centre, but it won't be ready for some time. We're the closest lodgings for at least forty miles.'

'Can I stay here then?' Ivy asked, suddenly worried. 'I know you're closed but you said you didn't have any guests at the moment – do you have an available cabin or room?'

'The resort is empty at the moment because this is what we

call our fallow period,' Bonnibell explained. 'We usually shut for half a week of every month. It gives us time to restock, repair and sometimes the staff have a day off. None of the cabins are meant to be occupied yet, unless you count the staff or people here on resort business.' She frowned.

'I see,' Ivy said. 'I don't want to bother anyone. I suppose I could sleep in my car...'

The comment was meant for herself, but Bonnibell's eyes widened.

'You can't.' She glanced out the window again, looking horrified. 'It's far too cold, you might get hypothermia.' The older woman shut her eyes and her mouth moved as if she were calculating a tricky sum. 'I could offer you Snowman Chalet. It's one of our new buildings and we've got no one coming to stay there for a week. It's yours if you don't mind staying out alone in the woods?'

'Not at all,' Ivy said, swallowing. 'If that's definitely okay, I'd love to stay there. It should only be for one night.'

Bonnibell smiled. 'In that case it's yours, hen. In the meantime, Connell will take your car to our charging unit so it'll be ready for when you leave.' She nodded, looking more relaxed. 'It'll be better if you stay at the resort. It'll give us more time to locate Ross and you'll be warm and safe until we do.' Bonnibell opened a drawer and gathered up a handful of leaflets. 'If you want something to occupy you until we find him, there are plenty of ideas in these.'

'Thank you,' Ivy said, taking them and nodding enthusiastically. 'That's so good of you – I won't be any trouble.' She knew she couldn't go back to the castle until she'd spoken to Ross. She could only imagine Miriam's reaction if she arrived without securing his imminent return, and she had to impress the older woman. Her whole future was hanging in the balance.

'That's grand.' Bonnibell's eyes sparked. 'We're hosting a

staff meal this evening in the main dining room. You're welcome to join us if you like.'

Ivy knotted her hands in her lap. 'Will Ross be there?' she asked hopefully.

Bonnibell pulled a sad face. 'As I said, the lad's not keen on socialising. Connell was going to invite him, but I doubt he'll come. You're far more likely to find Ross camping or tracking in the wilderness than you are at a get-together indoors.'

'Then I'll pass on the meal, but thank you for offering,' Ivy said, earning herself an indulgent smile. 'I've got snacks in my car; they'll keep me going tonight.'

'Ach, our housekeeper will deliver a hot meal to your cabin later. Guests never go hungry at the resort, it's a matter of principle. If you give me a moment, I'll arrange for someone to help with your luggage and show you where you'll be staying.'

'Thank you, although I don't have much stuff with me,' Ivy said, thinking of the small bag she'd packed this morning. She always took spare clothes when she went out in the Mini in the cold just in case the battery didn't last, but hadn't expected to stay over, so had only brought a few essentials. 'What will happen when your husband finds Ross?' she asked.

Bonnibell shrugged. 'You'll be the first person I call. In the meantime, try to relax and enjoy your visit. I'm sure whatever you need to speak to him about can wait until tomorrow.' She glanced out of the window at the falling snow. 'Hopefully the weather will have improved by then too.'

Ivy nodded as Bonnibell rose and began to fuss around the Aga. She took in the festive surroundings, wondering how long it might take Connell to track down Ross – and how easy it would be to convince him to speak to Miriam once he had.

3

ROSS

'Ach, dammit to hell,' Ross Ballentine cursed as his boss's red tractor appeared over the sharp incline at the top of the hill, close to where Christmas Resort's outdoor maze was located. He stood transfixed and watched the tractor glide downwards, making a beeline for him. For a nanosecond Ross considered climbing onto his snowmobile and making a run for it, but he guessed Connell Baker would just follow and track him down.

'Moose, Snowball, stay close!' Ross ordered, twisting to watch his boisterous golden retriever chase rings around the frisky wild boar the dog had adopted when it had been abandoned by its mother years before. He shook his head and patted his thick gloves on his coat, dislodging the snowflakes that had settled onto his chest while he'd been checking the water quality of the small lochan he was standing beside.

As both grounds manager and outdoor adventure specialist, his role at the resort was busy, varied, and meant he spent most of his time outside. Ross hadn't meant to stay in this spot for so long, though. After Connell had called him on the walkie-talkie last night to inform him that someone who worked for his grandmother had made an appointment to see him at the lodge, he'd resolved to avoid meeting them at all costs. It might be rude, but he'd assumed if he went AWOL for a couple of hours, Miriam's personal assistant would soon lose interest and go home.

He had no intention of speaking to anyone from Hawthorn Castle. He'd left the estate and parted ways with his family over five years ago. It had been swift and clinical, and while he'd dreaded losing touch, he'd found it easier and less painful the longer they were apart. He knew neither Miriam nor Simon wanted to see him again, they'd made it obvious how they felt when he'd lived at home. He was used to these infrequent attempts at contact – which he suspected were more a result of etiquette than any genuine desire to reconnect. Why would they want him in their lives after all this time? So he'd do them all a favour and steer clear.

It took almost five minutes for Connell's tractor to reach Ross. The vehicle offered good traction in the snow, but was painfully slow. His boss usually only got it out from the barn to pull guests in the resort's sleigh, but occasionally if the weather was particularly rough, he used it to visit Ross on the outer edges of the resort's land.

'I didn't expect to see you out in this,' Ross shouted into the wind as Connell parked and slowly dismounted.

The man was in his mid-fifties, with a white beard and round stomach that guaranteed he always played Santa to the visiting kids. Connell was always happy and quick to laugh, but the bulbous red cheeks and sparkling blue eyes hid a sharp and canny business mind.

'Bonnibell asked me to find you,' the older man said as he approached, just as a white husky scampered out of nowhere and immediately joined Moose and Snowball in their running game. 'Ach, Claus, please make sure you don't fall into the lochan. If you do Bonnibell will push me in too,' Connell joked, shaking his head and chuckling when the animals stopped to greet each other before charging off again. 'Did you forget our chat last night, lad? You were supposed to be at the lodge to meet your visitor almost an hour ago.' He raised an eyebrow at Ross.

'I lost track of time,' Ross said, feeling uncomfortable. 'Besides, I didn't actually say I'd be there.' He flushed, aware the excuse was below him.

'It was implied,' Connell said gruffly. 'And Bonnibell baked extra mince pies for you to take back to your cabin after the meeting.'

'Dammit.' Ross's shoulders sagged. 'I'm sorry, I'll find a way of making it up to her.'

The older man patted his shoulder. 'She's organising a feast up at the lodge this evening to welcome a journalist who's come to write an article about what we offer at the resort. It's a good way of advertising to potential new guests and she's keen to interview everyone on staff over dinner tonight.'

'Aye,' Ross said reluctantly. Promoting the place was a part of his role, but that didn't mean he had to like the idea.

'Bonnibell asked me to persuade you to join the meal,' Connell said, his voice loaded with meaning.

Ross sucked air between his teeth then brushed snowflakes from his cheeks when a gust of wind blew into his face. 'I'm not—'

'Yep.' The older man nodded. 'Don't worry, lad, I already told her you probably wouldn't come.' His expression turned serious. 'But you can't avoid humanity forever. Someday there's going to be somebody you have to engage with. Humans aren't meant to be islands – someone far cleverer than me once said that.'

'It was John Donne,' Ross murmured, thinking about the book of sermons in his grandmother's office. He'd regularly sneaked into that room to borrow novels when Miriam wasn't in there. He thought wistfully of the multiple shelves of books, most of which his mother had collected over the years. Did anyone touch them now? His chest ached at the memory. 'I'm not sure I agree with him...'

'Colour me surprised.' Connell shook his head, looking disappointed. 'I also wanted to talk to you about taking on someone else.'

Ross pulled a face.

'Before you say no to that again, the adventures you run are popular and I think there could be a real opportunity to grow this side of the business. You've been working on your own for years now – and looking after the resort grounds is a two-person job.' He wagged a finger. 'It would free you up so you only had to focus on the adventures if that's your preference. You're spread too thin, Ross.' He scratched his chin. 'You need to give yourself time to enjoy life.'

Ross shuffled on his feet. 'I'll think about it...' He tugged his scarf up from his neck so it covered the bottom of his face, which was starting to freeze. The material also prevented him from agreeing to anything on impulse when he already knew he was going to turn it down. He didn't want to work with anyone else. There was nothing wrong with being an island – at least that way you couldn't get hurt.

'Think hard.' Connell stared, his grey eyes penetrating. 'You don't want to end up like your friend Grizzle McGregor,' he murmured.

'Aye.' Ross's shoulders hunched. This wasn't the first time he'd been compared to the hermit he'd befriended years before, despite there being no similarities between them.

Connell nodded. 'I'll head back to the lodge now. What shall I say to Bonnibell about your visitor when she asks?'

'That you couldn't find me,' Ross suggested hopefully. 'That I'll be hunkered down somewhere, unavailable, uncontactable – at least for now...'

Connell took in a deep breath of air before nodding. 'You'll owe me for that, lad.' He glanced up at the sky and his expression softened. 'Ach, I expect your visitor will be getting ready to leave soon anyway... Anyone with half a brain will be back at home, wrapped in a blanket beside a fire.' He rubbed his stomach. 'If they're lucky, they'll be eating mince pies.'

'Sounds like a good plan for all of us,' Ross muttered. 'Let's catch up later in the week. Moose, Snowball. Home!' he barked and watched his pets snap to attention before he patted Connell on the back in lieu of a goodbye and tramped towards the snowmobile.

'Ach, I almost forgot,' Connell said, following so Ross could hear him above the wind. 'There's a tree with a branch that's looking a wee bit wobbly out by the cabins to the north-west of the resort. It's just across from Snowman Chalet if you need a better idea of location. When you get a moment, please can you check it out?'

Ross nodded and then winced as he glanced at the sky. If the forecast was correct, there was going to be a storm blowing in tonight. It might be safer if he looked it over before heading home. At least if he did it today, when the resort was effectively closed, he'd be unlikely to run into any stray guests.

'Sure,' he said, watching Connell start the tractor and slowly make his way up the hill. The white husky shook himself before breaking into a sprint and overtaking. Ross nodded at his pets. 'We just need to make a quick detour, boys,' he instructed, before climbing onto his snowmobile and starting it up. Hopefully the branch would only take a few minutes to deal with, then he'd head back to his cabin and stay out of the way of Bonnibell and his grandmother's mystery employee.

4

IVY

Ivy stood at the threshold of Snowman Chalet and placed Bonnibell's leaflets and the bag she'd brought with her from Hawthorn Castle onto the bed, before unpacking her two favourite cacti plants. 'Okay, Prickles and Needles, I'm going to put you right here,' she said, unwrapping the cacti carefully from the bubble wrap she'd used to transport them and placing them on the windowsill which offered stunning views of the woods. She rearranged the succulents until she was happy and then spun around so she could take in the accommodation.

The cabin was beautiful, with a large open fire, king-size bed and an en-suite bathroom that had a shiny walk-in shower and large bath. Christmas decorations were peppered across the ceiling, wardrobe and walls, and the iron mantlepiece above the fireplace glittered and shone. A Christmas tree sparkled in the corner of the room, and someone had hung a fresh sprig of mistletoe above the main door. The whole space smelled of cinnamon, oranges and fir trees and Ivy took in a deep breath and shut her eyes.

'Isn't this wonderful?' she murmured to the plants. She knew if anyone saw her talking to them, they'd think she was weird – but since her father had given them to her on her twelfth birthday, Ivy had insisted on taking them everywhere she went. They reminded her of him and were a guilty secret she couldn't bring herself to give up. 'Enjoy the view while I get my bearings,' she said as she continued unpacking.

Her mobile suddenly began to ring and she shuffled to the bottom of the bag and picked it up just before it rang off.

'Ivy,' her mother said, sounding weary.

'Is everything okay?' Ivy immediately jumped in. Her legs jellified and she slumped onto the king-size bed, sinking into the soft mattress.

'There's nothing wrong,' Faith Heart said, her voice kind. 'You ask me that every time we speak. I just wanted to have a quick catch up before I headed to the operating theatre.' Ivy's mother was a revered heart surgeon and called infrequently because she was usually too busy working or lecturing to talk. 'It's time you got over what happened, darling,' she advised.

Ivy scraped a hand through her hair, trying to calm herself. 'You nearly died, Mum,' she said sharply. It would take her years to get over it, especially since it had all been Ivy's fault. The sudden call from the hospital about the heart attack had been terrifying and was the second-worst moment of Ivy's life. Only upstaged by the day her father had died.

'Heart attacks are more common than you'd think,' her mother soothed.

'I know,' Ivy mouthed. It had been what had killed her dad.

'And people recover from them and lead long lives afterwards. I should know, I operate on enough of them,' her mother joked.

'Not everyone survives though,' Ivy said softly.

She was met with a heavy silence.

Faith let out a long breath. 'I know that too, darling. But *my* episode was a one-off. I'm being checked regularly by my colleagues, so if there were any concerns, I'd know immediately and take corrective action.' She paused. 'You know the cause was too much stress.'

'Yes.' Ivy swallowed because she also knew she was the one responsible for causing it. She'd been fighting with her mother about her non-existent career just a couple of hours before. 'If they find anything, you'll take a break, won't you?' Ivy begged.

Her mother chuckled. 'Perhaps for a day or two,' she said.

But Ivy couldn't join in with her merriment. Her mum had recovered from the attack and subsequent operation quickly, then she'd insisted on going back to work within two fraught months. After almost six, she seemed to be doing well, but despite that, each time Ivy got an unexpected call she felt as if her world was about to come crashing down.

Something buzzed in the background and Faith tutted. 'Sorry, I've not got a lot of time to talk,' she apologised. 'I was just calling to find out how you are.'

It had been almost two weeks since they'd spoken. Ivy looked up and her attention strayed to Prickles and Needles, as if in search of an anchor, and she felt herself relax.

'Firstly, I'm so sorry darling but I'm going to have to work over Christmas again,' her mother said.

Since this was the tenth year in a row Faith had worked, Ivy guessed she'd probably volunteered.

'I hope you understand. So many of my colleagues have young families. Perhaps we can meet up in London in the new year?'

'Sounds good, Mum,' Ivy murmured. Her contract with Miriam stretched up to the end of December so she'd probably just spend the time in her small cottage in the castle grounds. It would give her a chance to prepare for her new role, assuming she got a place.

'The second thing I was calling about is to ask how everything is going with Miriam.' Her mother paused. 'I didn't want to ask her directly, but has she agreed to get you on the training programme? You know that's why I recommended you for the maternity cover?'

Ivy hummed her assent. Her desire to make up for what had happened after their argument was the only reason she'd taken the job and stuck it out.

'The contact is a relation of hers, so if she recommends you, a place is guaranteed.' Faith's voice raced with excitement. 'Last time we spoke she assured me you were doing really well.'

'I doubt that,' Ivy said under her breath. Until their conversation yesterday Miriam had seemed entirely underwhelmed. Even Ivy's work on the Christmas party hadn't passed muster most of the time. Instead, her boss had complained that Ivy was spending too much time choosing the right plant accessories for the event...

Then again, if things went well with Ross today, she could be on her way to a new life in London in just a few weeks. Ivy's attention shifted to the cacti on the windowsill and she let out a long sigh.

'I'm aware I keep nagging, but you know how important it is to me that you have a proper career to sustain you,' her mother said in her most serious tone.

'I know,' Ivy murmured.

'You never know what the future will bring... We've both lived through the worst, and you understand why good prospects are vital. You have to be able to support yourself, Ivy... I know I've said it a thousand times.'

'And that's why I'm working with Miriam.' Ivy bit her lip. 'I'm not going to let you down.' *Not again.*

'I don't want you to ever feel helpless – and I *never* want you to have to worry about losing your home.' Her mother sounded upset.

'I know,' Ivy said. 'And I have good news about the training programme.' She knew her mother would be happy to hear this. 'Miriam asked me to track down her youngest grandson yesterday. She promised if I found him and persuaded him to return to Hawthorn Castle that she'd get me onto the programme.' She tried to make sure she sounded enthusiastic, though her heart sank as she thought about the new job and moving to London. Then she shook her head. This wasn't about her.

'Really?' Faith asked.

'Really. I'm already in Christmas Resort where her grandson works and I'm expecting to meet him tomorrow.' Ivy was determined to speak to Ross, whatever it took. 'As soon as he's agreed to return to Hawthorn Castle, the job's as good as mine.'

'That's wonderful news!' Faith said, her voice booming. 'And it sounds like you're already halfway there.'

Ivy grimaced, trying to ignore the fact that she hadn't even met the elusive Ross. 'I'm going to get the job and make you proud,' she promised.

'Call me as soon as you have news,' her mother said, her voice racing. 'I can't wait to have you settled. You know how much I worry—'

Her mother stopped abruptly and Ivy felt sick.

'Oh, I know,' she said guiltily. 'I'll email as soon as I've spoken to Miriam's grandson.'

Hopefully once she had, she'd be on her way to a new career and her mother would finally be able to relax.

5

ROSS

It was quiet in the woods, and while multicoloured lights twinkled prettily on the roofs of the cabins, the buildings were unusually dark inside. Ross skidded the snowmobile to a stop and took a moment to study the trees, squinting through the snowflakes falling from the sky as they played Whac-A-Mole with his eyelids. A few metres ahead, he spotted the spruce he guessed Connell had been concerned about. One of the thick higher branches was swaying at an odd angle and Ross suspected if it got caught in a gust, it might go flying. If he could get up to it now, it would probably be safest to either strap, trim or chop it off.

'Moose, Snowball, stay close!' Ross ordered, climbing off the vehicle. He heard them scamper behind as he followed the narrow track towards the tree so he could get a better look. As he approached, he noticed there were lights glowing inside Snowman Chalet. Was Innes Gibson, the resort's housekeeper, getting it ready for guests? A robin landed directly in his path and immediately flew off as Moose sprinted forwards, barking excitedly, desperate to make friends.

'Careful, boy,' Ross said, leaning down to pat the dog's

glossy pelt as he whined and was quickly joined by Snowball who snuffled sympathetically at his face. As Ross stood, he noticed the door to Snowman Chalet swing open and a woman with long straight hair the colour of midnight peered out. Was someone staying in the cabin? Was it the journalist Connell had just told him about?

'Is anybody there?' She gripped the edge of the door as if intending to somehow use it as a weapon.

Usually Ross would have seen the appearance of a stranger as a sign that he needed to beat a hasty exit, but there was something in her voice – a wobble – that made him pause.

'I'm just checking on a tree, I work for the resort, nothing to worry about,' he shouted over the wind. 'Stay inside, I'll be out of your way soon.' He tracked closer to the spruce as Moose and Snowball scampered towards the cabin and this time he heard the slam of a door – and guessed the woman had taken his advice.

Obviously unimpressed that the visitor didn't want to play with them, the animals detoured and went charging into the woods. Ross continued walking until he was under the spruce – then he glanced up to get a better look. Could he climb onto some of the lower branches to get to the problem one? He was carrying tools in the snowmobile and had a small hacksaw and some ropes in there somewhere.

When he glanced back at his vehicle, he saw the door to the cabin was open again and this time the woman strode out. She was dressed in a silky green coat and red boots that were more suited to a night on the town than a snowstorm. When she started to slip on the decking, Ross heaved in an irritated breath – hopefully he wasn't going to spend the next hour strapping up a broken arm or leg.

'You should stay inside!' Ross yelled, letting out a regretful grunt when the woman righted herself and joined the narrow pathway at the bottom of the steps that would lead her to him. 'I'm only going to be here a minute,' he muttered, shaking his head and turning again when she didn't so much as hesitate. He noticed she was slender, relatively short and had a musical sway to her hips that made something between his ribs unexpectedly perk up. He shook his head and hooked a foot onto one of the lower branches so he could raise himself. He'd get a better look at the damage before deciding what to do next. If he was lucky and worked quickly, the visitor would grow bored and he'd make it back home before he lost the light.

'Sorry, I just— Do you work with Ross Ballentine?' the woman shouted a few moments later from somewhere below. Ross heaved himself further up until he was nose to nose with the damaged limb.

'Sometimes.' Ross grimaced, eager to change the subject. If the journalist wanted to quiz him about what he did at the resort, she could do it some other time. Preferably in better weather and when Connell was around. 'I do odd jobs for him,' he shouted without looking at her, hoping she'd get the hint.

'What are you doing?' she asked after a pause.

'There's a branch here with a break in it. If it gets caught by a gust it might fall. You should move away from the area; you'd be much safer indoors. I won't be long.'

Silence fell and Ross let out a relieved breath as he imagined he heard the pad of her footsteps and the sound of a cabin door being closed and locked.

'How are you going to cut it without any tools?' she suddenly called out.

Her voice was fainter, and Ross suspected she'd at least moved out of range. He momentarily shut his eyes and then started the careful climb back to the ground. When he arrived, she was still waiting – and it took him a full five seconds to breathe. The woman was beautiful; there wasn't another word he could think of to describe her – and since much of his childhood had been spent escaping into books in Hawthorn Castle's library, he usually had at least three words for everything.

But beautiful also seemed inadequate somehow. Her hair was glossy and straight. It sat just above her shoulders so even when she turned her head it barely moved, and it contrasted with her skin, which was ivory pale. Despite that, Ross had never seen so much colour in a face. Perhaps it was because of her eyes, which were vivid green and reminded him of the resort's lochan in mid-summer – of that moment when the sun shone straight through the water and all he could think about was stripping off and diving in...

The woman suddenly cleared her throat and wrapped her arms around her torso, and Ross realised he'd been staring at her.

'I've got tools to chop it – the branch I mean,' he babbled like some kind of eejit teen, before dragging his eyes away. 'I just need to go back to my snowmobile, but I can't do it if you're standing there,' he added vaguely. He considered encouraging her to go back into her cabin again. But that was pointless. She hadn't listened the last three times he'd asked.

'I'm Ivy Heart – I'm staying here for the night. Sorry, I hope you don't mind me asking, but do you look after all the trees?' she asked, sticking out her arm and shoving a hand under his nose. She wasn't wearing gloves and her fingers were almost puce.

Ross took them in his gloved hands and felt her squeeze. She looked into his eyes and he was suddenly glad he'd kept the scarf wrapped around his mouth because there was something unsettling and strangely affecting about her gaze.

'Um, yes, sometimes. Good to meet you,' Ross said stiffly, deliberately avoiding giving her his name, hoping she wouldn't think that was strange. 'Look, it's getting really cold, you should go back to your cabin and I really ought to be getting back to mine.' If he stayed any longer, he suspected he'd get pulled into a conversation about the resort. Maybe Ivy would ask if he was planning on going to the staff meal too? If Bonnibell found out they'd had a conversation, things could get awkward when he didn't turn up.

'What about the spruce?' she asked, looking up. 'I thought you said it might be dangerous?'

'It's not as bad as I thought,' Ross lied.

'Will it really be okay in this wind?' Her forehead squeezed as she looked around.

'It'll be fine.' Especially since he planned to return later to fix it when he knew Ivy would be eating at the lodge. It would be dark but he'd bring a head torch and it wouldn't take long.

Ross pulled off his glove, whistled between his fingers, and heard a familiar bark and the thunder of paws and rustling in the undergrowth as Moose and Snowball came running. He turned as Ivy's eyes widened as the dog and wild boar sprang into the open, hurtling towards them.

'What is that?' she squeaked, pointing a shaky finger at the brown bundle that was Snowball as he sprinted on his stubby legs, trying to keep up with his fluffy friend.

'That's Snowball. My wild boar – he won't hurt you, he's really very shy,' Ross promised as Moose thundered past them, skidding on the path. But as the boar was about to pass too, Ivy tried to hop out of the way. Whether she was trying to avoid Snowball or hoped to stop him, Ross didn't know.

'No!' she yelled as the full force of the speeding animal slammed her into Ross's outstretched arms.

He had enough of his wits about him to grab her and hold on as they both went flying backwards before slamming unceremoniously into a nearby bramble bush. Then Ross found himself lying face upwards trying to remain still as a curvy bottom pressed into his crotch – and spikes from the plant he'd landed on punctured his torso and bum.

'Ouch,' he hissed as Ivy squeaked and wriggled before trying to climb off.

'I'm so sorry. My hair,' she yelped as she tilted her body to the side, landing on her hands and knees. 'Ouch,' she echoed him, trying to push herself up with the bare hand now pressed into a bed of thorns. At the same moment, she gripped a bunch of her hair with the other and Ross realised she'd got badly tangled in a bramble branch. 'I can't get loose,' she complained, jerking the strands as Ross carefully squatted beside her to see if he could help.

He dragged off one of his gloves and placed it under her palm, protecting it from the brambles, which were obviously digging in. 'Stay still please,' he ordered gently, trying to help untangle the mass of hair as Ivy continued to crouch low, unable to move. 'It's really stuck in there,' he murmured, twisting the shrub and trying to get the hair loose. He eased closer to Ivy as he tried to see better. He could feel her breath on his cheek and smelled something floral through his scarf, felt the corresponding thump of his heartbeat as it shuddered and then sped up. 'Um, it's really stubborn and there's a lot of hair caught in here, I'm not sure if I'll get it free.'

He looked up and met Ivy's leafy-green eyes. The sudden searing need to ease himself an inch closer and rip the scarf away so he could kiss her made his whole body freeze. They stared at one another for a few seconds and Ross was sure Ivy knew what he was thinking. So why wasn't she pulling away? Instead, she seemed to tilt her chin, moving their heads a fraction closer. Blood surged through him and he swallowed before dragging his eyes from hers, trying to regain control.

'Um, I could cut the bramble off at the root,' he said roughly. 'But—'

'I'm going to have a *Rubus fruticosus* hair accessory,' Ivy joked. There was enough of a catch in her voice for Ross to wonder if the attraction he'd felt hadn't been one way. She'd moved closer, hadn't she? Had she wanted to kiss him too? She hesitated before taking in a long shuddery breath. 'Just cut the hair off, but please be quick, I'm freezing,' she said.

As Ross's brain finally released itself from the grip of his raging hormones, he realised she'd used the Latin name for brambles. He wanted to ask why, but this wasn't the time for conversation. Besides, did he really want to encourage her to talk more?

'No problem.' He sprang to his feet and sprinted to the snowmobile before digging around in his toolbox and running back. 'Hold still.' Ross bent beside Ivy again and cut the hair off at the spot where it had tangled. Then he helped her to her feet and watched as she frowned at the big knot of hair she'd left behind.

'Does it look awful?' she blinked, clasping at the left-over stump that remained of the sleek locks that framed her face.

'Not awful,' Ross lied. 'But are you okay?' he asked, spotting a bubble of blood as it dripped from her palm into the snow. 'You're hurt.' The wild thump in Ross's chest surprised him and he reached out to take her hand, examining the tears and scratches across the centre of her palm.

'Oh,' Ivy said, noticing the blood for the first time too. She stared at it and seemed to sway. 'Sorry, I'm not good with injuries. Especially my own,' she joked weakly.

'We need to get you back to the cabin. Moose, Snowball, follow,' Ross yelled. He took hold of her elbow and quickly turned and guided Ivy round, placing a hand around her waist so he could encourage her to move more quickly and also to ensure she didn't fall if she passed out.

The door to her cabin wasn't locked so he swung it open and signalled that she could step inside, and he then ordered his pets to wait for him on the decking. The room was sparkly, and a fire was burning in the grate. A Christmas tree, heavy with decorations, sat in the corner and the lights had all been switched on. The large bed at the far end of the room had been made up and there was a pile of leaflets on top of it alongside a bag that was mostly unpacked. Even from here, Ross could tell Ivy's packing had been negligible – it didn't look like she'd come prepared for snow or expected to venture outside for long. Ross quickly marched inside the en-suite and searched through the bathroom cabinet over the sink, hoping to find the first aid kit all the cabins at the resort contained. He silently cheered when he found it.

'I'm really fine...' Ivy insisted as he returned. 'It's just a scratch.' She wandered to the large mirror positioned above a dresser and her hand shot to her hair. 'Oh no. I look awful,' she gasped.

'It's really not that bad,' Ross lied again, coming to stand beside her.

'Don't you want to take your scarf off?' Ivy asked, looking confused as she stared at his reflection in the mirror.

Ross pressed a hand over the scarf, surprised he was still wearing it – it was still covering his face, but he was reluctant to remove it. Somehow baring his nose and mouth would just make this moment feel more intimate. 'I'm fine,' he said roughly. 'I'm still a little cold.' He held her eyes when they met in the mirror. 'You should sit so I can dress that wound.' He forced himself to drag away his gaze, registering the rough grate in his voice. He really needed to leave before he did something stupid like try to kiss her.

'I'm okay, honestly. Sure you can't give me a haircut instead?' Ivy joked, sinking onto the edge of the bed.

'I specialise in trimming plants and trees so I'm not sure you'd thank me if I tried,' Ross murmured as he began to clean and treat the wounds on her hands.

Ivy remained silent and Ross tried to ignore the heat fizzing through his limbs as he touched her skin. He didn't look up even as he tied off the bandage, but he could feel Ivy's breath on his face, knew she'd leaned closer as he'd tended to her.

He felt his whole body protest as he shot to his feet and stepped away from her. 'You can probably take that off tomorrow,' he advised.

'You've done that before,' Ivy said, catching his eye and giving him a half smile. Her cheeks were a little flushed and he was grateful she didn't look so pale anymore. 'Do you do all the first aid at the resort?'

'No, but we're all trained in it.' Ross shoved everything back into the medical box. He could feel Ivy watching him and he knew it was past time to leave. She was having an unexpected effect on him. Perhaps it was because of the feelings that thinking about Miriam and Simon again had stirred up?

'How long have you worked at the resort?' Ivy asked, rising from the bed and stepping closer to him.

'A while,' Ross said, backing away. He went to pop the medical box back into the bathroom before glancing at the front door. He could still feel something coursing inside him, desires he hadn't allowed himself to feel in years, feelings he hadn't known he was still capable of. 'I should go,' he said abruptly, nodding towards the door. 'If those cuts get worse—'

'I'll be sure to ask for you,' Ivy said, blushing. 'Only...' She cocked her head, her face registering surprise. 'You didn't tell me your name.'

'Oh, um...' Ross muttered something unintelligible under his breath as he strode to the door. He looked up momentarily and spotted a sprig of mistletoe hanging above him. Something in his chest thudded and he quickly swung open the door.

'Sorry, I didn't catch that,' Ivy shouted as Ross charged onto the decking and down the steps.

When Ross was halfway along the path that led to his snowmobile, he thought briefly about grabbing the hacksaw and sorting out the branch. But when he turned, Ivy was standing on the decking again still wearing her flimsy green coat – this time looking confused.

'Thank you,' she cried when she realised he was watching her. 'What's your name again?'

Ross patted a palm to his ear to indicate that he couldn't hear, then he waved and turned away, wishing for the first time in a long time that he was brave enough to go back.

6

IVY

Ivy stood on the decking, shivering, and watched the man climb onto his snowmobile and disappear into the woods. He'd been in such a hurry to leave – perhaps he was worried about making it home? As the large flakes of snow fluttered to the ground, she admired how they sparkled in the trees, pulling her flimsy coat tighter. It was getting frostier outside – and she needed to head back indoors.

She should have asked him what he knew about Ross Ballentine – they worked together. If her brain hadn't been so scattered by him, she might have actually thought of it while he was here. Ivy wished she'd seen his face – that the scarf hadn't obscured most of his features. Somehow, she knew he was handsome. Perhaps it was his whisky-coloured irises, which she'd found herself sinking into whenever he'd caught her watching him.

Groaning, Ivy went to stare at herself in the mirror again. She winced at the shorn off stump of hair, wondering if she'd imagined that moment in the woods when she'd thought he was about to kiss her. There'd been a look in his eyes, a tension across his shoulders, and she'd almost stopped breathing. Then she'd found herself leaning into him until he'd jerked away. She shook her head, irritated. She was supposed to be here to find Ross Ballentine, not lust over a random stranger in the woods.

Ivy slumped onto the edge of the bed, immediately upsetting the pile of Bonnibell's leaflets, which she'd dumped beside the pillow. Ivy watched them all slide to the floor and was about to collect them up when her mobile pinged, reminding her to check the motivational quote on the coaching app her mother had subscribed her to for her twenty-ninth birthday. A few months after the heart attack that had almost claimed her life.

As soon as she launched it, the welcome screen declared:

'Whatever you need could be under your nose.'

Want to bet? Ivy huffed, scrolling to the menu and selecting *Daily Goals*, then frowning as she considered what to add before starting to type.

1. Find Ross Ballentine.

2. Convince him to move back to Hawthorn Castle.

3. Get a haircut.

When Ivy bothered to use the app, she tried to include goals she knew she could achieve because it made her feel better about herself. She closed the app and put her mobile on the bed, then glanced around the room. It was pretty here – a stark contrast to the chilly, austere cottage where she'd been staying in the grounds of Hawthorn Castle.

Her mobile began to buzz and Ivy picked up, wondering if Miriam had somehow tuned into her thoughts when she saw it was her boss calling.

'Hello, Mrs Ballentine,' she said crisply.

'Ivy. Have you spoken to my grandson yet?' the woman instantly shot back, foregoing any pleasantries and launching straight to questions.

Ivy puffed out a breath as she considered her next words. 'Sorry, not yet. He didn't attend the meeting we organised,' she said carefully. 'I understand he often gets distracted when he's working at the resort. But I'm trying to organise another appointment for tomorrow.' She gulped.

Miriam remained silent for a few moments and Ivy's insides grew heavy as she wondered if she was about to be reprimanded.

'Well I didn't expect it to be easy. I told you he could be stubborn,' Miriam said eventually, her voice snippy. 'But don't forget it's essential that you get Ross on board. I want to announce to everyone that he's returning so they have plenty of time to spread the word. Have you booked yourself into the resort then, girl?'

Ivy glanced around the room and nodded. 'I've got a place for as long as I need it. Not that I think it'll take me more than a day to find him,' she added quickly as the weight in the bottom of her stomach grew heavier.

'Well, if you can't find my grandson and get him to move back here to become Laird, you're not going to make a very good trader. You've got to be hungry and enterprising to make a success of a career like that. I know you'll do your best because if you want that job you have to succeed,' Miriam warned. 'Send regular updates and don't forget to remind my grandson when you finally track him down that he's part of the Ballentine bloodline – a lineage we can trace back over six hundred years. Stepping up when asked is his duty. There are no choices or decisions involved here.'

'Of course, I'm sorry,' Ivy said. As Miriam hung up, Ivy let out a long sigh, wondering if she'd bitten off more than she could chew.

Whatever you need could be under your nose.

The message on the coaching app swam into her mind and Ivy quickly dialled the resort's number. Perhaps someone would be able to direct her to a local beauty salon so she could book an appointment. She might not have any idea of how to achieve the first two of her daily goals, but she might be able to work it out while she accomplished the third...

AFTER Ivy's call the previous afternoon, Bonnibell had booked her a morning hair appointment in a local beauty salon, and then dropped her off on her way to pick up some shopping. Ivy tugged the thick coat the older woman had loaned her tighter as she tracked along Christmas Village's high street, admiring the knitted bunting and shimmering lights swinging between the snowflakes. She passed The Corner Shop first and stopped momentarily to peer at the queue lined up in front of the main counter. The post office situated a few doors down was closed, but a few buildings further on Ivy passed Rowan's Café and glanced through a steamed-up window to see a scatter of pretty tables filled with people sitting in huddles and groups. She briefly contemplated popping in to pick up a takeaway hot drink, but didn't want to be late.

The Workshop beauty salon was empty when Ivy walked in. She could smell a combination of lavender, bergamot and frankincense as she wandered up to the desk at the far end, immediately noticing an essential oil humidifier puffing out fragrant steam. She pressed the shiny bell, taking time to admire the small Christmas tree perched on the white counter and various pots and tubes of beauty fare on the floor-to-ceiling shelves. Someone had wound tinsel around the products and Ivy jumped when Christmas music suddenly began to play and she heard the tap of spiky heels.

'Oh, I'm so sorry, I've been out back,' a voice rang out.

When Ivy turned her breath caught because the woman was gorgeous – with a movie-star face and figure more suited to Hollywood than the Highlands.

'You must be Ivy Heart. I'm Kenzy Campbell,' the woman said in a musical American accent. 'It's awesome to have you here. I believe Bonnibell booked you in for a haircut?' When Ivy nodded, Kenzy scowled at the stump of hair hanging limply by Ivy's cheek. 'She said it was an emergency and she was right. Don't worry, hon, we'll sort that out.' Kenzy led her into a small hallway. 'You can hang your coat there and make yourself comfortable. Do you want coffee? I always forget to buy tea.' She shook her head.

'Please. White, no sugar.' Ivy took off her coat before settling herself onto the cream leather sofa Kenzy had pointed to.

'Do you have anything particular in mind?' Kenzy asked as she returned and set the hot drink on the small table in front of the sofa.

'Not really, just something that will work with this,' Ivy said, patting the stump. 'While I'm here, could you put a colour on my nails too, please?' She wriggled her fingers and Kenzy beamed. It had been years since Ivy had bothered having her nails done – mostly because gardening and polish didn't work well together. But if she was going to fit in in London, she knew she had to look the part. She examined the cuts and scratches on her palms, which were already healing, and her mind drifted to the man in the woods.

Kenzy interrupted the daydream. 'It's all about red this season. I've got a few options to show you and I'll fish out some hair magazines so you can flick through them too. Unfortunately my usual stylist is off sick today, but I'm experienced. It just might take a little longer to get everything done.'

'That's fine,' Ivy said. She had nowhere else to be and

perhaps Kenzy might be able to give her a clue as to where she could find Ross.

'Oh hon, I can already tell we're going to get on.' Kenzy grinned. 'I've got another customer due soon; she's booked in for a simple wash and set. I hope you don't mind if I switch between you? She's an absolute doll, I'm sure we'll all get along.'

'Of course I don't mind,' Ivy said easily, sipping some of the hot drink as Kenzy gave her a stack of magazines. 'I've got a few things to work out in my head so I'm not in a hurry.'

When Ivy had spoken to Bonnibell the evening before, she'd asked if Bonnibell knew how she might find Ross, but the older woman had told her she had no idea. Apparently her husband Connell hadn't been able to locate him on the resort grounds, although Ivy suspected he hadn't looked very hard. Or perhaps Miriam's mysterious grandson had asked him not to tell?

The bell at the front of the salon rang out and Kenzy immediately dashed to the door. When she returned, a woman who looked to be in her mid-seventies with grey hair wearing a ruby tiara followed her in.

Kenzy quickly introduced Ivy to the older woman. 'And this is Edina Lachlan. She lives in Evergreen Castle which is situated just outside of the village,' she explained. 'Don't mind the headwear, Edina is very fond of jewellery,' she added, probably noting Ivy's surprise.

'Ach, life's better with some sparkle,' Edina said, her cheeks glowing. 'Good morning, lass,' she added, removing her coat and sitting beside Ivy. She was spritely despite her age, slim with an intense way of looking at you that suggested she missed nothing. 'I've heard all about you from someone at my knitting club. Apparently you came to find Ross Ballentine and are staying in Snowman Chalet at Christmas Resort, is that correct?'

'Um, yes,' Ivy said, a little taken aback. She'd heard news travelled fast in small communities, but nothing had prepared

her for this. She'd barely been in the area for a day. She leafed
through one of the magazines Kenzy had given her without
looking at the pages as Edina studied her with wily green eyes.

Then Kenzy returned from the small kitchen. 'I just over-
heard that you're looking for Ross. Have you any clues as to
where he might be?' she asked, placing a mug in front of
Edina too.

'Unfortunately not...' Ivy pulled a face as her mind filled
with the man she'd bumped into yesterday and the unusual
effect he'd had on her. Wishing again that she'd asked him about
Miriam's grandson. Perhaps if she had, she'd have had a chance
of seeing the mystery tree cutter again. 'We had a meeting
booked, but Mr Ballentine didn't turn up.' Ivy swallowed,
unwilling to give away any more. 'Bonnibell doesn't know
where Ross is at the moment – Connell promised to book me
another appointment with him, but I'm thinking I might try to
find him by myself.'

After yesterday, Ivy suspected Ross wouldn't turn up to any
of the meetings they organised, which meant her promised job
from Miriam was in danger.

'I'm still figuring out how, though.' She smiled, trying not to
look bothered. Her mother had recently told her that success
was about faking it until you made it – no one was ever going to
want to hire someone who had no faith in themselves...

'Ross can be elusive sometimes,' Edina said, winking.

'It's true,' Kenzy agreed, looking sympathetic. She gathered
up two black gowns before handing them to Edina and Ivy.
'Let's move into the salon so I can get working on you both,' she
said, helping Edina to her feet.

'Does Ross have any friends?' Ivy asked.

'He keeps himself to himself. We rarely see him in the
village and I know Bonnibell has almost given up on getting him
to join in with any of the staff meals or events she throws at the
resort,' Edina shared as she sat in the shiny chair by the sink and

lifted the tiara carefully from her head. 'The only person I know he sees plenty of is—'

'Old man Grizzle,' Kenzy filled in, nodding as she put the sparkly jewellery on a counter and settled Ivy into another chair before handing her the pile of magazines she'd been looking through earlier.

'Who's that?' Ivy asked, looking up.

'Grizzle. I've no idea what his real name is.' Edina smiled. 'He befriended Ross when the lad moved into the area and they've stuck together since.' She leaned her head back in the white sink so Kenzy could start shampooing her hair.

'Where does Grizzle live?' Ivy asked, flicking absently through one of the magazines as her mind whirred. Could this man be her route to finding Ross?

'In a cabin in woodland on the outskirts of Christmas Resort land. He's been there for as long as I can remember,' Edina explained.

'But why so remote?' Ivy queried. She loved being surrounded by plants and trees, but couldn't imagine being so isolated. Although she might prefer that to living in London... She frowned. She knew parts of it were leafy, but would that be enough? Her stomach squeezed uncomfortably.

Edina shrugged. 'Grizzle had a falling out with one of the women in the village when they were dating years ago.'

'Who was the woman?' Kenzy asked, her curiosity obviously piqued.

'Mairi Gibson,' Edina said. 'She's a widow now and lives alone – her son and his wife have just moved into their own place. She keeps herself busy and works at Christmas Resort part-time and in the optician's just off the high street on the other days,' she explained to Ivy. 'Grizzle's not that fond of people in general, but rumour is he moved out of the village to avoid her.'

'Odd,' Kenzy muttered.

Edina shrugged. 'The old bampot has a good heart, but he's not that easy to get to know.' Ivy nodded. She'd heard the term before and knew it meant fool – guessed from the older woman's tone that she was fond of Ross's friend. 'I've heard he's happy living out in the middle of nowhere with just his dog for company. Well, aside from Ross who calls in every day.'

'Ross visits him every day?' Ivy repeated. 'Could I find Grizzle's house by myself?' Perhaps if she did, she could wait and speak to Ross when he popped in.

'That's nae likely lass,' Edina said. 'Not without knowing your way around. Grizzle lives deep in the woods. You'd probably need a guide to find it. The only people who know the exact location, aside from Grizzle, are Ross and Connell.'

'And my honeypot Logan Forbes,' Kenzy said. 'He chops wood for him sometimes.' She beamed, her eyes shining. 'But Logan wouldn't give the position away even to me, the man's as tight-lipped as they come.' She smiled dreamily.

'Aye. And Connell probably wouldn't tell you either. Everyone in the village is very protective of the curmudgeon,' Edina said.

Ivy tapped a finger on her magazine. The message on her coaching app the day before had definitely been wrong. There was nothing under her nose, aside from another dead end. Then again, if she could track down the mystery man she'd bumped into yesterday, perhaps he could help.

Edina suddenly sat bolt upright, her wet hair dripping onto her gown. 'Why don't you register for one of those adventures Ross runs?'

'Good idea.' Kenzy encouraged the older woman to lower her head again so she could start rinsing.

'Adventures...' Ivy repeated slowly. She remembered Miriam mentioning something about what Ross did at the resort, but hadn't focused on the details. 'What kind of adventures?' Did those leaflets Bonnibell had given her, the ones she'd cleared from the floor and placed onto the desk in her cabin late last night thinking they were junk, include information about them? Was that what had been under her nose all along? For the first time since Ivy had arrived, she began to feel hope.

'Ach, could be anything,' Edina said as Kenzy finished rinsing her hair and started to dry it with a towel. 'My grandson and his girl bought me a reindeer-spotting trip last year. Mind you, we only saw my donkey Bob, but I think he scared everything else off with all his hollering.' She chuckled.

Ivy shook her head. Donkeys and tiaras? This woman was a strange combination, but she couldn't help liking her.

'Ross teaches people how to chop wood, spot birds and he regularly runs snow safaris – they're really popular,' Kenzy explained as she guided Edina to another chair and fussed about, making sure she was comfortable. 'My honeypot has booked us into a mystery adventure later this week.' She winked as Ivy absently turned another page on the magazine and saw a hairstyle she liked so folded the corner.

'There are people who regularly go camping with him in snowstorms then take midnight walks in the wilderness.' Kenzy shuddered, her pretty blue eyes twinkling. 'Including Logan. Ross is an amazing guide. He knows everything there is to know about the land, local flora, fauna and animals. If you buy an adventure, it would be a good way of spending time with him. Come on—' She indicated that Ivy should lean her head back in the sink. 'It's your turn.'

Edina chuckled. 'Aye, he'll have to meet with you then.'

'I thought the resort was closed at the moment,' Ivy said, gazing up at the glittering Christmas lights which had been strung across the ceiling as Kenzy soaked her hair.

'Ach, if people register, Ross will run an adventure anytime,' Edina said. 'It's not just the resort guests who book, people from the village do it all the time – and I've heard tales of folks coming from as far away as Edinburgh to experience a day with him. He's got a good reputation.'

'That could work,' Ivy said, shutting her eyes as Kenzy started to massage shampoo into her scalp. She'd go through the leaflets in the cabin later – if she was quick and paid extra, perhaps she'd be able to persuade Bonnibell to book her in for a one-to-one adventure?

A full day with Ross Ballentine would give her enough time to tell him about Miriam's plans for him and could be the first step to convincing him to move back to the castle to become Laird.

7

ROSS

Ross approached Grizzle's ramshackle cabin and immediately heard a dog start to bark. He was used to his friend's demonic pug and had worn extra thick socks under his snow boots just in case it tried to nip him today. He'd had to have a tetanus booster last summer when he'd popped in at random to check on the older man and had been unexpectedly pounced on as he arrived – so was extra wary now.

'It's me,' he called out, carefully pushing the door with one arm and shaking his head when it swung open, off kilter, suggesting one of the hinges had started to come loose. 'Stay,' he called back to Moose and Snowball, who were still standing beside his snowmobile, too wary of the pug to venture any closer. *Cowards.*

'Is that you again?' a voice with a strong Scottish lilt complained as the fawn four-legged fiend launched itself at Ross's leg, trying to gain traction on the thick rubber of his boots, still yapping between nips. 'I hope you've been to the post office?'

'Of course. I picked up the package you asked for,' Ross said, glaring at the dog. 'Bowser. Seriously, you know who I am

– I come here every day,' he protested, trying to dislodge the dog's tiny jaws. Ross arched an eyebrow when he heard Grizzle's gravelly laugh. 'I swear you trained him to bite me,' he muttered.

'When you're my age you have to get your kicks somewhere, lad.'

The older man continued to chuckle as Ross glanced around, checking for stray balls, dog bones and sticks that may have been abandoned and that his friend might accidently trip over.

The cabin was compact, with two bedrooms and a bathroom accessible at the far end, and there was a large space that served as Grizzle's sitting room, kitchen and dining area combined. Ross shivered, and then carefully lifted and closed the damaged door to stop the cold air blowing in.

He spotted the older man who was wrapped in a blanket and hunched in the rocking chair positioned beside the large red-brick fireplace to the right of an oak kitchen area. The logs and kindling Ross had laid out inside the grate last night hadn't been lit.

'Aren't you cold?' Ross asked, staying out of the older man's eyeline and dodging the dog as it continued to playfully grab and nip at his boot. He made his way to the small fridge, opened it and unpacked the bag, placing a small Pyrex dish with a casserole he'd made onto one of the empty white shelves, along with a pack of butter and loaf of sliced bread.

'Ach, getting cold is for Jessies,' Grizzle sneered. 'Did I just hear you open my fridge?' He turned and squinted across the dimly lit room, the wrinkles on his face deepening. 'You know there's nowt wrong with my ears?'

'I was just checking for milk because I fancy a hot drink. Looks like someone's left you a casserole again and some bread.'

Ross shuffled towards the large table set dead centre of the room. It was piled high with the muddy and discoloured treasures Grizzle had bought online or gathered on his daily walks. Less than a year ago, the older man would have already cleaned and fixed them up ready to sell in his online antiques shop, but it had been a while since he'd done much more than collect and bring them home. Ross wriggled his leg again as Bowser renewed his attack, this time jumping higher and snapping around his knees, making Ross fear for his manhood. He might not have used it in a while, but that didn't mean he was ready to lose it.

'Down boy,' he murmured.

'Leave the lad be.' Grizzle finally relented and Bowser whined before scampering across the room to his master. 'It'll be that harridan, Mairi Gibson, again. The woman's always sneaking in and leaving food,' he complained, his cheeks flushing. 'Although...' The old man's forehead crinkled in confusion. 'I don't know how she gets in here without me knowing about it – my hearing's as good as it was when I was twenty-three.'

Ross winced, feeling guilty – he knew Grizzle enjoyed his daily visits, but also knew the older man would be horrified if he realised Ross was cooking for him and leaving meals. They'd been friends for over five years now, but it had only been a few months since Ross had realised Grizzle had stopped using his beloved recipe books and was surviving on sandwiches instead of hot food. Ross had contemplated coming clean but knew his friend was proud. So he'd decided to remain silent when the hermit had speculated that the mystery cook was his nemesis from Christmas Village.

Mairi had a reputation as a busybody and when she'd been younger, she and Grizzle had been close, before they'd fallen out. Despite that, the older man complained to Ross about her relentlessly – accusing her of everything from stealing logs from his wood pile and overwatering his plants, to sewing buttons on his shirts. With any luck Grizzle would continue to believe his ex-sweetheart was the culinary culprit and never learn Ross was the mystery cook. Since his friend hadn't ventured into the village for years, it was unlikely he'd bump into Mairi and learn the truth.

Grizzle suddenly tugged off his glasses and rubbed his fists into his eye sockets and squinted before fixing his attention back onto Ross. 'Did you get my new specs from the post office?' he demanded.

The hermit's eyesight had been getting worse recently and Ross was concerned soon he might struggle to see at all. Instead of visiting the optician, the older man had been ordering spectacles on eBay in an attempt to fix his vision problems for himself. Ross had called him out on it, but Grizzle had always been too independent for his own good.

'Aye,' Ross said, handing him the parcel he'd picked up earlier. 'Did you book an optician's appointment?' he shot back hopefully. 'You know I'll take you if you want?'

'I'm not an invalid.' Grizzle bristled. 'And I've nae got time for any of that claptrap. I'm nae gonna have some wee boy or lass who's barely out of nappies telling me I need glasses when I'm perfectly capable of figuring that out for myself. It doesn't take a genius to know I'll hit on the right pair in the end.' Ross watched as Grizzle ripped open the bag and pulled out his latest pair of spectacles, looking triumphant. Then he whipped off his old pair and slid the new ones on. Ross kept his face straight as Grizzle adjusted the enormous pink frames and squinted down at his dog.

'Do they work?' Ross asked, trying not to chuckle.

'Maybe, lad,' Grizzle said, screwing up his nose. 'I'm sure once my eyes adjust, I'll be able to see.' He blinked a couple of times as he peered across the room, then stood abruptly and almost knocked over the coffee table. 'They're not perfect so I might order another pair later – which means you'll have to go to the post office again for me this week,' he said, trying to focus on Ross.

'That's okay,' Ross said. It would give him the perfect excuse to visit again.

'You might as well make yourself useful and look for the TV remote before you get out from under my feet,' Grizzle continued, still squinting. 'I know it was beside me on the sofa when I went to bed last night, but I can't find it anywhere now.' He sniffed. 'It was probably that Mairi tidying up when she dropped off the casserole,' he confided. 'She's always clearing up something. I'm constantly losing things.'

'I know,' Ross said, his voice dry.

Grizzle grunted and sat down again before placing a blanket on his knees, sliding the huge glasses back up his nose as they slid downwards and almost fell off.

Ross glanced around and immediately saw the remote where he'd left it the night before, stacked on the coffee table to the left of Grizzle's chair. He wandered across the room, and knelt to pick it up before pressing it into the older man's hands. 'I'm sorry, I think I might have tidied it when I was here yesterday,' he said, earning himself a growl.

'I *knew* it wasn't me,' Grizzle griped, switching on the TV. 'And before you say anything, I know the front door's halfway off its hinges. It wouldn't budge last night when Bowser needed to pop out to do his business and I had to shove at it. I might be older than Moses but I can still break down an eejit door.' He puffed up his skinny chest and flexed one of his arms proudly. 'Don't you go trying to fix it.' Grizzle wagged a knobbly finger in Ross's direction. 'I don't need your help – I've told you that a thousand times.'

'Fine, I'm not staying long enough for that anyway,' Ross shot back. He'd have to return later on some other pretext and mend the door while Grizzle was otherwise occupied. He didn't want to blame that on Mairi too, so perhaps his friend Logan could take the fall? 'I've got someone booked in for a wildlife spotting adventure this afternoon,' Ross explained. According to

Connell, who'd called on the walkie-talkie late the evening before, the client had reserved a place last minute and wasn't going to be in the area for long enough to wait for more people to join. They'd paid a premium for a one-to-one excursion, so Ross really had no choice.

His mind drifted to the woman called Ivy as he thought about today's adventure and he shook his head. It was unlikely to be her – if it was, Connell surely would have mentioned something about him taking the journalist out. Besides, if she was here to scope out the resort, she'd be more likely to be quizzing someone at the lodge or taking photos of the maze, cabins or the rest of the grounds.

'Can I make myself a coffee before I leave?' Ross asked suddenly, tramping to the butler sink which he'd scrubbed the evening before until it gleamed. It was already stained again and there were dirty cups and dishes piled in the bottom along with a saucepan he'd left in the fridge filled with his speciality beef stew. Grizzle might complain about the mystery meals, but he always ate every last bite.

Ross ran the tap and ignored the older man when he started to mutter. 'Coming here, using all my stuff. If you're going to make yourself a hot drink, you might as well do the same for me.'

'No problem. I've got milk in the snowmobile – I'll just go and get it.' Ross glanced back at the door. 'Bonnibell made some cinnamon buns for my breakfast. That woman always packs enough for four. You'll be doing me a favour if you agree to share some with me.'

Grizzle slowly rocked in his chair as if considering, then he shrugged his bony shoulders, catching the pink glasses as they slid down his nose. 'Fine, I'll do you a favour. I haven't had a chance to eat this morning yet. Besides, that woman's got a magic touch when it comes to food.' He quivered. 'Unlike Mairi. I swear that woman could sour carrots if she got the chance – which is odd because she used to be an excellent cook. But that stew last night...' He shuddered.

Ross blew out a breath, his temper simmering as he left the kettle to boil and stomped out of the front door towards his snowmobile so he could collect the milk and cinnamon buns.

'Sour carrots,' he echoed darkly. 'I'm an excellent cook.' He looked at Moose and Snowball who were still waiting beside the vehicle as he approached, clearly listening to every word. The dog cocked his head, his brown eyes filled with sympathy, and beside him the wild boar let out a low disbelieving grunt. 'What do you know?' Ross snapped, grabbing the food before turning and stomping away.

8

ROSS

Bonnibell swung open the front door of Christmas Lodge as soon as Ross pulled his snowmobile up in front an hour after he'd left Grizzle beside the fire, muttering complaints in his sleep.

'Afternoon, you're just in time!' she sang, her red velvet skirt swishing as she joined him on the porch before bending to greet Moose and Snowball as his pets bounded up to say hello.

'Where's your journalist today?' Ross asked lightly and peered into the hallway.

'The article's all done so she's already gone,' Bonnibell said.

'Oh.' Ross's shoulders sagged, wishing he'd had one last peek at Ivy before she'd left.

'It's such a shame you didn't get a chance to talk to her your-self.' Bonnibell's tone was disapproving. 'However, the client booked in for your adventure is waiting in the kitchen. She's already filled in all the relevant health and safety forms, and I've loaned her one of the resort's coats, some boots, gloves and a hat, but you might want to make sure you're happy with the number of layers she's wearing before you leave. I've made up a small picnic including a flask of hot chocolate for you to take out so you have supplies. I'm not sure of your exact plans today and' – her brows knitted as she glanced across the decking into the trees – 'I've heard there's a storm coming.'

'There's always a storm coming. I don't think they forecast anything else around Christmas Village this time of year.' Ross chuckled. 'I'm sure the clothes you've provided will be fine,' he said mildly, stamping his feet on the rug and dislodging a flurry of snowflakes as Moose and Snowball bounded ahead.

Bonnibell led them all across the hallway, and Ross followed her into the kitchen, trying not to think about the woman who kept invading his thoughts. Then he stopped in his tracks as his heart swooped into his throat. Sitting on a chair at the breakfast bar, wearing a coat, hat and gloves and sipping from a mug of hot chocolate, was Ivy.

'It's you,' he said, surprised, instantly regretting it when Bonnibell let out a strange choking sound. 'I mean, hello again.'

What was Ivy doing here? Hadn't Bonnibell just told him she'd left the resort?

'*You're* Ross Ballentine?' she squeaked, her eyes rounding. 'Of course,' she said as she studied him. 'You've shaved off the beard but I still would have recognised you the other day if it hadn't been for the scarf.'

'You've met already?' Bonnibell's gaze bounced between them.

Ross winced as Ivy nodded.

'I bumped into Mr Ballentine in the woods beside Snowman Chalet yesterday afternoon,' she explained. 'He didn't manage to introduce himself though.' Her tone was mild. 'Why is that?' she murmured.

But Ross decided not to reply.

'Well that's brilliant.' Bonnibell clapped her hands. 'Ross, Ivy here's been looking forward to meeting you. Especially since you missed your appointment.' She gave him a look that told him she knew that had been deliberate. 'She's got news from your grandmother which I'm sure you'll be excited to hear.'

'Miriam sent you,' Ross said slowly as everything clicked into place. Ivy wasn't the journalist – she was the woman his grandmother had sent to speak to him. The person he'd been trying to avoid.

'That's right.' Ivy hopped from the barstool and Ross saw she was wearing a thick black coat that skimmed her ankles and almost touched the floor. 'And I'm *really* looking forward to spending time with you today. There are so many things we need to talk about, it'll be the perfect chance for me to fill you in on what Miriam wants.'

Ross made a face as he tried to come up with a reason not to stay. His eyes skimmed her outfit and he nodded. 'Well I'm sorry but you're going to have to change if you're getting on the back of a snowmobile. That coat is far too long which means you'll have to unzip the bottom. There's a bad storm coming and you have to wrap up properly. Do you have salopettes or a snowsuit?' From the look of the negligible luggage he'd seen on Ivy's bed when he'd been in the chalet, she didn't have anything warm.

'But I thought—' Bonnibell began, her forehead crevassing.

'I've had a rethink,' Ross jumped in. 'I apologise, but I can't take you out if you're not properly equipped,' he said to Ivy. 'It's not worth the risk to our insurance. I hadn't anticipated the change in weather and I really can't risk you getting cold. Perhaps we could reschedule or you'll accept a refund for the trip? Now I really must be going.' He began to turn.

Ross knew they had guests due to move into most of the cabins at the resort in a few days which meant Ivy's time here would surely be limited. So he'd just make sure he wasn't available to run any new adventures until he was sure she'd gone. Okay, so he might be being unfair, but he didn't want to talk about his grandmother. Didn't want the uncomfortable emotions he could already feel stirring in his chest. Whatever Ivy was supposed to tell him, he already knew it wasn't something he wanted to hear.

'I don't have anything else to wear,' Ivy said, sounding unhappy.

'Oh don't be dafty, hen.' Bonnibell quickly recovered. 'I've got something in my wardrobe you can have.' She glanced down at her curvaceous figure. 'The outfit is a few years old and doesn't fit me anymore, but...' She eyed Ivy critically. 'Aside from being a bit long in the leg they should fit you perfectly, and I've got an underlayer that will keep you extra snug. I'll get them now.' She gave Ross another odd look as she marched from the kitchen, leaving them alone together.

The silence stretched until Ivy cleared her throat. 'I've got news and a letter from your grandmother. I wanted to explain everything to you at our meeting.' The look she gave him made it clear she'd been surprised when he hadn't turned up. Which meant Miriam hadn't filled Ivy in on the details of their relationship. 'Why don't you want to talk to me?'

Ross cleared his throat. 'Because unless you're here to tell me she's not well...?' He waited and felt a rush of relief when Ivy shook her head. 'I'm really not interested, and I think you'll find my grandmother isn't that invested in contacting me either.'

He watched her forehead crease as she digested his words. Felt a sliver of guilt, but his life at Hawthorn Castle was in the past. He wasn't sure what game Miriam was playing but he did know he wasn't really wanted there – and there was no reason to open old wounds that had healed years ago. He stepped closer so he could look into Ivy's eyes, steeling his wayward hormones as they began to race.

'Look, you might as well save time and cancel this trip. I'm not interested in hearing what my grandmother has to say. I'm sure she's paid you a lot of money to track me here. Now you can tell her we've met, and you told me what I had to know and we can leave it at that.'

Ivy studied him, her eyes wide. 'I would have recognised you if you hadn't been wearing that scarf,' she said, her voice husky. 'You look a little like Simon, but not an exact match. You're more... rugged.' She flushed. 'I mean less polished.' She gulped. 'But I can see it's you because you still look like you did in the photo from Miriam's office.'

'Photo?' Ross murmured. As far as he was concerned, when he'd left the castle, his grandmother had removed all traces of him. The happy flutter in his chest was irritating.

'I can show you,' Ivy said, turning around.

'No!' Ross snapped before she could get to her bag. 'Look, I really don't think this is a good idea.'

Ivy looked hurt. 'Will spending one afternoon with me really be so awful?' she asked quietly. 'Can't you at least give your grandmother that?'

Ross opened his mouth to tell her she didn't understand just as Bonnibell came trotting back into the room, clutching a pink snowsuit and matching underlayer.

'Here you are,' she sang, handing the clothes to Ivy. 'I'm sorry both, but Innes, our housekeeper, just called. Apparently I have to meet with her now – there's some kind of linen emergency.' She winked. 'Have a good afternoon, I hope you get plenty of time to talk, I'll catch up with you soon.' She nodded at Ivy, then pointed to the small backpack on the table. 'And don't forget your picnic.' With that Bonnibell was gone.

Ivy studied Ross silently, until she started to unzip and remove the long, puffy coat she was wearing and tugged off the hat too.

'You fixed your hair,' Ross said, surprised as the dark bob slid into place – and immediately regretted the observation as crimson flames shot across her cheeks.

'It's different, but it looks a lot better than it did before,' she said shyly, tugging at the new fringe, playing with the jagged edges that had been trimmed to cut in around her cheekbones.

The style was whimsical and very flattering. It made Ivy's green eyes impossibly large and drew attention to the curve of her mouth. Ross stared until she moved and hung the coat over a chair then began to take off her boots ready to pull on the snowsuit.

'I'm sorry,' he gulped as she tugged on one of the legs and he realised he was still watching, his pulse revving hard. Alarmed, he took a wide step backwards towards the door. 'Why don't you finish changing and I'll wait for you outside.' He turned abruptly, then realised he'd forgotten the picnic, so grabbed it without looking back and stomped into the hall. 'Moose, Snowball!' he barked as he reached the front door and realised neither of them had followed, and were most likely still gawping at Ivy too.

Both animals appeared as he made his way onto the porch and carefully shut the door, feeling out of sorts. As he got to his snowmobile and secured the picnic onto the back, he heard footsteps crunching in the snow.

'Ross!' Connell shouted as soon as he turned around. 'Good to see you made it to the meetup this time.' He pointed to the lodge.

'You didn't mention the client who'd booked in for the tour was the same one I've been trying to avoid,' Ross grumbled.

'Ach, lad, you couldn't dodge her forever,' the older man said. 'I don't think Ivy was planning to give up and I couldn't get away with fibbing to Bonnibell again. I felt bad about it the other day. Just do the trip – I'm sure all the lass wants to do is talk, and hearing a few words from your grandmother surely won't hurt, will they?' He pulled a face, his rosy cheeks reddening.

'Let's hope not.' Ross didn't add that the wrong words might stir up all kinds of uncomfortable feelings. He'd avoided talking about his family for years and didn't particularly relish having to do it now.

The door of the lodge suddenly opened and Ivy walked out and spotted them immediately. Bonnibell's snowsuit was long, but the hot pink outfit hugged her frame, drawing attention to a delicate figure and impossibly small waist. Suddenly Ross wished he'd left her wrapped in the shapeless black coat.

He dragged his eyes away and grabbed a helmet as Connell greeted her. 'Well I'd best be off, have a smashing day.' He gazed into the sky. 'Word is there might be a storm coming,' he repeated Bonnibell's warning. 'Make sure you take extra care. That said, Ivy, you're in really good hands.' With that the older man gave her a merry wink and headed for the woods.

'You look warmer,' Ross said gruffly, handing Ivy her helmet.

She glanced down. 'It's a surprisingly comfortable fit. I'm glad you agreed to let me come.' She pulled the helmet on and tried to fiddle with the clasp but her gloves got in the way.

In the end Ross stepped in and pulled off his, taking care not to brush his fingers across Ivy's chin, but failing, which meant the surface of his skin began to fizz. He stepped away and swiped his hand on his clothes, before pulling the gloves over his fingers again.

'I only have a few things to say. I promise it won't take long and I think you'll be happy once you know why I'm here,' she said quietly.

'Can we do this later?' he said stiffly. 'You've paid for a resort adventure and it's my job to deliver that this afternoon.'

'Sorry, of course.' Ivy gave in. 'Where are you planning on taking me first?'

She tried to meet his eyes but Ross dropped his gaze to her mouth, quickly adjusting it again when he found himself tracing the plump curve of her top lip.

'That depends on what types of wildlife you want to see,' he said. 'There're all kinds around the resort. If you've a desire to spot a particular species, it might change where we head to first. Unless you don't care?' he added hopefully.

If she didn't – if this really was just an excuse to deliver a message from his grandmother – then he knew exactly where to take her. It wasn't far and the trip wouldn't take long. He could let Ivy talk for ten minutes and with any luck he'd have her back at the lodge in a couple of hours.

Ivy unzipped a side pocket in the snowsuit and pulled out a piece of paper before handing it to him. 'I did some research into local wildlife when I booked the tour last night. Then I created this chart and Bonnibell printed it for me this morning.' She cleared her throat as Ross studied the page, his eyes widening.

'It's colour-coded,' he said, stunned.

'I've ranked the species I'm interested in seeing using colours.' She pointed to one of the columns. 'Everything high-lighted in red is in my "must-see" column. I've always fancied seeing a reindeer, but donkeys, otters, mountain hares and eagles are also on my wish list. I also really like vegetation and I know you get all kinds around there.' She blinked. 'So there's another spreadsheet just in case we have time for that.'

Ross cleared his throat as he perused the pages. 'Are you always this efficient?' he asked, studying the charts, reluctantly impressed. Understanding why Miriam had asked Ivy to track him down and why she hadn't been so easy to put off.

'It's not my happy place.' Ivy pursed her lips. 'But since I've been working for your grandmother...' She winced. 'Well, she likes things done in a very particular way.'

'Her way or the highway.' Ross nodded, remembering her saying from his teens. He quickly scanned the list as his heart sank, because some of the plants and animals could take a while to find. It also meant he'd have to travel to the far corners of the resort, which meant any chance of a quick afternoon out had just disappeared. 'We'd better get on. If we're going to find any of these species, we're going to have to hunt for them, but I can't promise we'll see them. I'm sure you read that in the resort's terms and conditions.' He kept his eyes averted so they didn't accidently meet hers again. 'We'll do a circuit around the far edges of the property to see what we can see, and there are a few places where we can sit out of sight to wait. If the animals are shy, I know a few tricks that might draw them out. I laid down a few treats earlier today.' He hesitated, wishing again that Ivy would change her mind.

'Should I get on?' She nodded at his snowmobile. 'Or do I get my own?'

Ross looked resigned. 'As it's only you on this trip we'll stick with mine. Just climb on the back and put your feet in those stirrups.' He pointed to the metal bars. 'There are also special places where you can hold on.' He showed her those too. 'If you don't feel secure you can put your arms around me.'

Ivy widened her eyes and nodded before swinging a leg over the back of the snowmobile and making herself comfortable. Ross was pleased when she opted to grasp the handles, which meant he wouldn't have to try to ignore her while she was holding him.

'Did you learn about the wildlife when you were living in Hawthorn Castle?' she shouted. 'It's a beautiful place, you must miss it?' Ross swallowed down a frisson of annoyance. Then he grunted and tugged his helmet over his head and signalled that he couldn't hear. As Ross fired up the engine, he felt Ivy slide forwards on the seat so she could place her hands over his hips.

Dammit, he thought as he slid the snowmobile forward, realising spending the day with Ivy Heart was going to be even more difficult than he'd imagined.

9

IVY

Ivy gripped Ross's hips and rested her head on the curve of his back, trying to work out how to approach what she needed to tell him. She still couldn't believe that the man who'd troubled her dreams again last night was the same person she'd come to Christmas Resort to track down. But why hadn't Ross wanted to talk to her? What had happened between him and Miriam? It was a mystery – but she suspected once Ross finally heard why she was here, understood his grandmother wanted him to take over as Laird, he'd be eager to hear all about her plans. *Why wouldn't he?* It would be a chance to reconcile with his family and the start of an incredible vocation. He'd be titled, wealthy – people would revere him and he wouldn't have to worry about money or security for the rest of his life... If she had the same opportunity, she'd grab it with both hands.

The snowmobile suddenly shot over a large bump on the icy hill they were travelling down and Ivy shifted further forward, winding her arms around Ross's waist before she could talk herself out of it. It wasn't professional, but neither was flying off the saddle seat into a ditch.

'Are we almost there?' she shouted at the back of Ross's

helmet, wincing when the snowmobile hit another hump, and hoped the words would carry on the wind. When he didn't reply, she leaned her head onto his back again. As they accelerated, she watched the bushes and trees, which were bulging with snow, fly past, and tried to work out each of the species.

'*Follow your dreams, they know the way,*' she whispered to herself, quoting the daily lesson from the coaching app she'd read that morning. Hopefully today the quote would be accurate again – and the new three daily goals she'd set, involving number one, speaking to Ross and two, convincing him to return to Hawthorn Castle, would be easy to achieve. She'd already nailed the third, which involved tracking down the mystery odd-job man, which she'd added on a whim because she'd wanted to see him again.

Ivy frowned as they headed into a forest of trees, a few of which had been decorated with bunting knitted in multi-coloured wool. Then, after a few more minutes, the vehicle pulled to a stop and she reluctantly unwound her arms from around Ross's chest.

Ross climbed off and undid his helmet before dangling it over the handlebars, then he zipped a finger over his lips when Ivy took hers off too. He bent suddenly and wagged a finger at Moose and Snowball before whispering 'Shhhhh,' and tipping his head to the side to offer them a few silent blinks. The animals must have understood because Moose whined.

'There's a clearing further ahead where we can sit and wait,' Ross whispered. 'I've seen a herd of wild reindeer in the area this week and sometimes they congregate here. We'll have to stay hidden and it's vital we don't make any noise.' He paused, perhaps to give her time to digest the directive. 'Leave the helmet on the bike beside mine, follow me closely and don't forget to be quiet.'

He pressed a finger to his mouth again, drawing attention to the sexy contour of his lips, and Ivy averted her eyes.

She gulped as she followed Ross along the icy pathway, taking in the array of ferns, mosses and shrubs decorated with tentacles of ice, trying to remember the names, which she'd once been able to recite without thinking. She stopped so she could take in the view and felt herself still. The sparkling duvet of snow and the glimmering flakes fluttering through the trees made it magical. She could have stayed here all day, absorbing the stunning vista and smells, the gorgeous trees and shrubs.

Ivy picked up her pace, snapping a few twigs under her boots as she caught up with Ross, who kept turning, checking she was still there – and frowning each time he realised she was. When they drew closer to a round snow-covered clearing, he stopped and jabbed a finger right where a series of long bushy branches had been rested against a tree, creating a den which Ivy guessed acted as a camouflage. Ivy followed Ross behind the screen, then sat on one of the four stubby tree stumps on the ground when he indicated to them and mimed sitting. She watched as he sat too, and then signalled to his pets to take their places at his feet. Both Moose and Snowball slumped onto the ground beside him, then watched transfixed as their master opened his backpack and tossed them both rewards.

'Do you want hot chocolate?' Ross whispered.

Ivy nodded. 'I thought we couldn't talk?' she said, her tone hushed.

'Instructions and animal-related conversation are fine if we keep it to a minimum,' he murmured.

As Ivy's mouth pinched in annoyance, Ross looked away. Then he poured them both a mug from the flask and handed her one before pointing to the gaps in between the branches.

'Keep a lookout over there,' he said, leaning closer. 'I saw the reindeer in the area yesterday and left out some treats before I came to pick you up. Hopefully they'll come looking round here for food. If the wind blows in the right direction, they should catch the scent.'

'What did you leave them?' Ivy asked, sipping some of the drink. She leaned closer, catching a whiff of balsam fir and pine needles, and wondered if the smell was just the trees or Ross.

'They like carrots and slices of apple,' he said, his eyes still fixed on the gaps between the branches. 'It usually attracts them – it just depends on how close to the area they are.'

'Isn't there a herd of wild reindeer that visits the Hawthorn Castle Estate?' Ivy asked, frowning when she noticed Ross's shoulders tense. 'I've never been lucky enough to see them, but is that how you learned about what they like to eat?'

'I'm not—' he started.

Then Moose's ears suddenly pricked up and Ivy heard rustling in the undergrowth.

'Steady, boys,' Ross warned roughly, as he leaned towards the screen and encouraged Ivy to do the same.

That's when she saw them. Three fawn-coloured reindeer, one with antlers, sniffing their way along the snowy pathway and heading straight for their hiding spot. One of the reindeer put its head up and took in a deep breath of air. They were magnificent. Ivy felt something inside her click, felt the fast pitter-patter of her heart as the reindeer continued to draw closer and one of them spotted the food Ross had left out.

'They've found it,' Ivy gasped, almost falling off the tree stump in her excitement. This beat sitting in an office, hands down. She stopped breathing as one of the reindeer glanced up again as if it had heard. Then Ivy felt Ross gently squeeze her shoulder and let herself relax, watching as the creatures crowded around and gobbled the treats noisily, seemingly oblivious to their audience.

'This is incredible,' she rasped after a few minutes as the reindeer finished the snacks and nudged one another's necks, before turning their backs on the den and disappearing into the woods. The whole thing probably only took five or six minutes, but Ivy felt as if she'd been watching them for days. She couldn't tear her eyes away.

She remained still, enjoying the peace and tingles that had travelled down her neck while she'd been sitting. 'I understand now why you love it here so much,' she said quietly. For the first time in almost a year, she felt relaxed. There was nothing nagging at the back of her mind, no guilt that she should be doing something more productive. She took in a deep breath and revelled in the scent of trees and shrubs, imagining she could identify some of them just from their smell.

She turned and looked straight at Ross, who immediately looked away. But before he did, she caught an odd look on his face – one that told her he was battling with himself about something.

'You should finish your drink,' he said roughly, pointing to her mug which was still half full.

'Can I show the letter from your grandmother?' she asked, digging into her bag without waiting for his response. When she couldn't immediately find it, she pulled out the picture frame she'd taken from Miriam's office and handed it to him to hold.

Ross stared at the picture, his forehead creasing. 'This is from just before I left,' he said, roughly rubbing a finger over the glass. 'One of the gardeners at the estate took it and gave it to Miriam. I never thought she'd keep it. I always thought she'd remove any traces of me.' He sounded shocked.

Ivy didn't tell him that it was the only photo of him she'd seen in the castle. She could see he was affected, realised this was her best chance of getting him to listen. 'I'm here to tell you your brother, Simon, has decided to...' She paused, straightening. 'Well, for various reasons he doesn't want to become Laird.'

'Simon?' Ross glanced up, looking surprised. 'But that's all he's ever wanted. It was his dream, the only thing that mattered to him. What happened?'

Ivy shrugged. 'I'm not sure. I just know he had a huge fight with Miriam and stormed out. I don't know where he's gone.'

Ross blinked, his cheeks flexing. 'My grandmother put Simon under a lot of pressure from a young age, but he was always happy with that. Being Laird was his destiny.' He looked confused.

'The letter Miriam wrote for you will probably explain everything – you should probably read it now.' Ivy dug into the bag and pulled out the crisp cream envelope with the embossed red wax seal that Miriam always used. When Ross didn't take it, she continued to hold it out. 'Your grandmother wants you to come to the castle as soon as you can.'

Ross's lips knotted and Ivy shuffled closer. She understood they'd fallen out, but surely this news would change everything?

'I don't think you understand,' she said gently. 'She wants you to return to Hawthorn Castle so you can take over from Simon and become Laird.' When he didn't react, she added, her voice a little desperate now, 'You'll inherit the land, title, everything...'

She waited for him to smile, but he just went back to staring at the photo.

'There's going to be a party on Christmas Eve and she wants to reintroduce you into society. It's a huge honour.' She paused again, still watching him, and her stomach sank. This wasn't the reaction she'd been hoping for. 'Why aren't you excited?' she asked, baffled.

'Because I'm not interested. And I really don't think my grandmother wants me to return.' Ross shook his head. 'I'm not part of the family anymore. This is just protocol. I have to be the first person she contacts, it wouldn't be right otherwise. I'm not sure how long you've been working for Miriam, but I'm sure you're aware everything is about appearances.' His voice was dull. 'You should have gathered that my grandmother's not that invested in me returning because she didn't come herself.'

'What do you mean?' Ivy asked.

Ross gave her an assessing look. 'She sent you, didn't she?'

'Well, she's very busy,' Ivy said quickly, realising the excuse sounded weak. Miriam had had years to visit her grandson – why hadn't she? And if this was so important, was it a little odd that she'd asked Ivy to visit instead of coming herself?

'I'm really very sorry about Simon,' Ross said, suddenly rising to his feet, his large body stooping under the canopy. 'But I'm not the person to take this on and Miriam knows that. She doesn't really want me.' He shook his head. 'I have a cousin once removed, Frank something.' He tapped his temple. 'I can't remember his full name, but the family are part of the Ballentine bloodline. Miriam will know this... I expect she'll ask you to speak to him next.'

'I... I don't...' Ivy started, bemused as Ross plucked the unopened letter from her hand, then put that, along with the framed photo, into her backpack.

'You should finish your drink,' he said, pointing to the mug.

Ivy wasn't sure what to say so she drank it and handed it to him. This wasn't what she'd expected. She knew they'd fallen out, but this was a huge opportunity – an honour for Ross. What had happened between him and his family that was so awful?

Ivy knew something about fractured relationships and the misery of living with words you wished you'd never said – and the idea that whatever had happened was still festering between Miriam and her grandson made Ivy even more determined to get them to talk. Getting the job in London was vital too, of course, but somehow getting them to reconcile felt even more important.

Ross kept busy while Ivy considered what to do next. He zipped the flask and their mugs back into the backpack before pointing towards the opening to the den. 'The reindeer are unlikely to return now. There's somewhere a few miles from here where I've seen mountain hares a few times, we might as well go there next.' He slung the bag over his shoulder and shot out of the small enclosure first, as if he couldn't bear to be inside with her.

'This isn't over,' she muttered as she joined Ross outside and looked up. The canopy from the trees protected them from most of the snowflakes, but even from here Ivy could see that the storm raging above them had worsened.

Ross followed her gaze and scowled. 'We should head back to the lodge soon,' he warned.

'Can we see the mountain hares first?' Ivy begged. She knew this was probably her last chance to speak to Ross alone. Once he'd dropped her off at her cabin, it was unlikely she'd be able to trick him into spending time with her again. There was still so much to talk about, so much she wanted to know. 'They're one of my favourite animals,' she lied.

'Which is why they were number nine on your colour-coded chart?' Ross asked dryly, although she detected a spark of humour there. 'Fine. We can take a look, but I'm not sure if we'll see any today. They tend to burrow when it's cold and can be difficult to spot because they camouflage themselves in the snow. There's some of the heather you were interested in seeing up there too.' He glanced up again. 'But after we look, we're going to head back to the lodge before we get stuck out here.' He took off at a fast pace, eating up the ground, with Snowball and Moose bounding ahead, dipping in and out of the trees as they played games with each other.

Ivy broke into a trot trying to keep up. 'Is there something I should know about you and Miriam? Why are you estranged?'

'Still?' Ross stopped and turned so he could face Ivy. He stared down at her for a few moments, his eyes flickering across her face, then he nodded as if he'd made a decision. 'I'm going to tell you something about my grandmother. I don't normally share but perhaps this will help you understand my position and leave this alone.' He let out a long breath. 'Miriam Ballentine became my legal guardian when I was twelve, after my parents were both killed in a sailing accident,' he said, his voice low and even.

Ivy took a step towards him, saw Moose and Snowball do the same. It was as if they could hear something in his voice, something that told them what he was saying hurt.

'I heard about the accident, I'm very sorry.'

Ross frowned. 'It was a long time ago,' he said. 'Although on days like these when everything gets stirred up it feels like yesterday.'

Ivy could understand that. She swallowed, feeling guilty.

'I was...' He hesitated. 'On the boat with them. Simon was meant to come but he ended up going to a party with some of his friends, so it was just the three of us.'

'I had no idea,' Ivy said, her cheeks paling. 'Miriam hasn't really talked about...' She waved a palm and Ross nodded.

'She was never that good at discussing it. I think she believes expressing her feelings is beneath her. In her world, it happened and we all had to move on and focus on what was important.'

'What happened exactly?' Ivy asked, partly because she wanted to know, but partly because she sensed Ross needed to tell her.

'We hit a storm,' Ross said, as a gust of wind blew through the trees, making them both flinch. 'It came out of nowhere. Mam and Da were experienced sailors but we must have hit something that had been drifting because the boat started taking on water.' His eyes fixed on something behind Ivy as if he'd travelled back in time. 'They sent a distress signal, made sure I had a life jacket – but, somehow, it had lost its buoyancy.' He winced.

'That's awful,' Ivy said, her tone low.

He jerked his head. 'The boat went down really fast and I only realised the life jacket was useless when we hit the water and I began to go under the waves.' Ross swiped a shaky hand across his mouth.

Ivy wondered if he was recalling how it had felt to have the water rising above his nose, how terrified he would have been when he couldn't breathe. She considered telling him to stop, but she wanted to hear this. Suspected Ross needed to get all of it out too.

'My mother gave me her life jacket and my father tried to use his for both of them.' His voice lowered. 'I can only guess what happened because I don't remember much from that point. I only know the storm was so bad the rescue helicopter almost didn't find me. When I got winched to safety, I begged them to keep looking for my parents, and they did, for a while... but their bodies were never recovered.'

'I'm so sorry,' Ivy whispered.

Ross paused as if steeling himself. 'I wasn't a good swimmer,' he said flatly. 'Simon's always been far more competitive than me, better at that kind of thing. I often wonder what would have happened if he'd been in the boat with us too.' He shut his eyes.

'What could he have done? He wasn't that much older than you,' she said, her voice almost a whisper.

'We'll never know.' When Ross spoke again his voice was toneless. 'All I know is I was a young boy at the time. Devastated from the loss, in need of affection and guidance through my grief and guilt. But Miriam...' He shook his head. 'I think she blamed me. All that seemed to matter was my brother Simon and the legacy he was going to inherit. It felt like he was the only important one.'

'I'm sure that's not true...' Ivy trailed off, thinking about the older woman and how the estate did seem to mean everything to her – that and maintaining the family lineage. She was very focused on running the estate, on managing the grants and business accounts, and ensuring Simon was doing everything he should. Ivy had even heard Miriam talking to Simon recently about marrying into the right circles, preserving the bloodline. She hadn't heard the outcome of the conversation but there had been a few slammed doors. Ivy couldn't imagine Miriam finding time for a grieving child.

Ross cleared his throat, seemingly working his way through the emotions swamping him. 'My parents used to take us everywhere together, but Miriam left me behind. As she groomed my brother for his duties, took him away on trips, I was left to my own devices.'

The edge of Ivy's mouth twisted. 'That's... I'm so sorry.'

He shrugged. 'After a few years it became normal and I honestly didn't mind. I stopped trying to connect with my family, and realised it was better for all of us if I spent my time with the groundskeeping team. The staff changed regularly but whoever was working let me hang around.' He lifted a shoulder. 'Maybe Miriam encouraged it because it meant I wasn't there as a reminder of what had happened, or perhaps she really wasn't interested in me being under her feet. But they taught me about trees, native flowers and shrubs, helped me develop an interest in what I do now...' He looked around and his face cleared. 'I love being outdoors, it's the only place I feel... right.'

Ivy nodded. She understood that too, although this was the first time in a year that she'd let herself admit it. Not that that would change anything. She let out a breath. 'What about your brother, what about Simon?'

Ross looked weary. 'He was very tied up with learning to be a Laird. He had to keep our grandmother happy and there wasn't time for a younger brother.' He gazed into the trees, the lines at the edges of his eyes deepening, and Ivy thought she could see pain etched into the crevices, wondered if anyone had ever tried to smooth them out. 'I often wondered if they both blamed me. I think in their place I would have.' He nodded.

'Why? It wasn't your fault,' Ivy said, shocked.

'Wasn't it?' Ross murmured and there was something in his voice that made Ivy ache for him. 'In the end I forced myself not to care and stopped wondering why they'd essentially abandoned me. After university I left and didn't return. It was better that way.' His voice was firm. 'Better for all of us.'

Ivy stared at him, unsure of what to say.

'I hope now you know everything, you'll understand why I'm not interested in returning to the castle. I didn't matter then and I'm not interested in suddenly mattering now. I don't want those feelings stirred up and I'm very sure Miriam doesn't really want me to be Laird.'

'I... I'm... I'm sorry for what you went through but—'

'You still think there's a chance of a happily ever after?' Ross asked gently, gazing at her, his eyes wide.

'Perhaps.' She looked pensive. 'I wonder if you and your grandmother are more alike than you realise. Years can change people, make them see the world in a different light. I don't believe in leaving something festering like this for so many years.' She stared at him. 'Surely you'd like to see Miriam and your brother again?' They were his family, the only family he had.

'I really wouldn't, Ivy,' Ross grunted. 'I appreciate what you're trying to do but some things really can't be healed. You need to go back to the castle to tell Miriam I'm not interested. I think you'll find if you do, she'll be relieved.'

He held Ivy's eyes and she fought to contain her breath. She could see hurt in his expression but had no idea how to ease it or make it right. Had even less idea of why she wanted to. She opened her mouth and Ross shook his head. Then he turned away and started walking again.

'I didn't share my story with you because I wanted sympathy,' he said, his voice hard. 'I'm explaining why I'm not going back to the castle. My grandmother doesn't really want me and there's nothing for me there.'

'There's your family,' Ivy blurted before she could stop herself.

He turned and his whisky-brown eyes narrowed, making Ivy wish she could swallow her words.

'I have no family.'

They finished the walk in silence, and Ivy mulled over what she'd learned, looking for a clue as to how she could find a way through the tangled mess of hurt. Perhaps Miriam had changed her mind – maybe she regretted the way she'd treated her youngest grandson. Things might work out if they could only have a conversation – and perhaps Simon and Ross could be reunited too.

Then again, was she wrong to force this? She hated the idea of leaving a family in pain. But if bringing it up over and over would hurt Ross, shouldn't she leave it alone?

Ivy contemplated this as Ross handed her the helmet and then pulled off his gloves so he could help her fasten hers. This time she could tell he made sure their skin didn't brush.

'I can see your mind whirring,' he said gruffly, as he stepped away and got ready to pull on his helmet. 'I sense you're not someone who likes to give up.' Through the shield in Ivy's helmet their eyes caught and held. 'On one level I admire that about you. But please don't ask me to see or speak to my grandmother again.' With that he shoved on his helmet and tugged it over his head.

Ivy climbed onto the back of the snowmobile and clutched the handles, mute, realising perhaps sometimes it might be better to leave things as they were – even if that meant she'd have to wave goodbye to the job in London and making her mother happy once and for all.

10

IVY

The ride across the fields to the place where the mountain hares roamed was stunning. Ivy held on tight as Ross carefully navigated the ground, travelling more slowly, perhaps because she'd chosen not to hold on to him this time. She didn't feel comfortable wrapping her arms around his chest again. After what he'd just shared, she needed to regroup and digest. She did take time to admire the landscape, smiling and cooing when they slid past three metal reindeer ornaments shimmering prettily on a hill. The snow was still heavy and everywhere Ivy looked, she saw mounds of it, covering fences, gates, shrubs, trees. Even the large wooden barns they slid past were enveloped in white.

Ross pulled the snowmobile to a stop beside the bottom of a large hill. He waited while she climbed off too, watching his pets explore the ground in between the rocks. 'There's a heath just up from here but be careful please, the path is gravelly,' Ross instructed, taking the helmet from her and placing it beside his. 'I'll bring the picnic Bonnibell made – there's somewhere close by where we can shelter while we wait.' He hesitated as he took a closer look at her face. 'Are you okay? You look a little pale.'

'I'm okay,' Ivy insisted, clearing her throat. She didn't want to tell him how much his story had affected her, suspected he might decide she was trying to manipulate him. 'Let's go, these mountain hares aren't going to find themselves.'

Ross studied her for a beat, his mouth twitching at the corner as if he were trying to appreciate her weak attempt at humour. 'Fine, but after we see them, we're going to go back to the lodge. The weather's definitely worse and it's a long journey – we're as far north of the grounds as we can get.' He whistled and his pets thundered towards them and then over-took, following a narrow pathway along the edge of the bottom of the hill, clearly well-versed with where they were headed.

'They love it here,' Ivy remarked.

He grunted, then perhaps thought better of his answer because he added, 'Yes.'

'I didn't realise wild boars could be pets,' Ivy said, speeding up when the path opened out again so she could walk with Ross side by side. 'How did you train it?'

'Him,' Ross filled in. 'And that wasn't me, it was Moose. He found Snowball when he was a piglet, just a few weeks old. He'd been abandoned by his mother for some reason and was close to my cabin, out in the woods. Moose brought him home.' He chuckled. 'I had no idea what to do at first, but they bonded. Snowball thinks of Moose as his mam, da, brother, and every-thing in between. They sleep, eat, play together and Snowball does whatever Moose says. Snowball is housetrained, although I've built him his own den near my house. He's really affec-tionate and fairly obedient. When he doesn't listen to me, Moose steps in.' The smile he gifted her was open and quite stunning.

'You love them,' she said, her insides warming.

'I suppose you could say they're my family. I'm it for them, I don't have to question my place,' he said as his smile fell, and he glanced ahead. 'It's not far now, there's a small cave where we can shelter and sit.'

He tracked upfront and Ivy followed. All the while her mind was whirring. She knew she wasn't going to try to persuade Ross to speak to Miriam again, but the thought of returning to Hawthorn Castle empty-handed was making her anxious. She swallowed, imagining Miriam's reaction and her mother's disappointment when the promised new career didn't materialise. She'd fail her mum again, condemn her to a life spent worrying about her... She had no idea how to come to terms with that.

Pausing for a moment, Ivy breathed in, relishing the icy freshness of the air, feeling herself calm, as if she was being anchored. Then she nodded – she'd just have to figure out something else.

Ross pointed to a cave and guided Ivy inside, before indicating a series of tree stumps on the floor. He stroked Moose and then Snowball before taking a seat.

'Do you want something to eat?' Ross asked. He opened up the backpack again and drew out the picnic Bonnibell had made.

Ivy could smell mince pies and her stomach grumbled. 'Sounds lovely,' she said and watched as he put a mince pie on a plate and poured out more hot chocolate, before handing the food and drink to her. Snowball got up and wandered closer, his brown nose catching the tempting scents.

'Moose, why don't you two take a walk?' Ross suggested firmly and the golden retriever got up and immediately trotted out of the cave. Snowball took one last yearning look at Ivy's plate before following. 'Keep your eyes on the meadow,' Ross advised as he bit into a mince pie and swallowed. 'If you look carefully you'll be able to see the mountain hare from their long black ears. They tend to bury themselves in the snow so you'll have to look carefully. I've got binoculars, if you'd like to use them?'

Ivy nodded and Ross handed them to her. They fell silent. She wanted to ask him more about Miriam and what had happened, but it didn't seem fair. She concentrated on her search but couldn't see much through the lenses aside from snow – and somehow, she didn't want to spot a hare yet because it would mean Ross would want to take her back to Christmas Lodge. She wasn't ready to be parted from him yet.

Then she heard a high-pitched yelp and Ross shot to his feet. 'That's Moose!' he said urgently, sprinting out of the cave.

Ivy put the mug and plate on the ground and followed. Ross had already reached the dog as she ran to catch up. The retriever was licking his right paw.

'He's hurt, I think he cut himself on something,' Ross said, crouching so he could see better. 'It's bleeding.' Scarlet droplets bloomed across the snow. 'I think I can treat it but I need to get him back to the cabin so I can bandage it.' He glanced over his shoulder and his forehead bunched when his eyes met Ivy's. 'You're going to have to come with me. It's too far back to the lodge and my place is only a few minutes from here. I don't want to leave this wound open for longer than necessary.' The dog whined again and Ross pulled a face. 'He's going to need to ride on the snowmobile with us – are you okay with him sitting on your lap? I'll need you to hold onto him. I'll go slowly,' he added quickly, worry in his voice.

'Of course,' Ivy said. 'If it's easier, I could walk?'

Surprise flickered across Ross's face. 'That's not necessary,' he murmured, rising to his feet and scooping Moose into his arms before nodding back up the track that would lead them to the snowmobile.

. . .

IT TOOK ALL of ten minutes on the snowmobile to reach Ross's cabin from where they were parked. He'd carried the dog to the vehicle and then driven slowly as Ivy had kept one hand on the handlebar and the other wrapped around Moose. The dog had whimpered a few times and kept checking over his shoulder to make sure Snowball was still in sight. When they'd travelled a few metres inside some dense woodland and drew up in front of Ross's house, she felt him expel all the pent-up anxiety he'd been holding.

Ross's cabin was beautiful outside and Ivy could see the building consisted of two floors with enormous windows that would probably offer stunning views of the surrounding wildlife and trees when it wasn't snowing. There was a shed to the right of the structure and a small clearing in front, where Ross obviously chopped firewood.

'Let's get inside,' Ross said, hopping off the vehicle and lifting Moose from Ivy's lap, dodging Snowball as the wild boar trotted ahead, zigzagging between his legs, clearly stressed. Ross opened the front door and strode inside, leaving it ajar so Ivy could follow him.

The hallway was large, with black coat hooks set across the right wall and rows of wooden racks laid out underneath where shoes, wellingtons and various footwear had been arranged. Ivy quickly pulled off her snow boots and put them beside a pair of large walking boots, before hanging up the snowsuit too. Then she turned and stopped when she noticed the multiple framed pictures which had been hung on the opposite wall. There were a series of black and white photos of the facade and grounds of Hawthorn Castle; a couple of relaxed shots of Miriam by herself, one where she was reading a book; a small picture of a couple Ivy presumed were Ross's parents; one photo of Simon and a painting of the Ballentine coat of arms.

Did this mean Ross wasn't as immune to his family as he'd said? If the man really didn't care about reconnecting with

Miriam and Simon, surely he wouldn't want the constant reminders of them? The fact that these pictures were hanging in his house made Ivy pause. Did he miss them? Was his desire to walk away more about fear of rejection? Should she reconsider and have another shot at convincing Ross to speak with his grandmother? She knew Miriam could be cold and unsympathetic, but surely she must have missed her grandson to have sent Ivy here. She didn't believe her boss was entirely without feelings, or that this whole errand to find Ross was simply born from a desire to tick an etiquette box.

Ivy wandered through the hallway into what was obviously the main room. It was open plan, with high ceilings, a huge brick fireplace at the far end framed with a long sofa and mismatched chairs, some of which had been turned to face the view. A jumble of cushions and blankets in sunny oranges, reds and yellows had been spread across the furniture, and multiple mismatched lamps were dotted on random tables, which she could imagine throwing a cosy glow across the room when it grew dark.

The kitchen was situated at the opposite end of the large room to where Ivy was standing, with grey cabinets under a long black granite counter. There was a breakfast bar set to the side with a scatter of cooking implements on it: knives, chopping boards and a large saucepan which looked like it needed washing up. Ivy wandered to the counter, contemplating filling a bowl with soapy water, and spotted a bottle of whisky on the sideboard, realising it was the same brand as the one Miriam drank.

Had the man subconsciously filled his home with as many reminders of his life at the castle as he could?

It was then Ivy spotted three small picture frames on a round oak table to the left of the fireplace. One of them contained a family shot of Miriam, his parents, and two young boys who she presumed were Simon and Ross. Another was of the brothers hugging beside a large lake, and there was one of just Simon, standing outside of the castle. She stared at them before nodding. Whatever Ross had told her, it was obvious he hadn't really put his family behind him. That they mattered to him more than he'd said.

'I think Moose is going to be okay,' Ross said, sounding relieved as he strode from a room connected to the kitchen. The dog hopped after him, putting all his weight on one leg, his right paw covered in gauze and bandages. Snowball followed too and they both went to slump on the fluffy rust-coloured rug in front of the fireplace.

'We should get you back to the lodge,' Ross said. He wandered to the window to peruse the view. 'That weather doesn't look good though.' He pulled a face and put his hands on his hips.

The snow was so heavy now it was impossible to see more than a few metres ahead. Even the snowmobile, which had been parked for barely fifteen minutes, was buried under a few inches already.

Ross hissed as he turned to look at Ivy. 'I think we might have to wait this out.' He grimaced. 'At least until the snowfall slows. I can leave Moose and Snowball here for a while, but I can't risk dropping you back and getting stuck at the lodge – and I don't want to take either of them out in this. Moose's bandage needs to stay dry at least for tonight to give him the chance to heal.'

'I'm happy to wait out the weather,' Ivy said, slumping onto one of the chairs. Perhaps she could find some way of winding their conversation back to Miriam.

Feeling tired suddenly, she shut her eyes and leaned her head back on the sofa. She must have fallen asleep because when she woke, the fire was glowing and she had a blanket draped across her knees.

Mortified, she sat straighter and blinked herself awake. 'Sorry,' she said through a yawn, swiping her face.

'You were obviously tired.' Ross poked at the fire before squinting outside to where the sky was now an inky black. There was a long string of white lights shimmering in the darkness, bouncing in the wind. 'The weather's not let up at all. If anything, it's got worse. I contacted Connell on my walkie-talkie while you were asleep and told him we're both safe but stuck. I'm going to try to take you back to your cabin later if things get any better, but...' He pulled a face. 'In the meantime, I have to pop out. I've a friend...' He cleared his throat, his cheeks reddening, and Ivy felt an odd sensation – as if there was a screw suddenly tightening in the middle of her ribs. 'Someone I try to visit a couple of times a day. I need to check on him.'

Him. The screw loosened an inch. Ivy realised he was probably talking about his friend, Grizzle.

'Will you be okay if I leave you here?' Ross asked.

'No!' Ivy shot up from the sofa. 'Sorry, but absolutely not, I'm going with you.'

'I can't take the snowmobile,' Ross warned. 'I'm planning to walk. It's almost a mile – I'll be leaving Moose and Snowball here,' he said.

'I've watched enough horror movies to know what happens to young women who get left alone in a strange house in the middle of nowhere. Besides, this could be some ploy to scare me into going back to the lodge on my own.' Ivy shuddered.

'I wouldn't do that,' Ross muttered.

'Whatever, I'm not staying here by myself. If you won't let me come, I'll just follow you.' Ivy didn't want to be left here alone and if they stayed together, she might be able to find her way back to the conversation about Miriam.

Ross looked unhappy. 'If that's what you want.' His eyes flickered down Ivy's body, making the surface of her skin vibrate.

'You're going to have to dress up again. If anything, it's colder than it was when we were outside earlier. I don't want anything to happen to you.' His lips pinched. 'Also, you should know, my friend is... not always welcoming. You should probably be prepared. His bark is worse than his bite, but he's got this dog...' He hesitated then winced. 'And *his* bite is definitely much worse.'

'Are you trying to put me off joining you?' Ivy asked, suspiciously. 'Because you should know that's not going to work.'

Ross studied her for a few moments before his shoulders slumped and he nodded. 'Then stay close and don't get lost.' With that, he turned and headed towards the hallway, leaving Ivy feeling even more confused – because this was a man who wouldn't speak to his own grandmother, but who'd brave bad weather to check on a friend.

Suddenly Ivy had no idea what kind of man Ross Ballentine was. She only knew that with every hour that passed, she liked him a little more.

11

ROSS

Grizzle's cabin looked dark when Ivy and Ross approached, but there was enough of a glow from one of the side windows to suggest the older man was probably still awake. It had been a difficult walk, especially since Ross had been carrying tools and had needed to take Ivy's hand a few times, aiming to guide her along the safest route so she didn't trip or fall. He didn't want to deal with any more injuries. He just wanted this over with so he could get her back to Snowman Chalet and avoid any more questions – and yet another tsunami of guilt.

After hearing about Simon leaving Hawthorn Castle, he was confused. Why had Miriam sent Ivy to see him? Did his grandmother really want him back? He shook his head, quieting down the flicker of hope swirling in his chest which was driving him crazy. He just needed to check Grizzle was okay and get Ivy back to the lodge as quickly as possible. But the snow was still falling in thick icy flakes, and the longer they were outside, the more he was giving up on the idea of delivering her home. He'd kept a safe distance from his family for years, barely thought about them from one day to the next. Now they were seeping into his thoughts and everything he did or saw seemed to remind him of them. How in hell had he got himself into this situation?

As they drew closer to the door of the hermit's cabin, the pug began to bark and moments later, the four-legged beast shot out, yapping and vaulting across the snow, making a beeline for Ross's boots. Then, he sniffed, seemingly catching Ivy's scent. All of a sudden the dog stopped yelping and its ears pricked up. Ross tried to step in front of Ivy, aiming to protect her from the miniature fiend, but the woman side-stepped him and bent down as Bowser skidded up.

'Protect your face!' Ross shouted, trying to step in between them again.

'Is this the scary dog you warned me about?' Ivy asked dryly as the hellhound stuck its nose into her gloved hand, then put a paw on her thigh and tried to lick her cheek.

Seriously?

'That's not a dog, it's a demon from hell,' Ross grumbled, watching him carefully. 'A contrary one at that. I brought treats last week and he still tried to nip my leg. You bring him nothing and...' He gaped, shocked by the creature's reaction. 'Bowser, this is so embarrassing.' Ross shook his head in disgust as his arch enemy continued to slobber all over Ivy while simultaneously eyeing him with a menacing expression.

'I'll leave you two lovebirds alone,' he huffed once he was sure Ivy was safe. He shook his head as he marched to the porch and carefully opened the damaged door. He'd brought tools in the bag, guessing it would only take a few minutes to rehang the hinges. Perhaps Ivy could distract Grizzle while he worked? 'It's just me,' he called out as he entered.

'Here again?' the older man growled. 'I thought at least the storm would keep you away.'

He was still in the same chair and the fire which Ross had

left burning this morning had gone out. The air was freezing again and there was an odd scorched smell.

'Did something catch fire?' Ross asked, striding inside, his heart hammering. He switched on another lamp and felt his whole body slacken when he saw everything was intact.

'Ach, it was that casserole you saw in my fridge this morning. Mairi must have overcooked it before she left it there. I put it in the Aga, but it was burned when I took it out,' he snorted.

'Didn't she include cooking instructions?' Ross asked, aware he'd taped the information to the edge of the container.

'Lad, I didn't bother reading those,' Grizzle said. 'I threw the lot in the bin, along with the dish. That woman...' he complained, although the mere mention of her had brought a flood of colour to his neck and face.

Ross shut his eyes and took in a deep, calming breath. The meal hadn't been burned when he left it, which meant the hermit had ignored the instructions, or not read them at all. Ross would have to fish the meal out of the bin later when Grizzle was otherwise occupied to see if the casserole dish could be saved.

'You must be starving. Shall I fix you some pasta?' Ross knew there were a couple of packs in the cupboard along with a tin of tomatoes because he'd left them there himself. 'I know I could eat.'

'*I'm* not hungry and I'm perfectly capable of cooking for myself. You should go back to your own place if you want to be fed,' Grizzle snapped as the door nudged open and Ivy walked in with Bowser, who was gazing at her adoringly. 'Who's that?' The older man sniffed. 'Smells better than you, lad.'

'I'm Ivy Heart,' Ivy said, as she took in the dim room and wizened old man hunched in front of the fireplace.

She didn't say a word, but Ross could tell she was taken aback. He felt a twinge of regret that he hadn't warned her about what to expect. He wasn't used to sharing, didn't feel comfortable unpeeling layers of his life. Perhaps he was just worried Ivy wouldn't like what she saw? The thought had him taking a step away because he shouldn't care.

'I'm a friend of Ross's,' she said, widening her eyes.

Ross stared at her standing under the bright overhead light, and was weirdly reminded of the lush summer leaves that grew on the oak trees dotted around the resort. He could almost smell them as he gazed at her, remembering how they looked when dappled sunlight slid between the branches. His heart thumped. Annoyed, Ross looked away and shook himself as Grizzle let out a surprised cough.

'Ach, well the lad could do with a few. He's obviously lonely because he's always barging in here annoying me,' Grizzle complained.

'And delivering your eBay purchases,' Ross reminded him, his tone teasing.

Grizzle sniffed again and waved a hand. 'Come closer lass.'

When Ivy complied, the older man stood so he could get a better look. He would have been taller than Ivy once, Ross realised with a jolt, but his hunched shoulders meant they were now almost the same height. His friend was getting old, and suddenly the idea of him living out here alone bothered Ross. What would happen to Grizzle if Ross wasn't around?

'You're nicer looking than the lad.'

At Bowser's sharp bark of agreement, Grizzle chuckled. It was the first time Ross had heard that sound from his friend in a while. Ross knew how it felt to be lonely, but the older man insisted he wasn't – despite that he'd recently begun to manufacture a stream of excuses to ensure Ross visited every day.

'You can stay,' Grizzle declared to Ivy. 'Do you want something to eat?' He rubbed his stomach. 'I'm hungry.'

'You just said—' Ross said sharply.

'I could eat,' Ivy jumped in, pinning Ross with another odd look. 'Shall I cook something?'

Grizzle shrugged, his face brightening. 'I'm sure whatever you make will be tastier than anything Mairi's been leaving,' he growled.

Ivy gave Ross a quizzical look.

'I've not got much in,' Grizzle continued as Ross widened his eyes at Ivy and shook his head, holding his breath until she nodded. 'There's pasta, some tins of tomatoes, chilis, garlic and a few herbs on my windowsill.' He counted the ingredients on his fingers and Ross was surprised his friend had any idea about what he had. 'It would be nice to eat something edible for a change.'

Ross fought the desire to correct Grizzle – his cooking was great.

'An arrabbiata then. That's one of my favourite dishes.' Ivy pulled off her hat and gloves and started towards the kitchen. Then she stopped and pulled a horrified face when she spotted the pots of herbs beside a drooping cyclamen Ross had given Grizzle and an azalea Bonnibell had gifted him too. 'These could all do with some water,' she admonished, sounding upset.

'Ach lass, I've never had green fingers when it comes to anything indoors. In my world plants are meant to live outside,' Grizzle said. 'You feel free to do whatever you need to revive them. I'll bet some of them are starting to look as wrinkled as me.' He watched intently, sliding his new pink glasses up his nose as Ivy went to tend to them. Her movements were almost reverent as she carefully took each plant from the windowsill before picking off the dead leaves and filling the sink so she could place the pots in it.

'Watering them from the bottom usually works best,' she murmured.

Ross realised she was talking to herself. He could have watched her all day, but instead he carefully put down the bag of tools and went to work on the door, quickly changing the screws on the hinges and adding a few extras to make it more secure. He took special care not to make any noise in case Grizzle noticed and ordered him to stop.

When the pasta and sauce were bubbling on the stove, Ivy checked the plants again. The leaves were perking up and she offered them a smile and carefully put them back on the windowsill before setting to work lighting the fire. Ross was about to offer to help, but she must have realised because she shook her head. Instead, he took a seat on the chair beside Grizzle, and linked his fingers when Bowser eyed them speculatively.

'It's been a while since I had any proper visitors,' Grizzle confided, watching Ivy work.

'What does that make me?' Ross asked grumpily.

Grizzle shrugged. 'The lad visits every day, but he only comes to see me because he's got nowhere better to be,' he said to Ivy, his tone conspiratorial. 'It's not normal for a man his age to spend so much time alone or with a *bodach* like me.'

'*Bodach?*' Ivy asked, a smile lighting her face and making something inside Ross's chest bounce.

'Ach, it means a grumpy old man,' Grizzle translated, chuckling before his attention turned to Ross again. 'Perhaps now you're here you'll be able to keep him out of my hair.'

Ross let out a heavy breath as Ivy raised a speculative eyebrow in his direction. 'I got the impression Mr Ballentine wasn't keen on my company. He seems perfectly content keeping himself to himself,' she said lightly as she returned to the small kitchen to check on the bubbling pots.

Ross could see she found the cantankerous old man amusing – although he wasn't sure he liked that it was at his own expense.

'Ach that's all blather and nonsense,' Grizzle mumbled, squinting at Ross and shaking his head. 'Dig deeper and you'll discover he's lonely. Living in the middle of nowhere on his own. It's not natural.'

Ross grunted, although his friend's observations hurt. He wasn't lonely all the time, and spending time by himself was better than the alternative. Besides, he liked his life. Didn't he?

'But *you* live out here on your own, don't you?' Ivy probed, adding more seasoning to the pan before she knelt to put another log onto the fire.

'Yep, I've been here for almost forty years,' Grizzle said proudly, puffing up his chest as he slumped back into the rocking chair, making himself comfortable. Ross had never seen him so relaxed around company. It was fascinating and baffling to watch the transformation.

'Why?' Ivy asked.

The question had the older man swinging back in his seat.

'Because I dinnae like people,' Grizzle blustered, calling Bowser over and taking his time fussing over the dog. 'The lad's tolerable,' he said cheekily. 'But I've always been happy with just me and my dog.'

'Always?' Ivy pressed.

The older man considered that for a moment.

'Aye, perhaps not always. There was someone once.' His eyes shifted to a smattering of framed pictures on the mantlepiece.

Ross stayed perfectly still. Grizzle wasn't usually one to confide. What was it about Ivy that made usually taciturn people open up? He watched as she rose and went to look at the photos. He'd never paid much attention to them. Most featured Grizzle when he was younger, with a variety of men and women – people Ross had assumed were friends. There were some of the older man with his family, none of whom were alive now.

'But some of us are meant to live alone.' Grizzle's eyes slid away from Ivy, who was still studying the pictures, and he glared at Ross. 'While others are too *bucksturdie—*'

'What?' Ivy asked, sounding confused.

The older man chuckled. 'Obstinate,' he clarified. 'To realise they need more than an old man and a couple of pets to bloom.'

'I've always found plants thrive in company,' Ivy said, turning away from the pictures. 'I believe people are the same.'

'I like my life,' Ross muttered to himself, although he could hear the lie in his voice. It was easier when he didn't think about it. But having Ivy here meant he was starting to see through the cracks.

'You might like it more if you had people in it,' Ivy said lightly before glancing around the room. 'You could really do with some Christmas decorations in here,' she said to Grizzle.

The subject change was welcome and Ross felt himself relax a notch.

'Aye, there's a box of them in my back bedroom, but my eyes aren't as good as they once were so I can't find them.' Grizzle pushed the glasses back up his nose. 'Besides, I've nae got anyone to put them up.'

Ross tensed. 'I'd have done it if you'd asked,' he said, exasperated. He wasn't trying to impress Ivy, but he didn't like looking bad in front of her either.

The older man snorted and waved a hand towards the door on the opposite side of the room. Ross hadn't been in there for months, but he knew it was a spare bedroom, understood that was where the older man usually kept the treasures he collected and cleaned before selling them on.

'I'm not sure we should do it now,' Ross jumped in, glancing out the window and wincing as a gust of wind suddenly battered the glass. Sheets of snow billowed past on squalls, obscuring everything in their path. 'We're going to have to leave as soon as we've eaten, I can see the wind's picked up and I think the walk back to my cabin is going to be challenging.'

'Tomorrow then?' Ivy suggested, beaming at Grizzle, her eyes suddenly sparkling. 'I'm happy to return and do it for you.'

'I can do it,' Ross insisted, his lips pinching.

'Ach, Christmas decorations need a woman's touch, lad,' Grizzle said, glancing between them, his eyes lighting up, clearly enjoying stirring things.

'I thought you'd be heading back to the castle tomorrow? I think we've said all we need to,' Ross said to Ivy. The longer she was here, the more he was going to mull over things he didn't want to think about. And yet the thought of her leaving gave him an odd burning sensation in the centre of his chest.

'I'm happy to stay for a few more days.' Ivy gave Ross a thoughtful look. 'So it won't be any trouble for me to come back,' she said to Grizzle.

Ross let out an irritated grunt.

'That'll be grand, lass,' Grizzle declared. 'The lad will bring you.'

'I'm working tomorrow,' Ross said quickly.

'The day after then.' Grizzle chuckled. 'You don't know how good it is to have fresh company. There hasn't been anyone in this house since...'

'I visited seven hours ago?' Ross asked innocently.

'It's nice that Ross comes to see you so often,' Ivy said, her tone protective.

Ross sat back in his seat, stunned to hear Ivy jump to his defence. Ross waited for Grizzle to shoot her down, but instead the older man shrugged and slowly nodded. Ross watched as Grizzle began to chatter with Ivy again, his expression animated as she headed back into the kitchen and took three bowls from a cupboard, ready to serve the pasta. His friend looked happy – the flush on his cheeks had turned rosy. For a beat Ross contemplated whether Ivy should stay at the resort.

Then he shook his head. He couldn't risk allowing her to hang around. He wasn't going to bring her back to Grizzle's. Instead, he'd do everything he could to get her to return to Hawthorn Castle as soon as he could.

She was only here to get him to speak to his grandmother. And whatever happened, however drawn to her he was, it was vital that he remembered that.

12

IVY

It was freezing outside and Ivy tugged her hat over her ears as the wind raged, hurling ice and snowflakes into her face. She carefully descended the steps leading from Grizzle's house and twisted around as Ross shut the door and checked it was secure, ensuring the hinges he'd just replaced held firm.

He gave Ivy a thoughtful grimace as he joined her and pointed right, nodding that she should walk ahead. She wanted to talk to him, to ask more about his friendship with Grizzle, hoping any titbit about the relationship might help her to understand him more. But the gale was now so loud she could barely hear above its windy shrieks. She headed for the woods instead, relaxing as the birches and firs began to take the brunt of the gusts and the air stilled a little. Ivy looked up and saw snowflakes sneaking between gaps in the canopy as branches got separated by the wild storm. She took in a deep breath and felt the cold air sting her throat, relishing the sensation. Was it odd that she felt more alive in this moment than she had in the last year?

'The weather's got worse.' Ross sped up until they were

walking side by side. 'But I'm still hoping I'll be able to get you back to Snowman Chalet tonight.'

Ivy felt the smile slide from her face. The man was determined to get her out of his hair. Yet after seeing the photos of his family at the house, and hearing Grizzle's take on how lonely Ross was, she was more resolved than ever to stay.

'I'm not sure I fancy our chances,' she said, looking up into the trees just as her right foot hooked into a stalk of brambles and she started to go over. Ross caught the back of the snowsuit and guided her to her feet.

'Careful,' he warned. 'I'm almost out of bandages.' He gave her a half smile as if to confirm he'd just made a joke.

She glanced up again soon after and this time her attention caught on an enormous oak tree with beautiful twisty branches and her foot snared on a rock. She cursed as she began to stumble forwards again. Ross grabbed her hand before she could fall all the way and held on.

'I'm not normally clumsy,' she promised, keeping her eyes on the ground as she gripped his large fingers through her glove. 'There's just so much to look at. It's stunning.' And it had been a while since she'd let herself get caught up – let herself appreciate anything outdoors.

'Not everyone thinks so,' Ross said, slowing a little. 'Or perhaps that's not true. I think many don't notice what's in front of their noses.' He stopped and pointed right to a small clearing. 'In the spring, that whole area is covered in Scottish primroses – Grizzle told me they've been growing here for over four decades.'

'I'll bet that's something.' Ivy shut her eyes as she tried to recall the Latin name. '*Primula scotica*,' she whispered, delighted the translation had come so fast. She tried to imagine how the flowers would look, wished she'd be here to see them bloom. She swallowed, pulling her mind away from the colourful images. 'Is Grizzle having trouble with his eyesight?'

she asked abruptly. 'When we were there just now, I could see you were worried and those pink glasses...'

'I know.' Ross pulled a face. 'His vision has deteriorated recently. But he won't visit the optician's to get himself checked out.'

'Why not?' Ivy asked.

Ross shrugged. 'He's never liked accepting help. He keeps buying glasses on eBay in the hope that he'll hit on the right prescription. I'll expect he'll have already ordered a dozen now we've left.'

'You worry about him?' she guessed.

'Only recently. I've been concerned he's not eating properly.' Ross fell silent and all Ivy could hear was the wind and crunch of their footsteps in the snow. 'It's why I've been leaving him food.' Ivy could hear guilt in his voice.

'Didn't Grizzle say someone called Mairi is cooking for him?' Ivy asked, as she followed, trying to recall exactly what had been said. She did remember the look on Ross's face when she'd been about to ask his friend about it.

It took Ross a drawn-out moment to respond.

'I'm the one preparing the meals, I'm just pretending it's her,' he finally admitted. 'I feel bad about it, but it's the only way I could think of getting him to accept the food. He complains, but he eats it. Besides, it's only temporary. Just until he goes to the optician's, or orders the right glasses. Sounds bad, doesn't it?' He winced.

'It sounds like you're a good friend,' she admitted. Ross was a kind man – and the more she got to know him, the more she wanted to know more. 'What will happen if Mairi and Grizzle ever meet up?'

'There's no chance of that. He avoids the village and as far as I know she feels the same way.'

'Have you known Grizzle for a long time?' she asked.

'Aye.' Ross seemed to relax as the subject changed. 'He took me under his wing when I moved to the resort, a few years after I finished university – over five years ago now.'

'How did you meet?' She wouldn't use the information against him, but understanding why the older man mattered so much might help with her quest to at least get Ross to talk to Miriam.

He snorted. 'That's an embarrassing story.'

'Tell me.' Ivy grinned.

'I bumped into him when I was camping out by the woods at the resort, testing an adventure I run most weeks now.'

'What did he do?' she asked. She could see lights in the distance and guessed they were approaching Ross's house. She tried to slow her steps because she wasn't ready for their conversation to end, suspected as soon as they got indoors, Ross would start talking about getting her back to Snowman Chalet again.

'He shoved a stick into my tent and asked if I'd lost my mind,' Ross explained. 'When I told him I was sleeping there on purpose he called me an eejit.' He grinned suddenly. 'Then he told me I was going to freeze to death and disappeared into the woods. I thought I'd never see him again, but Grizzle sought me out the next day.' He went ahead, guiding her along a narrowing track, still holding on tightly to her hand.

'Why?' Ivy asked, enjoying the story. 'To check you were still alive?'

He snickered. 'If I recall correctly, he brought a basket of firewood, a blanket and a loaf of fresh bread and some cheese to share. It was the start of our friendship.' Ross paused at a tree which was blocking their path and indicated that Ivy should climb over, letting go of her hand before hopping over too. 'I often wonder if that was the moment when I started to realise not everyone was like my family.' He caught her hand again.

'And you continued to see each other?' Ivy asked, keeping her eyes fixed on the pathway so she didn't trip as Ross continued to guide her.

'Most days,' he said. 'Grizzle used to find me on the grounds, enjoyed telling me I was wrong about almost everything. I have a degree in horticulture but he decided I knew nothing.' Ross chuckled. 'I think he was mostly right. He decided to teach me about the native flora and fauna, where all the animals' habitats are. He said he couldn't let me continue to embarrass myself. That if a man was going to work for Connell Baker, he at least had to know a reindeer from a brown hare.'

Ivy hooted. 'I can imagine that.'

'He wasn't even joking,' Ross said dryly.

'You're close though?' Ivy shot back.

Ross took a moment to answer. 'In many ways he's my best friend. I've known him a long time.'

'And you help each other out?' Ivy checked.

'I help however I can.' Ross let out a frustrated sound, stopping momentarily to breathe in the night air before he began to walk again. 'Grizzle's difficult to know. It's a fine line. I think he likes me visiting, but he doesn't want to admit it, which means I have to be careful not to appear as if I'm helping too much.'

'What would happen if you weren't around?' Ivy asked, suddenly concerned. What would become of the older man if Miriam got her way and Ross was persuaded to leave?

'If I didn't visit there are others in the village who would try, but he seems to tolerate me best. Aside perhaps from you.' The trees began to thin again, revealing Ross's house and the wide patch of sparkling white land in front. 'I don't know why I'm telling you all this.'

'Perhaps it's because after today you might not see me again?' Ivy said breezily, waiting for his reaction.

'Well, I...' Ross sobered and then his eyes caught on a lumpy shape to the right of the front door. 'Dammit, that's my snowmobile,' he complained, letting go of Ivy's hand and striding towards the vehicle, which had been completely hidden by a blanket of snow. He started to swipe at it, pushing the icy layers off. 'I put a tarp over it when you were sleeping earlier, but I should have parked it in the shed. It's totally buried. It's going to be hell to move now. I'll have to dig it out.' He cursed. 'The snow's a lot thicker than I thought.' He looked up and around as if the fact that it was still blizzarding was a surprise.

Hadn't he noticed? Had he been as captivated by their conversation as she had?

'Does that mean we're not going to be able to go back to the resort?' Ivy asked hopefully.

'I guess not,' Ross grunted, looking unhappy as he trudged towards the front door.

Ivy watched, wondering if the tingles swirling around the pit of her stomach were because she had more time to fulfil her task, or because she was about to spend the night with Ross.

13

ROSS

'It's so cold out there,' Ivy observed as she practically fell through the door of Ross's house. She slumped onto the ground and pulled off her boots and his over-large coat, simultaneously stroking Snowball and Moose and chuckling as they both arrived within seconds of them coming in to greet them, demanding attention. She looked relaxed and Ross realised she was getting used to the wild boar now.

'Yep!' he agreed, unsettled that he hadn't been able to take Ivy back to the resort. 'You can sleep in the spare room – it's already made up.' He sucked in a breath and saw Ivy nod as she pulled off her snowsuit, then got up, taking time to silently study the photos on the wall before making her way further inside. Ross followed after, taking off his coat, gloves and hat too, unsure of what to expect now they were alone and back in the warm. Would Ivy ask about Miriam and Simon again? Could he avoid talking about them?

'Do you want some whisky?' he asked, trying to relax as he made his way into the kitchen and pulled out a bottle of single malt.

'Yes please,' Ivy said, taking a seat on the long sofa and grabbing a blanket to rest across her knees. He handed her a glass and went to light the fire. He wasn't tired and wouldn't be for ages. The journey to and from Grizzle's and the feelings Ivy's visit had roused would probably keep him up for hours.

He watched her take a small sip and smile. 'This is the same brand as your grandmother drinks, did you know that?' she asked softly. 'Perhaps you're more similar than you thought.'

Stunned, Ross shook his head before turning his back, and started to add wood to the grate, his stomach tense. He'd spent years locking his family out of his life. Because it was easier. He wasn't sure how he felt about the comparisons Ivy was drawing. Was even less sure about the odd feelings of hope they were stirring.

Something suddenly buzzed and Ivy grabbed her mobile from her pocket, read the screen and tutted.

'What is it?' he asked.

She twisted the phone round so he could see. 'Your grandmother. She wants an update. She's asking when you're going to talk to her. I'm showing you so you can see how much she really wants you home. This isn't about etiquette, Ross. I genuinely think she wants to make amends.'

He reluctantly looked closer and then barked out an involuntary laugh. 'Her contact name is Cruella de Vil?'

'It was a joke,' Ivy shot back, her cheeks flaming charmingly as she started to tap on the screen. 'She just... sometimes... *Argh*. You weren't supposed to see that,' she fussed, obviously embarrassed. 'Sorry, look, I've changed it. Can we pretend you never saw it?' She showed him the screen again and this time the contact read *Miriam Ballentine*.

'I don't think I'll ever forget.' But Ross knew he liked Ivy more because of it. Because it meant she had seen a little of the woman his grandmother was. Hadn't blindly decided he was the bad guy here. Why that mattered, he didn't know. 'But I'm hardly going to tell her,' he said gently, as her blush deepened and he felt the barrier he'd erected between them wavering. 'The moniker is apt. I know she's my grandmother, but...'

Ivy nodded, recovering her composure. 'I'm sure she's a difficult woman to know.'

'You're being very diplomatic.' He shook his head. 'Miriam knows what she wants and she always gets it,' he said. 'She's not very forgiving and she doesn't know how to love.' He winced. 'Sorry, I don't want to speak ill of her. She's an impressive woman – she kept the castle and estate going after my parents died. That's important to her.' It was important to him too. His family legacy mattered even if he was only ever going to enjoy it from afar.

Ivy cocked her head, her forest-green eyes penetrating. 'Did you ever consider she might be different if you met her now?' She continued to gaze at him. 'Whatever happened between you... perhaps she has regrets. Maybe things between you can be fixed. If you spoke, don't you think you could find some common ground?'

Did he really want to put himself through that? Her rejection had hurt, why would he choose to open himself up again?

'You're very persistent,' he said.

'My mother always says things are impossible until they're done.' Ivy's lips pinched. 'And I do believe almost anything can be made better if you put your mind to it.'

Her voice grew heavy and Ross turned to look at her, suddenly realising there were a lot of things about Ivy's life she hadn't shared. He didn't know much about her, aside from she was kind, her mother was important to her, and she worked for his grandmother. Suddenly that didn't seem like enough.

'Like what?' he found himself asking, regretting the words instantly because getting to know Ivy better might just make everything worse. He wanted her to leave tomorrow, didn't he? If so, why was he encouraging her to share her stories?

She stared into her drink, looking troubled. 'I don't

know… But I think it's worth considering how you might feel if your grandmother wasn't around one day and you'd decided you wanted to make up when it was too late.'

'I…'

Ross rocked back in his seat. It wasn't something he'd ever considered. Perhaps he should have after what had happened with his parents. But Miriam had always been indestructible. A force of nature. Could he imagine a world without her in it?

Ivy nodded, reading him. 'It's something to think about, isn't it?'

'Did that happen to you?' he asked quietly.

'I…' Ivy stared at him as pain flickered across her eyes. 'Not exactly and this isn't about me,' she deflected.

He nodded, swallowing his disappointment, watching Ivy knock back the rest of her drink before shifting the blanket back from her knees.

'Just think about it,' she said. 'It's getting late and I'm tired. I hope you don't mind if I turn in?'

'The spare room's on the right at the top of the stairs,' he said. 'There are some of my T-shirts in the wardrobe and a new toothbrush in the en-suite. Please help yourself.' Then he watched her head for the stairs, feeling oddly disappointed and hollow all at once.

It was for the best though. He knew that. Tomorrow she'd go back to Hawthorn Castle to tell his grandmother he wasn't interested in being Laird. Then he'd go back to living his life. But as Ivy disappeared from view, Ross found himself gazing at the spot where she'd been sitting, wondering if things would go back to normal, or if she'd managed to stir up a whole host of feelings that he was going to find it difficult to forget.

SOMETHING CRASHED over Ross's head and he began to choke, *spewing mouthfuls of unwelcome liquid from his throat before it* got as far as his lungs. It was cold. Colder than the snow he loved to ski through in the winter. Chillier than the ice pop his brother had once shoved down the back of his T-shirt when they'd been fighting. But Ross wasn't shivering. Why was that?

He tried to curl his fingers under his life jacket but they wouldn't cooperate. Instead, the waterproof coat his mam had insisted he wore while they were sailing in the storm attempted to sink his arm like it was an anchor.

Every inch of his body wanted to give up and sleep – but he wasn't ready to admit defeat. He thought about his grandmother, imagined her barking orders, insisting that it was his duty to fight and stay alert, his obligation to survive – and he was too terrified of Miriam Ballentine not to do as he was told. More afraid of her than Mother Nature it seemed...

He squinted into the waves again, searching desperately for his parents who'd been swept out of sight as their boat sank. But it was so dark and he could see nothing but black waves the size of skyscrapers. Even the flashes of lightning that haphazardly lit the sky didn't pick them out. 'Mam? Da? Please answer me,' he screamed into the wind, hoping they'd hear, choking again when water forced its way down his throat.

Then Ross thought he heard a voice above the roar of wind. 'Mam?' He squinted, but the waves spat water into his eyes. Then, he could just make out something in the far distance, that looked like lights. Was it his parents? Or was it the white light someone had once told him about in school – the one you sometimes saw just before you died?

For a moment Ross wished his big brother was here, holding his hand. Even though Ross was far too old for that and would have punched his brother in the face if he'd tried to touch him at any other time. But Simon would know what to do, he was so like their da. He'd have fixed whatever was wrong with the boat, mended the life jacket and somehow got them all to safety. He wouldn't just be floating, alone, afraid for his parents, watching *the odd lights which seemed to be getting closer. He wouldn't be waiting to die.*

And Simon would never have taken the life jacket.

Ross swallowed the bile and self-hatred as it rose into his mouth. His parents had to be out there somewhere, he had to find them... Give his mother back the life jacket he should never have taken. He blinked as hot tears spilled from his eyes, mixing with salt water as he frantically searched the waves continuing to throw him up and down.

Where was she? Where was Da? What had he done?

Ross woke covered in sweat. He lay staring at the ceiling of his bedroom waiting for his heartbeat to settle, for the nausea to dissipate. He hadn't had 'the dream' in almost a year. Had believed he might never have it again. At least he'd hoped time had finally given him a reprieve and allowed him to put the past behind him. But perhaps all the talk of Miriam and his brother – of expectation and duty, of long-buried guilt and pain – had stirred up everything? Or perhaps it was just Ivy?

He studied the ceiling, imagining he could see a face staring down at him. Long ago he'd thought it looked just like his grand-mother giving him one of her long disapproving looks. He'd repainted it then, tried to emulsion over the shadows under her eyes, the regal nose that was bunched as if she were trying to avoid a bad smell, but it hadn't worked. Because she was there again, giving him that look – the one she'd tried to hide during the months after he'd been rescued from the water. The look that said it was all his fault. The same one he fancied Simon had given him every time he was caught off guard.

Even when Simon had crept into his bedroom to talk to him in the middle of the night to share his grief, Ross had known his brother blamed him. He'd seen the accusation in his whisky-coloured eyes, had heard it in his voice, even as Simon delivered words that said the opposite. It didn't matter how many times his brother had tried to deny it, Ross had *known*.

Neither Simon nor Miriam had ever said they blamed him, but the knowledge was there at his core, gnawing at his heart... It was the reason Ross had spent so much time outside. Why the gardens had become his solace, the place he felt at peace. And it was why he'd left Hawthorn Castle: because he couldn't bear to stay. Couldn't stand to be reminded of what they'd all lost because of him.

Ross felt disoriented as Ivy's words spun around his mind, confusing him, making him wonder for the first time if his version of events was true. Even if it wasn't – shouldn't he think about the very real chance of forgiveness? Ross pondered the idea as he continued to stare at the ceiling. Then he shook his head. His grandmother didn't want him; he had to stay away.

14

IVY

Ivy slumped in the velvet chair in Snowman Chalet and stared into the fire. Persuading Ross to hear Miriam out was proving more difficult than she'd imagined. But at least now she knew why he didn't want to return to the castle, and understood his reticence. She just didn't agree. There were wounds to fix here, she just had to persuade Ross they were worth mending. It was obvious he craved connection. His relationship with Grizzle proved it. The photos of the castle and his family in his home also told her that he hadn't really moved on and wasn't as immune as he pretended to be. She wouldn't leave that wound festering without trying to fix it.

She got up to check her phone, logging in to her coaching app, and sighed when she read today's lesson.

'It does not matter how slowly you go so long as you do not stop' – Confucius.

Ivy pouted at the screen. 'I'm not giving up, but it doesn't matter what I say to Ross, he's determined not to speak to Miriam.' She shook her head. 'He misses his family and needs to put things right or he could end up regretting it. ' She exhaled loudly, abandoning the app without filling in her goals, and went to stare at herself in the large mirror hanging over the sideboard, surprised when she noticed her wild, thick hair and glowing skin. She looked healthy – less pale and pasty than she had in a while. Like a long-neglected plant someone had finally remembered to water and feed.

When someone knocked on the door, Ivy's heart skipped, hoping it was Ross. But when she swung it open, she found Bonnibell on the front step holding a flask and a Tupperware box.

'Good morning, hen.' The older woman beamed, wandering inside the cabin as Ivy stepped out of her way. 'I heard Ross dropped you off earlier, so I thought I'd bring breakfast and see how you are. I'm so sorry you got stranded at his cabin last night. Did you manage to get any sleep?'

Ivy thought about the night she'd spent staring at the ceiling. 'A little,' she lied.

Bonnibell eyed her as if she knew. 'Did you two stay in the warm?' she probed as she placed everything on the dresser beside Ivy's makeup and unscrewed the flask, grabbing two snowman mugs from the pocket of her billowing red cape. 'There's coffee and cinnamon buns,' she added.

Ivy watched Bonnibell pour, and admitted, 'Not all evening. He took me to see his friend, Grizzle, for a while.'

'Aye.' Bonnibell handed Ivy a steaming mug and grinned. 'How is the curmudgeon?'

Ivy took a sip of the sweet drink and hummed. 'Okay.'

'Did he manage to order a pair of spectacles that work yet?' she asked, clearly well-versed with the older man's eBay purchases.

It seemed like everyone in the village knew everyone's business. Ivy wasn't sure why she liked the idea – maybe because it showed they cared about each other.

'Not exactly,' she said, thinking of the pink glasses.

'And is he eating enough?' Bonnibell passed Ivy a cinnamon bun.

She took a bite before answering, humming again because it was so delicious. 'Ross is cooking for him,' she admitted.

Bonnibell screwed up her face. 'But the lad's a terrible cook.' She scratched a hand through her wavy bob. 'I'll have to see if I can get some food to the old man or he's going to starve. We look after our neighbours – even if they don't want our help.'

Ivy wondered what Grizzle would make of that. Hopefully it wouldn't cause any trouble between him and Ross.

'Did you sort your business out with Ross?' Bonnibell asked next.

Ivy shrugged. 'He listened, but I'm afraid he's not really responding to what I have to say.' She cleared her throat, clasping her steaming mug before taking a seat by the fire. 'Has he ever talked about the Ballentines at Hawthorn Castle?'

'No, hen.' Bonnibell's mouth pinched and she opened the Tupperware box and grabbed a bun for herself. 'He moved here five years ago and he's always kept himself to himself. Believe me, I've tried to bring him out of his shell.' She looked unhappy. 'I often wondered if he was related to them, but Ross doesn't like to share and I wasn't going to pry. He's an important part of our resort family and I didn't want to annoy or scare him off.'

Ivy's mouth pinched, considering. 'Miriam Ballentine is his grandmother. I work for her and she sent me to speak with him,' she admitted. 'I can't really tell you any more without breaking a confidence. I probably shouldn't have told you that.' But she'd had to confide in somebody.

Bonnibell nodded as she chewed the bun and swallowed, her dark eyes reflective. 'I'm guessing she's sent you because she wants to connect with her grandson, hen?' She held up a palm when Ivy clenched her teeth. 'I'm just... hypothesising.' The smile she flashed was warm and just a little mischievous. 'I've known the lad for a while and it always seemed to me that he was escaping from something. I'd have predicted a broken romance, but family are just as capable of smashing our hearts.'

Ivy nodded slowly. 'In so many ways,' she blurted, regretting it when Bonnibell's eyes flashed.

'I'm not sure if you're talking about yourself or Ross, and I'm not going to ask, which is going to cost me.' The older woman's eyes twinkled and she stood suddenly and swiped her hands over her red velvet skirt. 'I will say I'd like to see the lad with a smile on his face. He spends too much time alone or with that cantankerous honeypot, Grizzle McGregor.' She shook her head sadly.

Ivy nodded. 'Ross told me to go back to the castle. He's not interested in meeting his grandmother, but everything I've seen so far tells me he's hiding from his true feelings.' Something in the pit of her stomach tightened. She wasn't sure if it was because she was afraid of Miriam's reaction if she returned without fulfilling her task; her mother's subsequent disappointment because she wouldn't get on the training programme; or because she'd be leaving Ross with an unresolved conflict in his family. She just knew if she left now, she'd feel she'd failed and worse, she'd be leaving someone she cared for in pain.

'The lad can be stubborn.' Bonnibell watched Ivy, her expression serious. 'Perhaps if you got another chance to speak with him, he'll be more open to what you have to say?'

'I don't know how I'm going to find him again.' She thought about the long trip across the resort back to the lodge this morning. She already knew there was little chance she'd ever be able to find Ross's house without directions. 'I'm guessing he's going to be trying to avoid me from now on.' The thought was depressing.

Bonnibell winced. 'I'd like to suggest you meet him at the resort, but even if I set something up, we both know he's unlikely to come – which means if you want to see him again, you'll have to go wherever he is.'

'I couldn't find his cabin on my own.' Ivy wouldn't find Grizzle's either, which bothered her a lot because she'd promised to help hang the older man's Christmas decorations.

'You know Ross is running a camping adventure later today?' Bonnibell said, her eyes glittering. 'Logan Forbes and Kenzy Campbell from Christmas Village are both booked on, and there's definitely room for one more. I could get Connell to pack an extra tent in the tractor. We don't necessarily need to warn Ross in advance that you're coming...'

'Camping?' Ivy asked, shivering.

'Aye, lass.' Bonnibell smiled. 'There's plenty of equipment to handle the cold weather and you've got my snowsuit and underlayer to keep you warm. I won't need them. I'm not planning on fitting in them again.' Her eyes tracked to the two remaining cinnamon buns in the Tupperware box, and she picked up and winked. 'See what I mean? I've got a couple of warm sweaters that the members of our local knitting club made, you're very welcome to have one of those too.'

It does not matter how slowly you go so long as you do not stop. The words from Ivy's coaching app filled her mind, and this time she heard her mother's voice. She wasn't going to achieve anything without talking to Ross again. He needed to reconnect with his family and put the past behind him. She was sure Miriam's intentions were good – she just had to give them both the chance to talk.

'I suppose going on another adventure might work,' she said, wondering if she'd be wasting her time.

'Can't hurt, hen,' Bonnibell declared, finishing off the bun.

'You're right,' Ivy said, steeling herself. 'Then how do I go about booking on?'

. . .

'You NEED TO STAMP, dance or jump on the snow before you pitch your tent,' Ross instructed, his voice matter-of-fact, demonstrating how to flatten the powdery ground with his large, heavy boots.

Kenzy and Logan chattered happily as they wandered to their allocated spot and began to imitate him, before grabbing each other and starting a sexy tango on the ice.

Ross cleared his throat and turned towards Ivy, his face impassive. 'It's important to create a flat and solid surface. Think rock hard, consider how secure you want your guide ropes to be. Your stakes are going to come flying out if the snow isn't firm enough.' He pointed upwards. 'You'll notice I chose this spot because it's close to the trees – there's a spectacular view over the valley and into the resort but we'll have protection from the wind.'

'Is it going to snow a lot?' Ivy asked, suddenly concerned. She was wearing the snowsuit and underlayer and had packed the extra sweater Bonnibell had given her but wasn't sure she had the right equipment to cope with a storm.

'I've been keeping an eye on the weather and it's not going to be as stormy as it was last night.' Ross's dark eyes skimmed Ivy's face as if he were reading her thoughts. 'But don't worry about the weather, we'll be perfectly safe.'

'We're not worried, we'll keep each other warm somehow.' Kenzy laughed, spinning Logan as they continued to dance.

The big man flushed, but was obviously too besotted with his partner to stop.

Ivy glanced around the clearing, wondering if she really should have come. It didn't help that Ross had looked horrified when he'd driven up to the resort in Connell's tractor, which was attached to a sleigh piled high with tents and food, and had spotted her waiting outside. He'd said very little as he'd pointed to the seat beside him on the tractor before handing Logan the keys to a snowmobile, but it was obvious from his expression that he hadn't been happy to see her.

Ivy felt something in her chest squeeze and fought to contain it. She'd thought they'd bonded last night, but perhaps she'd misread the situation. She knew Ross wanted her to leave, but had hoped he'd understand why she'd chosen to stay.

'You're going to need to set up over here.' Ross pointed to a spot to the right of the trees, a few metres away from where Kenzy and Logan were waltzing to the Christmas tune Kenzy was humming under her breath.

Ivy swallowed. 'Will I be in a tent on my own?' she asked. When Ross gave her a jerky nod, a swarm of bees took off and buzzed around her stomach and she wrapped her arms around herself.

'You'll be fine,' Ross said, stepping closer.

'You don't want me here, I can see it,' she said bluntly. 'It makes me wonder if you're going to feed me to something while I'm asleep.' She scanned their surroundings, checking for movement. Sleep would be unlikely until she got back to the resort. It was beautiful here though. All sparkles, Christmas decorations and fresh snow. The trees and shrubs were stunning – but what would it be like when the sun went down?

'That wouldn't be good for business,' Ross said briskly, but Ivy thought she saw the hint of a smile. He stepped closer. 'Tell me, are you really here because you want to experience the wilderness again, or is it because you still think you can convince me to speak to my grandmother?'

Ivy hesitated, contemplating lying. 'Both.'

He nodded. '*Cruella* would admire your tenacity.' His chest heaved. 'But I appreciate your honesty – at least I can deliver on one of those wishes.' He turned away. 'I'll help you pitch your tent. Bonnibell's made us dinner, all I need to do is warm it up, then we'll take a walk in the woods when it starts to get dark. There are some interesting creatures around here at night.' He gave her a half smile. 'None of them will want to eat you, but they might be curious enough to come out and take a look. We'll finish off the adventure by singing Christmas songs in front of the fire.'

'Sounds perfect,' Kenzy enthused from a few metres away as she stopped dancing and pulled Logan closer.

'Are we definitely going to be warm enough?' Ivy asked.

'Of course, but Moose and Snowball can sleep in your tent if you'd like?' Ross offered.

'Yes please,' Ivy said, looking into his eyes. 'I promise not to mention you going to see Miriam again – but if I happen to drop references to your grandmother and brother into conversation, I hope you'll forgive me?'

Ross held her eyes for a beat and nodded. 'Talk all you like, Ivy, but I won't promise to listen.'

She nodded, understanding him perfectly, and watched as he strode to the space he'd allocated for his tent. Watching those long legs and wide shoulders, feeling tingles of awareness slide through her again.

'He's impressive, isn't he? He rarely comes into the village so I can't say I often get to see him this close up,' Kenzy suddenly whispered.

When Ivy turned, she saw Logan was helping Ross to flatten the snow.

Ivy swallowed. 'Yes,' she agreed, because she suspected the younger woman would see through a lie. Besides, Ross *was* impressive. He was wounded though and if she could keep her nerve, find the right thing to say, she might be able to help with that. 'To be clear,' she said when Kenzy's eyes sparkled, 'I'm only here to talk with him – nothing's going to happen between us.' If she could achieve her quest to reunite Ross with Miriam then she wasn't going to be living in Scotland soon, so there was no point in starting anything beforehand.

'You keep telling yourself that, doll,' Kenzy sang. 'But I saw the way he looked at you just now. If you want me to touch up your makeup or style your hair while we're camping, just shout. No charge.'

'Here?' Ivy choked, looking around.

'I'm not going to let a silly thing like being in the middle of the Scottish wilderness get in between me and a makeover,' the younger woman chuckled. Then she winked before heading towards Logan, who was now unpacking their tent.

Ivy paced to where her tent was supposed to be erected and started to jump up and down, firming the ice. Then she stopped and tipped her face up, let herself take a moment and breathed in the cool, crisp air, drawing it into her lungs, feeling the cold tickle and tingle in her nostrils. She paused, smelling pine and fir trees, the faintest hint of winter leaves. Feeling the dull ache of longing, wishing she could freeze this moment and that she didn't have to move to London, before she shook the thought away.

A few minutes later, Ross arrived to check on her progress, carrying a bag. 'Here's the tent,' he said as both Snowball and Moose scattered tiny footprints on the snow surrounding the area she'd compacted. 'Have you ever pitched one?' he asked.

'Not for years. I haven't slept outside since I was a teenager,' Ivy admitted. 'Unless you count dozing on a sunbed.' She glanced around before looking at him: his skin was glowing. 'You love it here,' she said.

His cheeks reddened. 'I suppose...'

'Simon likes walking around the castle grounds in the afternoons,' she said, remembering him disappearing each lunchtime and returning with a similar flush on his cheeks. 'I used to think it was because he wanted to get away from Miriam, but he talks to the groundsmen, knows all their names.'

Ross let out a long breath. 'That surprises me. He didn't much enjoy being in the gardens when we were growing up and he rarely interacted with the staff.'

'Why do you think he's suddenly decided being Laird is too much for him?' Ivy asked.

'I...' Ross hesitated, looking concerned, then his eyes clouded. 'Couldn't say. I hardly know him anymore. Perhaps he really is just trying to take a break from my grandmother. She's very driven. Or maybe now that he's reached the point of taking over all the responsibilities of being Laird, he doesn't want them anymore.' His lips pinched. 'I can understand that.'

'He has looked stressed recently, and your grandmother has been very demanding.' Ivy unzipped the bag Ross had dumped on the ground and started to take out pieces of the tent, placing the poles, guide ropes and pegs in tidy piles.

'I'm sorry about that,' Ross said thoughtfully. 'I've considered getting in touch a few times over the years, but...'

'What?' Ivy turned to look at him.

'Nothing.' He shrugged. 'I suppose I thought he might not want to hear from me. We were close once, but after our parents died, we drifted apart. He tried to contact me a couple of times after I left Hawthorn Castle, but I never got the feeling he really wanted a relationship. I guess I thought he was just doing it because he thought he should.'

'Because of etiquette? You said the same about Miriam,' Ivy pointed out.

Ross's eyes held hers and she thought she saw something in the amber depths – was he re-evaluating? Before she could be sure, he glanced away, checking on Logan and Kenzy's progress with their tent.

'You've both done a good job of compacting the snow,' he observed, his tone now matter-of-fact.

It was as if their previous conversation had never happened – or the new reminder of his family had made him uncomfortable? Ivy's breath caught. Every time she thought she was making progress, Ross pulled away.

'Now check everything's out of your bags. In a moment I'll show you how to pitch your tents.' With that he strode away.

Ivy watched him as he bent to pet Moose and Snowball before grabbing more equipment, and she was suddenly glad she'd come. Because it was clearer than ever that Ross was hurting, and she was doubly determined to do what she could to fix that.

15

IVY

Ivy leaned forwards and warmed her hands on the large fire Ross had lit. It was still early – the sun was just setting over the valley in front of them and the views were stunning. Kenzy and Logan were snuggled on a log to the right of Ivy, while she and Ross had chosen separate stumps side by side.

The trip so far was proving a disaster. Each time she'd brought up Miriam or Simon since the moment she'd been pitching her tent, Ross had deflected the comment with an unhappy memory of his own. A huge part of her wanted to just give up and go back to Hawthorn Castle, but there was another part of her that couldn't bear the idea of leaving Ross feeling so alone. If she could keep up the momentum, she was sure she'd at least be able to convince him to talk to Miriam. She wanted him back, didn't she? Surely she'd know the right things to say.

Kenzy suddenly unwound herself from Logan and yawned. 'I don't know about you, hon, but I'm thinking of turning in.'

'It's barely half past four,' Ivy said, checking her watch.

'Ach, early to bed, early to rise.' Logan grinned, peeking over at the tent they'd finished pitching a couple of hours before. 'Thanks so much for the meal,' he said, glancing down at the empty metal bowl which until recently had contained stew. It had been a speciality of Bonnibell's: rich and full of flavour, the perfect antidote to the icy cold. The mince pies she had sent to finish off the meal were mostly all gone too, aside from a few crumbs. If she started cooking for Grizzle too, Ivy guessed the hermit wouldn't stay skinny for long.

'We're supposed to be trekking in the woods,' Ross reminded them, sounding unhappy.

Was he concerned about being alone with Ivy again?

'Sorry, hon, I don't think I can keep my eyes open.' Kenzy yawned again then winked before dropping a soft kiss on Logan's jaw.

'Aye,' he agreed, giving her a dopey smile. 'We'll be up early though, see you at dawn.' With that he snagged Kenzy's waist and they both made their way towards their tent.

'And then there were two,' Ross said edgily, picking up the four bowls, a couple of which still had food in them. 'I'll feed the leftovers to Moose and Snowball, best not to leave food around the camp. It might attract—' He stopped, clearly catching the dismayed look on Ivy's face. 'Mice,' he added before going to fill up the pet bowls.

There was a sudden squawk and giggling from Logan and Kenzy's tent.

'Perhaps we should start our trek now?' Ross said, as a blush bloomed across his cheeks. 'It's still light enough to see and we'll take torches for when it gets dark.'

'Good plan,' Ivy agreed quickly as Kenzy giggled again. She was still wearing her snowsuit and had put the jumper Bonnibell had given her on underneath. 'Will I be warm enough when the sun sets?' she asked as she rose.

'Yes, if you didn't get cold last night, you'll be fine.' Ross quickly grabbed a spade and shovelled snow onto the fading fire, waiting until it was out before heading to his tent to pick up torches and a backpack. 'The pathway's not too far from here,' he said, indicating that Ivy should follow. 'We'll go into the woods and see if we can track down reindeer. If we're lucky we might hear owls and there's a chance of spotting badgers, deer, foxes and squirrels out there too.' He sounded excited. 'The team at the resort have hung fairy lights around the trees – they'll flick on soon because it's almost dusk. You'll like it.' He smiled suddenly. 'It's very festive. A couple of our visitors have told us they spotted elves and one even saw Santa once the lights were on. Although he might have had one too many whiskies that night.'

Ivy chuckled. 'Do you like Christmas?' she asked. Twigs crackled under her feet as the snow thinned below the canopy of trees. She took in a deep breath and smelled pine needles, felt something inside her chest do a happy dance.

Ross took a moment to respond. 'I remember enjoying it with my parents before they died. We were a close family then.' He paused. 'What about you?'

Ivy shoved her hands into her pockets. 'We used to have family Christmases. But my dad passed when I was sixteen and that changed a lot of things.' She took in a lungful of air, waiting for the sudden burst of pain to ease. It had been years ago, but talking about it still affected her. 'Now Mum usually works the holiday shifts... She's a successful surgeon. I'm very proud of her.'

Ross must have heard something in her voice because he stopped and turned so he could study her face.

'If I'm not working, I might come to the resort next year. It's very beautiful,' Ivy garbled on, avoiding his eyes and looking around in case he asked her more about her family. She wasn't ready to share with him, and definitely didn't want the conversation leading to her potential new job in London, which seemed such a distant reality the longer she stayed. 'I really understand why you love living here.'

Ross gave her a dazzling smile. 'The outdoors has always

been my happy place. I'm not sure how I'd have coped if I'd been born into Simon's shoes.' His good humour faded as soon as he mentioned his brother and he turned and shone the torch beam on the decorations which had been hung onto the trees, making them sparkle and shimmer. 'We'll follow the bauble trail for a while. If you hear a honk, don't worry, it's probably only Bob.'

'Is that Edina Lachlan's donkey?' Ivy asked. 'We met at The Workshop,' she added when Ross gave her a quizzical look.

'Aye, Bob has been known to stray onto the resort's land. He's got big teeth but he hasn't eaten anyone. *Yet.*' Ross smiled.

'Ha, ha,' Ivy clucked.

They walked in silence for a few minutes, the only noises coming from Moose and Snowball as they hopped in and out of the shrubbery. Then something barked in the distance and Moose stopped, his ears pricking up before he glanced back at Ross and whimpered.

'That's odd,' Ross said, speeding up a little. 'I swear that sounds like the demon dog.'

He jogged ahead, with Snowball and Moose hanging behind, obviously reluctant to investigate in case their master was right. Ivy began to walk faster too, taking care not to trip, as they ventured deeper into the woods and the light dimmed.

Then suddenly the pug came bounding out from between a cluster of evergreens. He stopped, obviously catching their scent, and bared his teeth when he spotted Ross. But as soon as Bowser saw Ivy, he let out a delighted yelp and headed straight for her. She knelt as he reached her, fussing and soothing as she plucked random pieces of undergrowth from his fur. Bowser tried to lick her face, whimpering pathetically as he strained to get closer, obviously upset.

'Where's Grizzle?' Ross asked urgently as he lowered and tried to pat the dog too, quickly whipping away his hand when Bowser offered a low growl.

'Are we close to his cabin?' Ivy asked, looking into the darkness.

'A couple of miles,' Ross said, sounding worried. 'I didn't think he ventured this far since his eyesight started to trouble him. He's not reckless, even before that he'd never come this far after dark.'

'Maybe he's hurt and the dog decided to come and get help?' Ivy suggested, rising to her feet.

'The only thing that animal is usually interested in is trying to take chunks out of me,' Ross said dryly. 'But I'm going to have to check on Grizzle just in case.' He glanced back the way they'd come. 'You'll be better off waiting at the camp just in case he turns up there. I'm going to walk to Grizzle's house, then I'll check the tracks and pathways heading in this direction just in case he's got himself lost on one of those.'

'I'll come with you,' she quickly shot back.

Ross shook his head. 'I'll be much quicker on my own and I'd rather leave someone here to watch out for Grizzle in case he turns up.' His forehead squeezed and he looked concerned. 'I hope the old man was properly dressed, he could freeze in this weather, especially if he's fallen or got himself lost.' He puffed air between his lips, looking agitated. 'I didn't get a chance to visit him this evening...'

'I'm sure he'll be okay.' Ivy put a gentle hand on Ross's shoulder and felt the muscles underneath her palm flex. 'Should we get Logan and Kenzy to help look for him?'

Ross pulled a face. 'If I haven't found him by the time I return I'll wake them, but...' His eyes drifted back towards the dark woods. 'I don't want to worry everyone. There could be a simple explanation and he'll be furious if we make an unnecessary fuss.'

Ivy didn't know Ross well, but she could see from his expression that he didn't believe there was a simple explanation.

Bowser barked and wagged his tail, perhaps understanding their intention, before he nudged Ivy's leg.

'I need to get you back to the camp,' Ross said. 'If you can take care of Bowser for me while I look? I suspect if I take him along, he'll just try to eat me which would slow the search down considerably.' Despite the harsh words, she heard affection in his voice.

'Sure,' Ivy agreed, following as Ross quickly backtracked.

He was obviously uneasy about his friend. Despite his insistence that he didn't want to connect with anyone, his relationship with Grizzle proved just the opposite, which gave her hope.

They reached the edge of the woods in record time and Ivy kept her eyes fixed forward, ignoring any rustling in the undergrowth. She'd light the fire again and wait until Ross returned – no way would she be able to settle until he was back. If he was gone too long, she'd wake Kenzy and Logan and they'd follow. As they made their way out of the trees, Ivy spotted an orange flicker and then a haze of smoke billowing into the sky.

'Someone's lit the fire again,' Ross said, speeding up.

Bowser barked and catapulted his round body forwards, overtaking them. By the time Ivy and Ross caught up, the dog was nuzzling and barking excitedly, slobbering all over Grizzle. The older man looked exhausted: he was slumped on one of the logs, his hands hovering over the fire.

'Ach, I thought you'd gone for good,' he grumbled as he watched them approach, glaring at the tent where Kenzy and Logan were obviously sleeping. 'Whoever's in there hasn't put in an appearance, but I heard someone snoring ten minutes ago.'

'How did you get all the way out here?' Ross demanded, grabbing a couple of the thick logs he'd cut earlier and feeding them to the fire. He grabbed a thermos from his tent and poured the older man a drink without asking.

Grizzle snatched the mug from his hands and gulped it

down without comment. Ross filled a bowl with water and put it on the floor for the dog. Bowser growled as Ross drew closer, but when Ivy leaned down to pet him, he gave her a sweet doggy smile.

'That Bonnibell.' Grizzle hummed as the hot drink slid down his throat. 'I'd recognise the lass's hot chocolate anywhere. Scottish nectar I call it.'

'Grizzle?' Ross asked, patiently waiting for a response to his earlier question.

'Ach lad, don't fuss. I broke the door again and Bowser ran out.' He rubbed the dog's ears. 'He must have spotted something because he chased after it. I thought I'd follow and try to find him, but those stupid new glasses fell off and I couldn't see so well in the dark.' He scratched a hand over his eyes.

Ross's lips thinned. 'Don't you think it's time you admitted you need to see an optician?'

'I'll take care of it myself, lad. Which reminds me, I've got another two pairs arriving tomorrow. Will you pick them up from the post office?'

'Aye,' Ross grumbled.

'Where did you find Bowser in the end?' Grizzle shot Ross an accusatory glare.

'He was in the woods,' Ivy interjected. 'We were walking and he just appeared.'

'Ach, well it was clever of him to find you. I'm sure he'll be able to guide me home, so I'll be off in a minute.' Grizzle began to rise, then he groaned and lowered himself back onto the log.

'Everything okay?' Ivy asked, watching as Grizzle rubbed his eyes again and glanced around, squinting.

'Aye, lass. I just need to warm these achy old bones. I've obviously been on my feet for longer than I thought.' He sniffed. 'Have you any food? Mairi left a pie in the fridge but it smelled funny.' He shuddered.

Ross let out an irritated sound. 'I've got some of Bonnibell's beef stew in my tent. Why don't I warm it? After you've eaten, if you're feeling up to it, I could walk you back to your cabin?'

Grizzle's mouth pinched. 'I don't need a boy scout, I'm perfectly capable of finding my own way there,' he said grumpily.

'Bowser looks exhausted,' Ivy said as the dog looked up at her with rounded eyes. 'I'm not sure he's up to a long walk and Ross isn't going to be able to carry him without losing a limb.'

Bowser's low growl confirmed it.

'You can't carry the dog either,' Ross jumped in, giving Ivy a stern look.

'Then I'll wait it out,' Grizzle muttered, wriggling on the stump. 'I can sleep here beside the fire until morning. I've slept in worse places.' He gave Ross the evil eye when he looked like he was going to protest. 'Besides, if I'm not at home it'll spook Mairi when she tries to sneak in with another meal.' He chuckled, suddenly perking up, his cheeks flushing pink again and giving him a healthy glow.

'How about you sleep in my tent for a couple of hours?' Ivy offered gently. 'I'm guessing Bowser will appreciate it and I'm really not ready for bed.' She stretched her arms wide, trying not to yawn as the older man regarded her through suspicious eyes. 'Honestly,' she said. 'I told Ross I was planning to stay up – I want to see how many wild animals I can spot.' She turned towards the younger man and widened her eyes, encouraging him to agree with her.

His appreciative expression made her stomach swoop.

'Aye.' Ross nodded. 'Ivy's excited about the creatures we get out here in the wilderness.'

'You're not going to leave her out here on her own?' Grizzle asked suspiciously.

'Of course he won't,' Ivy said lightly. 'Ross has already promised he'll stay up too.'

'I assume the lad hasn't forgotten that he's bringing you to visit me soon,' Grizzle said, his expression wily. 'I need the lass's help with those Christmas decorations, don't forget.'

Ross's whole body stiffened and Ivy folded her arms and watched his reaction. He was obviously less than impressed with the idea of taking her back to the older man's house, but with any luck, it meant she'd get another day with him.

'If you want,' he grumbled. 'Tomorrow. We can pack up camp and all go together. But only if you agree to sleep here now...'

'Ach, well. I suppose Bowser could nap for a while.' The older man scratched his dog under the chin. 'The lad looks tired. But we'll need to be up and gone at first light and glasses or not, I'll show *you* the way.' With that, he stood and shuffled his way carefully towards Ivy's tent.

'Just a sec,' Ivy said, bouncing in front of him and retrieving her small backpack of clothes before sweeping a hand and guiding him inside. 'Sleep well,' she murmured before turning back to face Ross, unable to stop a yawn from escaping.

'Wild animals?' he asked, grinning at her, his expression one of delighted surprise. 'You've a way with people,' he added softly, making her heart skip. 'I can't believe how quickly the old man has taken to you. I'm beginning to understand why Miriam sent you to talk to me.'

Ivy grimaced. 'At least Grizzle listens.'

She watched Ross unzip his tent and grab a couple of blankets before indicating that she should sit on the log Kenzy and Logan had been cuddling on earlier. Then he swept the blanket around her shoulders and went to feed the fire.

'Oh, I listen, Ivy,' he said quietly before slumping beside her and turning to study the flames. 'I'm just not sure I'm ready to hear.'

16

ROSS

Ross was only aware that Ivy had fallen asleep when he felt the weight of her head pressing against the edge of his arm. She'd been sitting beside him, staring into the flames, and he'd been waiting for her to share another story about Simon or Miriam, probably hoping she'd finally hit on something that would resonate. He'd been steeling himself not to react to her tales, or to ask for more, knowing given half a chance he'd eagerly gulp down any news about his family. But he didn't want to open that particular wound again, so why was he finding it increasingly difficult not to ask about them?

Was it just the Ivy effect? Had he starved himself of company for so long that he'd risk anything to extend the conversation? Then again, the tales Ivy had shared so far had stirred something inside him, feelings he'd spent years trying to tamp down and ignore. If she stayed around much longer he might not be able to stop himself from promising to speak to his grandmother.

And would that really be such a terrible idea? Perhaps Ivy was right and she had changed; maybe she did want him back in her life?

Confused, Ross stared into the fire, trying not thing think until Ivy whispered something in her sleep and then stiffened when an owl hooted in the woodland behind them.

'What was that?' she gasped, sitting straighter, sounding half-asleep.

'Nothing,' Ross murmured. 'Do you want to turn in? My tent's empty. There's a spare sleeping bag inside it which you're welcome to use.'

She studied him, her eyes hooded, before turning to gaze at the fire. He'd been adding logs, keeping it ablaze until she'd dropped off. That had been almost half an hour ago and since he hadn't wanted to move and wake her, it was just orange embers now.

Ivy had surprised him today. She'd been so determined to help him find Grizzle, and her kindness when the older man was obviously too tired to walk back to his house had proved she was the sort of person who put others first. She'd offered Grizzle her bed without a second thought – leaving herself with nowhere to sleep, despite the fact that she was exhausted. Her selflessness and ability to open her heart to a virtual stranger had drawn out yet more feelings Ross didn't want to have. His life would have been very different if his family were more like her.

Ivy let out a loud yawn. 'I'll take the sleeping bag, but I'm not monopolising your tent. You go and get some sleep – you've got to get Grizzle to his home tomorrow, and you'll be the one driving the sleigh I'll be riding back to the resort. I'll stay here.' She looked around warily. 'Could you leave Snowball with me please? I'm guessing if anything comes looking for a handy snack, he's the one most likely to scare them off?'

Ross chuckled as she swayed sleepily on the log. 'You'd be better off with Moose. Snowball might look scary but he's a marshmallow – more likely to hum predators into submission than attack them.' As if to prove it the wild boar began to purr.

'How about we share the tent? The boys can sleep between us. They'll keep us warm and preserve your reputation.'

'I have a reputation?' Ivy smiled shyly, and the wicked curve of her mouth did odd things to his insides.

Ross cleared his throat and rose, snapped his fingers and indicated to his pets that it was time to go to bed. He shovelled snow onto the glimmering embers again before helping Ivy to her feet and guiding her towards the tent.

'Um, shall I wait outside while you change?' he asked, feeling awkward suddenly.

'It's too cold. I won't look if you don't. Besides, I'm not going to take much off,' she promised, disappearing underneath the flap when Ross unzipped it.

Moose and Snowball immediately joined her and Ross stood for a second, unsure. But the air was frigid and after a couple of beats he shuddered and climbed in too. Ivy was lying on her back. She'd already tugged off her hat, gloves and boots and was easing the snowsuit over her slim legs. Ross sat on the other side of the tent and began to take off his boots too, trying not to watch her progress, even though it was difficult because his eyes kept drifting to her. Ivy was beautiful and her kindness today had helped to turn what had once been fascination into an attraction that was surprisingly fierce.

'Can you help?' she asked suddenly. 'These damn things are stuck on my ankles.' She shoved at the bottom of the snowsuit but was obviously too weary to get it off. 'Just pull, I don't care.' She lay on her back and watched through half-open eyes as Ross shuffled across the tent and grabbed the bottoms and yanked, almost falling backwards out of the tent. She giggled. 'Smooth.'

Ross chuckled, relaxing a notch, trying not to watch as she unzipped the sleeping bag and wriggled inside.

'You can undress, I promise not to peek,' she said, sleepily shutting her eyes.

Ross tugged off his jumper, and as he did his T-shirt rose up, exposing the lower half of his stomach. Ivy hissed and then groaned as she turned over and ducked her head into the camping pillow she'd claimed.

'You looked,' Ross said, surprised.

He switched off the lantern and lay down too, felt his pets settle between them. Was Ivy attracted to him? And did he like the idea? He moved onto his back and stared at the ceiling, heard Ivy punch the pillow before turning over again. A few minutes later she turned back the other way.

'Did you mean what you said to Grizzle about taking me to his cabin to hang up the Christmas decorations?' she suddenly whispered.

Ross grunted. 'It's not like I have a lot of choice,' he complained, immediately feeling bad because it was so obvious that he didn't like the idea. 'I wasn't going to, but... yes I will if you still want to go.'

'Of course,' Ivy said.

'He likes you and there aren't many people I can say that about. I'm not even sure he likes me sometimes.'

Ross almost heard the crack of Ivy's smile.

'He likes you alright, he treats you like a son and I like him too,' she said. 'He says what he thinks, and that dog is adorable.'

'Adorable.' He snorted, shifting a little, trying to get comfortable. Usually he'd have gone out like a light as soon as his head hit the camping pillow. He loved sleeping outside, loved the freedom of knowing there was just a thin sliver of material between himself and the world. Life felt so simple that way, but he couldn't settle tonight. 'I think the word you're actually looking for is abominable.'

Snowball whined in his sleep, which Ross took as affirmation. 'I can't believe the old man was lost in the woods.' He felt dizzy as the implications suddenly hit him. 'I'm afraid one day I might not be there if something happens.' He swallowed. The risks of Grizzle living out in the wilderness were starting to feel very real. He'd never worried about him before, but with his diminishing eyesight, suddenly he wasn't so sure he'd be safe.

'That's a lot of worry to have on your shoulders,' Ivy said. 'Doesn't seem right.'

'I don't mind,' Ross said. 'But— I mean, even if I did go and see my grandmother, there's no way I could consider...' Now he was jumping ahead of himself, imagining how it might be to live back at Hawthorn Castle, away from his old friend.

'Are you imagining leaving him?' Ivy guessed. 'It wouldn't necessarily come to that. You wouldn't be that far away and he seems really independent. Also, perhaps there are other people who could check on him...' She fell silent.

'He doesn't let a lot of people into his world,' Ross confessed.

'Imagine that,' Ivy said.

He knew she was teasing, probably trying to shift him out of his sudden melancholy. It worked, because Ross couldn't stop the answering smile.

'Which means, there's no one else who can visit him,' he finished, rolling his shoulders, which still felt stiff with stress.

If the hermit hadn't accidently stumbled onto their camp, it could have taken hours before he was found. And if they hadn't found Bowser, Ross might not have known Grizzle was missing until sometime tomorrow afternoon. His stomach knotted. They'd been dancing around the subject of Grizzle's eyesight for months now, but it was a serious problem. What would he do if something happened to the old man? He hadn't realised how important the hermit was to him before now. He'd said Moose and Bowser were his family, but over the years Grizzle had become just as important.

'He might listen to me,' Ivy said suddenly. 'I mean, for some reason, he's taken a liking to me. I'm not sure why, and perhaps it won't last, but I'll talk to him if you want?'

Ross considered the offer, hesitating. 'I'm not sure.' He'd expected Ivy to be back at the castle by now. Could he ask for her help?

'I'm not going to ask you for anything in return, if that's what you're thinking,' she added, sounding hurt. 'I know how you feel about Miriam and Simon and I'll keep trying to convince you to reconnect, but talking to your grandmother is *your* decision. I hope you do, but I'm not going to blackmail you into having a conversation.'

'I wasn't thinking that,' he shot back, wondering what kind of person he'd become that the thought *had* crossed his mind. 'I just... I don't know much about you, that's all.' He shut his eyes, instantly regretting the comment. He was so out of practice with people. Opting out and spending time in a tent with just the trees and sky for company was so much easier. It was just him, the boys and the outdoors, he didn't have to worry about anything else. Now he wondered if that was the coward's way out.

'Okay,' Ivy said after a pause. 'It's fair of you to suspect my motives, I suppose. What do you want to know?'

Ross puffed out a breath, considering. He wanted to ask if she had a boyfriend, but since they were half-dressed and closeted in a tent together that seemed inappropriate.

'How about I think of something?' she asked after a pause. 'I know I told you that I haven't camped since I was fifteen.' Her voice was raspy. 'If I remember correctly, it wasn't as cold as this. I'm guessing it must have been summertime because I could definitely feel my nose.'

'Do you need another blanket?' Ross asked, grabbing his own and tugging it off, then shifting so he was resting on his side facing her, trying to work out how to hand it over. He wished there was more light so that he could see Ivy's face.

Moose made a snorting sound and Snowball wriggled between them, getting comfortable, and began to purr again.

Ross took in a deep breath and smelled something floral, but couldn't put his finger on what it was. He knew it definitely wasn't coming from either of his pets or him, so it must have been Ivy.

'No thank you. I'm warm enough. We've got our four-legged hot water bottles to make sure of that.' She chuckled and he heard her shift. 'Well, and to preserve a reputation I had no idea I had,' she added, sounding drowsy. 'I've just got a cold nose, but it's okay because I can hardly feel it anymore. This is just...' She swallowed. 'It's bringing back memories.'

'Good ones?' Ross held his breath while she considered the question, wondering if Ivy would tell him. He knew why she was at the resort, knew the only reason she'd insisted on joining him on the camp was so she could persuade him to speak to his grandmother. So he hadn't expected her to share her stories. Still wasn't sure if she would. Was it odd that he wanted her to, wanted to know more about this woman, to find out what was motivating her? Was she really as selfless as he thought?

She blew out a long breath. 'My dad was really into the outdoors. He owned a garden centre in Surrey, if you can believe that.'

'Really?' Ross said, surprised, then he remembered. 'Of course, you knew the Latin name for brambles...' He leaned back, making himself more comfortable on the sleeping mat, enjoying their conversation. He wasn't used to swopping confidences in the middle of the night. Found himself enjoying it.

'Yep. Dad taught me all the botanical names for plants and flowers.'

She fell silent and Ross wondered if she was going to continue.

'Is he the reason you're called Ivy?'

'Yes,' she said, the word disappearing into the darkness because her voice was so low. 'Dad originally wanted to call me

Clover because it was his favourite flower, but Mum put her foot down at that.'

'Tell me about him,' Ross prodded, keen to know more. 'How did your dad meet your mum?'

She sighed again. 'He had to visit a doctor after almost slicing a finger off with a set of shears. Mum was training to be a GP and she treated him – they were attracted to each other but he didn't make a move.' She paused. 'But then he dropped a spade onto his toe a couple of weeks later and almost lost a nail. I think he only did it so he'd have an excuse to see her again...'

'That was brave,' Ross said, wondering if he'd ever put himself out there like that.

'Dad asked Mum out a few weeks after what he called "the big toe disaster" and after changing surgeries and getting a new doctor, he proposed.'

'You were very close to him,' Ross guessed. He hardly knew her, but could hear it in her voice.

'He was... larger than life.' Ivy's tone was affectionate. 'Disorganised, terrible with money, often late – they couldn't have been less alike. But they loved each other and they were happy. When I came along Dad said he'd created a perfect garden filled with his favourite blooms.' Ross heard her swallow in the dark. 'When I was sixteen, he collapsed at work – his heart. And just like that, he was gone.' Her voice wobbled and she stopped, perhaps collecting her thoughts.

'Nothing was ever the same afterwards. It took me over a year before I could even look at a flower, let alone smell one. I think I deliberately forgot all the words he taught me. It's only since I got here that I've been remembering them... Despite the fact that I worked in a garden centre from the age of nineteen until about a year ago.'

'You did?' Ross asked, surprised. 'Is that because you wanted to follow in your dad's footsteps?' He remembered Ivy's expression when they'd been walking in the woods and how lovingly she'd tended to Grizzle's houseplants and herbs.

'That was part of it.' She paused. 'Mostly, I really love being around plants and I'm good at taking care of them. It's like it's in my bloodline.' She sighed again, a sad sound.

'So why are you working for my grandmother?' Ross asked, confused.

'That's a long story,' she said.

Ross stared into the darkness, wishing he could see Ivy's face. He could hear the in and out of her breath and knew she hadn't fallen back to sleep. He searched his mind for the right thing to say, the perfect question to ask. He was out of practice but wanted to try.

'I've got nowhere else to be,' he said eventually, shocked at how much he wanted to know.

'Okay.' She drew in a breath. 'Dad was a brilliant gardener but not so brilliant with the concept of keeping on top of mortgages, interest payments, or avoiding running up mountains of debt. It became obvious within a month of the funeral that we were going to lose the business and our home.'

'I'm sorry,' Ross said, wondering what that had to do with Ivy's career. 'What happened?'

He heard her sleeping bag rustle and Snowball wriggled again.

'Mum was a part-time GP by then, but she retrained as a surgeon, then worked day and night, holidays and weekends. It was hard but she eventually bought us a new house, provided everything we needed. Picked up the reigns and, honestly, she's never let go. Perhaps it was her way of dealing with what happened.' She paused. 'Since then, she's been fixated on me having what she thinks of as a dependable career. Something in the city, something, I don't know... important.' She fell silent.

'And she doesn't think you working in a garden centre is good enough?' Ross guessed. 'There are loads of jobs you could do – horticulturalist, botanist, conservation manager, tree surgeon, landscaper.' He paused.

'I've had the same conversation,' Ivy said flatly. 'She thinks it all amounts to the same.'

'That makes no sense.'

'I know it doesn't – but I think what happened with Dad means anything I do that's even slightly similar brings back bad memories and she's afraid.' She paused. 'Money's never been important to me. Then again, I've never earned much so she's probably right.' That sigh again.

'But is it really up to her?' Ross asked, baffled.

'That's easy for you to say,' Ivy said quietly. 'You've gone your own way.' She paused as Ross absorbed the hit of her words. 'That's not a criticism by the way,' she added quickly as if she'd guessed. 'It's just, Mum's all I've got.'

Ross let out an unsteady breath; it was hard not to draw comparisons and he didn't like the way they made him feel. Had he abandoned his family? Is that what Ivy saw?

He cleared his throat. 'You said you were working in a garden centre before. What made you change course?'

Ivy paused. 'I always thought Mum was unstoppable, but earlier this year she had a heart attack.'

'I'm sorry,' Ross said softly, jarred by everything she was telling him, trying to take it all in.

'It's okay. She recovered, then returned to work a few months ago and she's barely looked back,' Ivy said lightly. 'But... it changed everything. It's why I'm working for your grandmother now.'

'Because?' Ross asked.

'The job is a step on a ladder. Miriam knows Mum from uni and...' She hesitated. 'She promised to recommend me for a training programme in London. It's a really good move.'

Was it?

'You don't sound very sure about that,' Ross murmured.

'It's time I got on with launching my career.' Ivy's tone was determined, but Ross could hear something underneath. Misgivings, reluctance? Perhaps both. 'I don't want Mum to worry, and this role is a stepping stone to something greater, I hope. I've got plans; I just need to—' She yawned. 'Make them happen I suppose...' She trailed off. 'I don't want to let Mum down. I... It's really important I make her proud, that she stops worrying.'

'Why?' Ross asked. He could tell from her voice that this wasn't just some random wish, that there was something important she hadn't said.

Ivy remained silent for so long he wondered if she was going to tell him. 'I had a huge fight about my career – or in her words lack of – with Mum just before she fell ill,' she shared. 'I wasn't to blame for the heart attack, I know that, but—'

Ross heard an ache in Ivy's voice and wondered if she did. Thought about how easy it was to get tangled in guilt. To change the path of your life because of it. Then again, he'd walked away to save himself; Ivy was throwing herself into something it was clear she didn't want. The comparison shouldn't have bothered him as much as it did.

'It made me realise I could have lost her,' Ivy continued. 'That the last thing I'd remember about our time together would be all those angry words.' She cleared her throat. 'So now I don't sleep on a fight, and I will *never* walk away without settling an argument.'

'And it's why you've come to Christmas Resort to try to get me to heal my relationship with my grandmother,' Ross said as everything clicked into place. 'Because you don't want me to be left feeling guilty if something happens to her. Because if it did, I'd never be able to make things between us right?' Which would be the same way he still felt about his parents. He mulled the thought, unsure of how he felt about it. It was a new perspective, one he found troubling.

'I... yes, I suppose that's part of it,' Ivy said, her voice suddenly awkward. 'Although, I think...' She let out a long breath. 'I suppose I'd like to think that a part of you would like to make up with them too. You deserve to be happy, Ross.'

'Right.' He nodded and fell silent, listening to the rise and fall of her breath.

He had no idea how long it was until her breathing softened, suggesting she'd dropped off, and he shifted until he was lying face up again. He stared into the darkness and grimaced, realising he was beginning to like Ivy Heart a whole lot more than he really should.

Ross woke a few hours later and felt a hard lump by his feet, indicating Moose and Snowball had both shifted at some point to the bottom of the tent. Probably because it had been too warm where they'd been sleeping. Something snuggled into his side, though, and it took him a moment to realise it was Ivy. He could smell her scent again and it reminded him of the sweet jasmine he'd helped to plant around the portcullis at Hawthorn Castle. There was a hint of neroli in there too and if he dug deeper, perhaps a trace of ginger? He stayed perfectly still as Ivy mumbled something then swung an arm over his hip, and he ignored his body as it begged him to shift closer.

She's sleeping, he told himself darkly, and leaned his head away when he felt her breath on his cheek. He still couldn't see much but guessed from the warmth that her face was mere inches from his.

'Ivy,' he whispered as she moved closer to him. 'Are you awake?' he asked, and then almost jumped out of his skin as she began to dab gentle kisses along his chin. Ross ignored the surge of goosebumps that followed the touch of her lips.

'What?' she asked sleepily as she continued to caress her way across his jaw.

'Are you... awake?' he asked again, his voice strangled, hoping with every fibre of his being that she was going to say yes. She stopped then and he felt her jerk away, knew when she snapped her arm from his hip that she'd been dreaming. Was surprised at how disappointed he felt.

Less than twenty-four hours ago he'd wanted Ivy to leave Christmas Resort forever, now he wasn't sure what he wanted. He just knew everything about his life felt like it had begun to unravel.

'Ross?' Ivy whispered, her voice suddenly alert. 'Was I just kissing you? I was dreaming. I'm so sorry.' Her voice raced and Ross could almost feel the heat radiating from her cheeks.

He reached out and gently cupped one in his palm. Was a little surprised when Ivy leaned into it, but left it there.

'I'm not – sorry that you kissed me, I mean.' Ross paused, wondering why he'd just admitted that. When she didn't run from the tent screaming, he decided it was safe to say more. 'I was just hoping you were conscious. That you weren't...' He cleared his throat. 'Having a nightmare or something.'

She laughed softly. 'It wasn't a nightmare, but I *was* dreaming. You were there.' He heard her swallow in the darkness. 'It was a *really* good dream.'

'Was it?' he said, his voice suddenly deeper as his pulse kicked up. 'What was I doing?'

'Putting up a tent I think.' She puffed. 'Or chopping down a tree. You were definitely avoiding me; I can't remember all the details. Except, at the end of the dream, we were suddenly in a tent and...'

'What?' he asked, his voice suddenly raspy.

'Well, there were these noises outside and I was scared, or you were, I can't remember now,' she whispered.

He thought he felt her shuffle closer.

'I'm sure it was you,' he teased, his voice rough. He wanted to kiss her, but couldn't until he was sure she wanted him to. 'Soooo...'

'You kissed me,' she said. 'To take my mind off it.'

Something howled outside and Ross felt Ivy flinch, then she swung an arm back over his hip and nuzzled closer. An owl hooted.

'Well that's terrifying,' she said and her body shook as she began to giggle.

'It is.' Ross leaned closer. He couldn't see but despite that knew their mouths were mere millimetres apart because he could feel the warmth of her breath. 'Would you take my mind off it please?' he asked.

Ivy chuckled and suddenly they were kissing. There had been no slow glide in, no chance to catch his breath, or to question why Ivy had suddenly decided this was a good idea. He hardly knew himself. Perhaps it was being in the dark and all the stories they'd shared over the past few days – stories he was sure hadn't been revealed by either of them before now. Ross certainly hadn't told anyone how his parents had died or about how he felt about it. And somehow, he felt closer to Ivy than he had to anyone in a long time.

The kiss deepened and Ross felt himself shudder. He settled an arm over Ivy's hip so he could pull her closer. He was pleased the sleeping bags were between them because otherwise he suspected things might have moved faster. He had a sudden image of Ivy undressing him, of him doing the same to her and let out a low moan. He ran his palm down her cheek and across her shoulder, drinking her in. She hummed and nudged herself closer to him. It was Ross who eased back first when Moose groaned and Snowball stirred and nudged the bottom of his feet, bringing him back to earth. Ivy didn't say anything, but they lay facing each other, and she reached up and wound a finger around one of the curls of hair at the nape of his neck.

'That was perfect. Just like my dream,' she said, moving again until her nose was pressed into his neck.

He heard her sigh, felt the tremble of her body as she lapsed back into sleep. Then he pressed his lips to her forehead and shut his eyes, realising for the first time in a long time that he was in danger of opening his heart...

17

IVY

'All packed up?' Ross asked as Ivy finished helping Grizzle gather up his sleeping bag before bundling it into its sack. She felt shivers slip down her spine as he drew closer. Ross had already disappeared from the tent when she'd woken, and she'd lain staring at the canvas ceiling, knowing their kiss had changed everything. At least for her.

She'd come to reunite Ross with his family, but did their growing attraction mean she should tell him more about the job Miriam had promised in return and what she had to do to get his grandmother's recommendation? Ivy considered, wondering if the news would muddy the waters. She didn't want Ross suspecting her motives – he'd obviously been hurt by his family and she didn't want to hurt him anymore.

'We're ready to go, lad,' Grizzle said suddenly, picking up the bag before Ross could grab it, and limping towards the red tractor and sleigh Ross had borrowed from Connell.

'Careful,' Ross warned, just before the older man tripped over a snowy boulder on the ground he clearly hadn't seen.

'I'm fine, lad!' Grizzle snapped, just missing another rock as Bowser chased up to clamber at his heels. He stumbled forwards again and dropped the sack onto the ground. 'Are we going to leave soon? Kenzy and Logan went hours ago.' The older man turned to frown at the space where the couple had been camping. They'd both left early because they had to get to work and had taken Moose and Snowball ahead to the resort, so there would be plenty of room in the sleigh once the baggage had been packed.

'We can go now,' Ross said, sounding irritated as he walked up to throw Grizzle's sleeping bag, the tent and a couple of bags into the sleigh. 'Why don't you climb in?'

'I still don't know why I can't walk,' the older man complained as he signalled to Ivy to get in first.

'I told you, I'm not sure Bowser slept too well,' Ivy said, repeating the excuse she'd used to convince him to travel with them earlier. He'd taken a while to agree, but she suspected it was more about bravado than any genuine desire to get home on foot. There was a slither of space on one of the squashy red seats beside the equipment Ross had just thrown in and Ivy eased into it, beaming as she took in the tinsel and baubles that had been used to decorate the edges and sides. 'This is wonderful,' she said as Bowser and Grizzle clambered in too.

'Connell uses the sleigh to give rides to the resort guests,' Ross explained, shutting the door and holding her eyes, making everything inside her stomach unfurl like a flower blooming. Oblivious, he strode to the tractor and got on.

'Aye, you don't need to hold on, it moves slower than a tortoise in first gear,' Grizzle grumbled. 'Is there any food?' he shouted to Ross as Bowser sniffed one of the bags.

'Sorry, we ate everything at breakfast – but Bonnibell might have something for you when we get to the resort,' Ross promised.

Grizzle made a huffing sound and slumped in the seat, twisting so he could gaze out of the sleigh – although Ivy had no idea what he could actually see. She turned too so she could watch the landscape as Ross started up the tractor. They began to glide, sliding past fields of white which rolled downwards until they reached the horizon, probably continuing miles beyond that. Hedgerows layered in downy blankets of ice created a criss-cross pattern as far as the eye could see. Ivy could hardly contain her squeak of pleasure.

In the distance, her attention was drawn to a large, forested area and she wondered if the resort staff hung fairy lights on the trees inside, and if reindeer and donkeys roamed under the thick canopy ready to delight visitors. She smiled – this place really was magical. No wonder Ross didn't want to leave.

'There's a *Pinus sylvestris*,' she mumbled, pointing to the group of trees they were about to pass.

'Aye,' Grizzle said, sounding impressed. 'It's also known as a Scots Pine, lass – that's the national tree of Scotland. There's a couple of *Betula pendula* dotted in there too.'

'The Silver Birch.' Ivy turned to look at him and smiled. 'That was my dad's favourite tree.' Her mind flooded with multiple memories of him. This time, instead of ignoring them, she let herself remember, feeling an ache in her heart when she thought about how much she'd loved working alongside him – how much it had meant to her to follow the same path. She remembered her conversation with Ross the evening before when he'd questioned if she was doing the right thing by giving it up...

She shook her head; she wasn't going to let herself get distracted. Dad was gone, but her mum was still here and she had to protect her – family mattered, and Faith was all she had. Ivy fell silent and gazed at the landscape as they continued the journey, feeling more subdued.

Twenty minutes later, they slid into the small car park in front of Christmas Lodge. Bonnibell opened the front door as soon as Ross switched off the engine and he battled with Moose and Snowball who'd sprinted up to greet him, whining and barking, desperate for some fuss.

'Did you join the sleepover too?' Bonnibell asked Grizzle, looking confused. She shuffled in the pockets of her swirly velvet skirt and drew out some biscuits for Bowser as he bounced over, greeting her like an old friend. 'I'll expect you're *all* hungry,' she observed. 'Do you want to come inside?'

'I want to get back to my own place,' Grizzle griped. 'The lass promised to decorate it for me. Are you going to drive us all in your car, lad?' He eyed a Land Rover which was parked at the other side of the lodge.

Bonnibell raised an eyebrow. 'Why don't you come in while Ross finishes unpacking the sleigh first?' she suggested. 'I'm sure it won't take long and I'll grab some food for you while you wait.' She cocked her head as she regarded the older man. 'Unless you'd rather stand in the snow?'

'I suppose not,' Grizzle said, scowling at Ross. 'Don't be long, lad,' he demanded.

Grizzle didn't comment as they walked through the festive hallway – although he did stop to sniff one of the Christmas trees. Ivy slid out a stool for him at the breakfast bar in the kitchen, wondering if the older man would see it from where he stood. He looked out of place and uncomfortable and she wondered if he'd been inside the lodge before – if what Ross had said about him keeping himself to himself was true.

'Do you want some hot chocolate?' Bonnibell asked, kneeling to take a tray of freshly cooked mince pies from the Aga.

Grizzle sniffed the air, and squinted at her, before he seemed to deflate. 'Aye,' he said, his voice reluctant, and he didn't move from where he was standing.

'Why don't you borrow my reading glasses?' Bonnibell offered, picking up a pair of sparkly red spectacles from the counter and walking to Grizzle so she could place them in his hand. After a moment's hesitation he slid them on and Ivy had to suppress a giggle because he looked so cute.

'I've pulled out a stool for you,' she told him, and he nodded and went to climb on, taking a moment to drink in his surroundings. He didn't say a word as he picked up the steaming mug Bonnibell had just placed in front of him, alongside a hot mince pie.

'It's been a long time since I've had the pleasure of your company,' Bonnibell said lightly as she took a tin from one of the cupboards and filled it with mince pies and cinnamon buns. Then she grabbed a container from the fridge and slid everything into a canvas bag. 'I've put some of my speciality casserole in a dish, along with some treats.'

'There's no need for that lass, I can feed myself,' Grizzle mumbled.

'I had leftovers,' Bonnibell said briskly. 'You may as well humour me because I'm going to insist.'

Grizzle grunted. 'Fine, it'll be better than anything I've eaten recently.' He looked unnerved as he sipped the drink and continued to peruse the room. Ivy noticed he didn't complain when Bonnibell put a second mince pie on his plate.

She watched as the older woman grabbed a small bag from under the counter and plucked a handful of mistletoe sprigs from a pile on the kitchen table before placing them inside. She handed the bag to Ivy.

'Connell cut these fresh this morning to hang in the cabins.' Her bulbous cheeks glowed. 'If you and Ross are decorating today, they might come in handy.' Bonnibell gave Ivy a theatrical wink.

It made her stomach swirl. She was about to tell her not to bother when a woman's voice rang out and she shoved the bag into the pocket of her snowsuit.

'I'm here to get things ready for the knitting club!'

When Ivy turned, she saw a petite woman of about seventy

with silver-grey hair. She was attractive and wore fitted grey trousers and a pink cardigan with tiny sparkles that had been sewn on. She drew to a sudden halt halfway to the breakfast bar when she spotted Grizzle and her expression sharpened.

'It's you!' she gasped.

The older man squinted at her and his cheeks paled. 'No one said *you'd* be here,' he said, grumpily. He gulped down the rest of his hot chocolate and grabbed another mince pie before climbing from his seat. 'I need to go,' Grizzle said sternly, pulling off the spectacles as if he couldn't bear to see.

'You leaving is no surprise,' said the woman who had to be Mairi, shuffling closer and narrowing her grey eyes. 'It's been a long time, McGregor. You look old.'

Grizzle sniffed. 'If I could see you better, I'm sure I'd say the same.'

His response elicited the tiniest hint of a smile in her. 'Aye. Last time I saw you properly you were leaving my da's house after telling him you never wanted to see me again.' Her expression was blank so Ivy had no clue if she was angry or hurt by the memory. 'Although you failed to explain why.'

'It's been so long I hardly remember.' Grizzle moved past her as Bowser trotted over to sniff the woman's tights. Mairi stayed perfectly still and Ivy waited for the dog to bark. Instead he let out a low whine and nuzzled her knees.

'Come here, you eejit dog,' Grizzle grumbled.

'You're just as sunny as ever I see,' Mairi sang in her thick Scottish lilt. 'Then again, your bonnie disposition was one of the things I most enjoyed about your company.'

'I'd say it takes a grouch to know one – word is you're not exactly a sparkling wit yourself,' Grizzle snapped back.

Mairi's cheeks pinked. 'So you've been keeping up with me?' She sounded pleased.

Grizzle spluttered. 'I've not thought about you in over forty years, lass.' His face was flushed and his eyes had brightened –

if Ivy had to guess she'd have said he was enjoying the spat. He started to leave, then turned just before he reached the door. 'And I'll not be needing your charity anymore. Please keep your casseroles and pies to yourself from now on.' With that he turned and stormed from the room.

'What pies?' Mairi asked, looking at Bonnibell and then Ivy. 'If I was cooking for the man he wouldn't be as thin as that.' She shook her head.

'I've no idea, hen,' Bonnibell said, innocently. 'I believe Ross has been making his meals.' She raised an eyebrow at Ivy.

'Ross Ballentine?' Mairi pulled a horrified face. 'But the lad can't cook at all.' She turned back to stare towards the exit as the front door slammed. 'He might be an old crabbit, but that really won't do at all,' she said.

Ivy glanced at the two women before grabbing the bags Bonnibell had prepared. 'I'd better be going,' she said. Hopefully Ross would be ready to leave by now. She had a feeling things were already stirred up enough – and didn't want to get caught in the middle of any more angst.

As Ivy walked through the hallway, she put her hand in her pocket and felt the bag of mistletoe. What would Ross make of it – and if they found themselves alone, would they kiss again?

Ivy stroked the bag as she trotted out of the lodge onto the decking. It would be a terrible idea – but she couldn't help wishing they would.

18

IVY

The drive to Grizzle's house was quiet. Grizzle sat on the back seat with Bowser, Moose and Snowball, keeping the peace, while Ivy took the front seat in Ross's Land Rover. The roads were thick with snow but they managed to park close to Grizzle's cabin before negotiating their way on foot through a warren of snowy pathways and tracks.

Once they arrived, Ross took a few moments to check out the front door of Grizzle's house, which was hanging off its hinges – much like it had been the last time Ivy visited.

'Did someone break in?' she asked worriedly as she wandered inside and placed Bonnibell's casserole into Grizzle's fridge.

'Ach, no lass. I told you, the eejit hinge got stuck when I was letting Bowser out last night and I had to break it. It's the whole reason I got lost in the woods,' the older man explained, walking inside with his dog before taking in a deep breath. 'Finally home. I can smell my treasures and they're all here.'

He squinted around the sitting room before he went to a box he kept on the table and pulled out a pair of spectacles with oversized black frames and perched them on his nose. He looked almost owl-like as he wrinkled his forehead and looked slowly around the room, blinking. 'It's good to be back. Although I'll have to check the place for evidence of Mairi visiting. I wonder what atrocity she's left for me to eat today.' He looked towards the fridge with a strange light in his eyes.

Ivy shivered. Since the front door had obviously been swinging open all night, the whole place was freezing. She quickly put the kettle on and made tea then laid out some of Bonnibell's mince pies. Then she lit the fire while Grizzle went to change into something warmer and Ross took the opportunity to work on the door. It was then that Ivy glanced across at Ross and found him watching her. There was a look on his face that told her he was as confused as she was about their kiss. She was about to say something but Grizzle returned from his bedroom.

Ivy handed him his hot drink and put her hands on her hips. 'So shall I find these decorations?' she asked, glancing around. 'This room could do with some Christmas love.'

'Nae lass, I'll get them myself, I can see perfectly fine with these.' He patted the glasses, his eyes narrowing as he glanced across the room at Ross. 'And I can see well enough to know the lad's making a mess of a perfectly fine door,' he grumbled. 'When he's finished, he could do something useful and cut me a Christmas tree – with your assistance of course. There are plenty outside to choose from.'

'Aye, I've almost finished,' Ross said darkly from where he was working.

Ivy raised an eyebrow just as he glanced up and met her eye again. He nodded his understanding and she felt something jump in her chest. Being around Ross was complicated – the feelings he was arousing were confusing, especially after their kiss. She was supposed to have her mind focused on moving to London, on her new career, but being with him at the resort was unearthing so many conflicting emotions about what she wanted and the direction she was headed in.

A few moments later Ross put down the tools. 'Shall we get this tree?' he asked.

'Make sure it's a big one,' Grizzle demanded as he made his way into the smaller bedroom with Bowser, clutching a mince pie and his mug.

Ivy braced herself as she followed Ross outside. It was snowing again and the forest surrounding Grizzle's house was sparkly with ice. Her phone suddenly buzzed in her pocket and she pulled it out, frowning at the screen when she realised she hadn't seen today's motivational quote on her coaching app yet.

She quickly read it and huffed.

'You don't always get what you want, but if you're lucky you might get what you need.'

Ivy tensed. 'That's only helpful if I know what I need – because I know exactly what I want.' Ivy shut the app, ignoring her daily goals again, and checked her messages. She'd received two texts. The first was from her mother.

Ivy, sorry I've only got ten minutes before my next surgery. Just wanted to say I hope everything's going well with Miriam's grandson. I'm so excited about your new chapter, darling. It'll be wonderful not to worry about you anymore. Mum xx

Ivy puffed out a breath, feeling a little sick. She hadn't achieved anything. She sensed Ross was wavering about speaking to his brother and grandmother, which gave her hope, but wasn't sure if he'd go through with moving to the castle – although that relied more on his conversations with his family than her. She did worry that even if he did decide to move, that he wouldn't want to leave Grizzle. She pulled a face. The obstacles kept piling up. Was that a sign that what she was doing was wrong?

The second text was from Miriam and Ivy had to stop herself from changing the contact name back to Cruella de Vil because her boss's message was demanding and bordering on rude.

Ivy what is the latest with my grandson? I need an update on when he's due to arrive at the castle. Surely it can't be that difficult to impart the information? I hope I haven't made a mistake asking you. Remember your new career depends on your success. MB

Ivy let out a heavy sigh. She couldn't deal with either of the messages now. Half of her wondered how Ross would survive back at Hawthorn Castle with his grandmother. Would he be happy there? She winced because the more she got to know him the more she cared – and she wasn't sure where that left them both.

Feeling conflicted, she shoved the mobile back into her pocket and followed Ross into the woods. He'd already located an axe and was waiting for her with Moose and Snowball who were charging around the small clearing. 'I thought we'd go to the place where I usually get Grizzle's Christmas tree.' He paused. 'I always replace the ones I use and I know a few of them are a good size now.' He turned abruptly and paced away.

Ivy matched his steps as they headed right. The canopy of trees wasn't as thick here, so the snowflakes fluttered through it and settled on their coats, leaving a glittery glaze.

'Do you want to choose?' Ross asked as he stopped in a large clearing. He folded his arms and watched her, his brown eyes brooding.

Ivy shrugged and then looked around, almost tripping over Snowball as he began to race in circles around her. 'I think Grizzle will like that one,' she said after a few minutes' contemplation, pointing to a bushy blue spruce which looked the right size.

'That's a good choice,' Ross said, wandering up to study the tree. 'It's extra prickly which will suit him. You're a natural at this. I guess I shouldn't be surprised; it's in your DNA after all.'

He turned and smiled at Ivy, clearly unaware of how much the observation had affected her. Of the sudden longing for the path that was no longer open to her.

'It's the same variety I usually go for,' he continued, before his smile slowly dropped as he studied her and his eyes heated.

That's when everything flew from Ivy's mind and her blood thickened in response. Then just as suddenly, Ross broke eye contact and rolled his shoulders as if attempting to reset.

'Do you want to see if you can choose a tree to suit me?' he asked, his voice tense.

Ivy let out a quivery breath, wondering if this was a test. She folded her arms as she spun around to study the trees and consider. That was when she spotted a singular tree in the distance. It was taller than the others with broad, glossy needles. The branches were luxuriant and it was an almost faultless triangular shape. 'That balsam fir there,' she said, pointing. 'It's perfect.'

'Why?' Ross asked, taking a few steps towards it.

'Because it's growing apart from the others,' she said. 'And because it's absolutely stunning.' She took in a deep breath as she drew closer to it, almost losing herself in the scent. 'It smells like Christmas and being outside in the woods – and if I close my eyes all I can think of is you.' She felt her cheeks burn, suddenly mortified by what she'd just revealed. 'Um, and there are lots of branches so... um, you won't run out of space to hang your baubles.'

Ross cleared his throat but Ivy couldn't bring herself to look his way.

'Wow. Thank you,' he murmured, walking past her so he

could kneel at the base of the tree. He had his back to her now – perhaps because he needed some space too – and Ivy was grateful.

It gave her a chance to recover and she could also now scour his broad shoulders and long legs. She studied his profile, remembering how soft his lips had felt in the tent. Their kisses had been relatively chaste, but there had been heat there. Heat she'd really wanted to explore. She shook herself – that would be a terrible idea.

'Do you need any help?' she asked, keeping her tone bland.

Ross let out a shaky breath. 'Only if you can tell me how to deal with this...' He hissed, looking up, his eyes dark. 'Thing between us.'

Ivy cleared her throat, as every cell of her body seemed to rejoice. 'I've no idea,' she said, dropping her gaze to the ground. 'It's a bad idea on every level, but...'

'Aye. But that doesn't stop me wanting it,' Ross said finally, standing and facing her. 'It's like you've breathed life into me, Ivy.' He stared at her, looking baffled. 'Part of me wants things to go back to the way they were, when I barely thought of my family and I didn't want to get close to anyone again.' His voice was unhappy.

'I'm sorry—' Ivy started.

'Don't.' He held up a large palm. 'Because another part of me is happy you came. Terrified, but happy.' His face tensed as if he were struggling to find the right words.

Ivy stood, transfixed by the storm of emotions that raged across his handsome face.

'I just stopped feeling. For over fifteen years I've been paralysed by guilt.' He looked around, his face wonderstruck, like he was seeing his surroundings for the first time. 'Maybe I've been hiding in the wilderness. I thought I was content. But I was living like Grizzle. It's only now I realise how much I've let myself become like him.'

His gaze moved to the Blue Spruce. 'I'm prickly and unsociable – I never go anywhere, and I say no to every invitation.' He shook his head. 'If you hadn't come along, I'm guessing I'd have ended my days just like him. Too stubborn to go to an optician even when it's obvious I need one; contrary; crotchety and...' He hesitated. 'Lonely...'

His mouth pinched, drawing Ivy's attention to its edible curves.

'So...' she said, unsure. What was he saying?

'So, I need something to change, Ivy. I'm saying I'd like to let you into my world.'

She swallowed. 'I'm moving to London,' she murmured.

His face dropped.

'But—' She took in an unsteady breath. 'I...' She put her hands into her pockets, searching for the right thing to say, and felt one of the sprigs of mistletoe poking through the bag Bonnibell had given her. She drew it out and held it between them, wondering if it was a sign. 'I'd like to let you into my world too, at least for as long as I can.'

Ross stared at the plant as if he wasn't sure what it meant. But his expression was hopeful.

Ivy took a step towards him and held the mistletoe sprig in the air. She wasn't tall enough to reach above his head, so he plucked it from her fingers, took a step closer and suspended it above them both.

'Shall we start with a kiss?' Ivy asked, huskily.

When Ross nodded, she went onto her tip toes and pressed her mouth to his.

19

IVY

The kiss started slow. Ivy wasn't sure what she wanted. She'd known this man for less than a week, but somehow he'd rooted himself inside her and the feelings that were growing felt very strong, despite them being foolish and irresponsible. Ross must have dropped the mistletoe sprig, because she felt him gently press his gloved hands to the edges of her cheeks so he could tilt her chin upwards, then he bent lower so the kiss could deepen.

Ivy had never felt like this. She'd had boyfriends over the years – there had been one at the garden centre who she'd dated for over six months. But much like a sweet pea in mid-summer, the feelings had bloomed hot and fast, only to wither and die almost as rapidly. There'd been no animosity and no regrets – just indifference.

But her feelings for Ross already went far deeper and she wasn't sure what to do with them. The kiss grew hotter and her heart hammered as her blood pumped so fast Ivy felt light-headed. Her knees began to go and she wrapped her arms around Ross's neck and pressed their bodies closer, feeling the evidence of his arousal. Wishing suddenly that they weren't in the woods just a few hundred metres from Grizzle's house.

She broke off the kiss and stared into Ross's face. Saw confusion slide across his eyes before he pulled back too.

'Okay,' he murmured as if returning to sanity. 'That mistletoe should come with a warning.' He cleared his throat.

Ivy found herself smiling. 'I'll let Bonnibell and Connell know.' She swallowed before taking in their surroundings. 'We've been a while. I suppose—'

'Aye – we should get the trees.' He didn't sound particularly happy about it.

Ivy drew in a breath, still trying to get her wayward hormones to still. 'If we don't, Grizzle might come looking for us.' Was she trying to convince herself or Ross?

'Or worse, he'll send Bowser.' Ross pulled a face before he bent to pick up the mistletoe he'd let fall to the ground. 'Shall we revisit this later?' he asked, looking hopeful.

Ivy nodded. It might be a bad idea, but she knew she wasn't going to be able to refuse. Was this how her parents had felt when they'd met? Had the connection between them been just as compelling? It was madness to let herself fall further into it, but even as Ross went to pick up the axe, Ivy knew she wasn't strong enough to walk away.

THE BALSAM fir Ivy had selected for Ross's house was perfect. She wiped the snow from her hair and jumper as he finished setting it up to the right of the fireplace.

'I've never bothered putting a tree in this house before. There never seemed much point because it was only me and the boys,' Ross admitted as he shifted so he could light the fire.

'Have you got any decorations?' Ivy asked, wishing she'd thought about it earlier. Then again, her brain had been occupied since they'd left the forest with the two trees. Even decorating Grizzle's house hadn't stopped her mind from mulling over and over what had happened. As if it were trying to settle on an excuse for why their kiss had been so powerful so it could dismiss it. But Ivy knew if she pressed her fingers to her lips they'd still be tingling and wishing for a repeat.

'Aye,' Ross said as the fire began to crackle and glow. 'Bonnibell's been giving me baubles, pom-poms and bunting these past five years in the hope that I'd use them. She told me as an employee of Christmas Resort it was in my job description to decorate.' He chuckled. 'I haven't – but I know where it all is.' He paced into the utility room and returned carrying a large box and placed it on the floor beside the tree. 'Do you want to get started and I'll make us both a hot drink?'

Ivy nodded, then knelt and began to shuffle through the decorations as Snowball wandered across the room to help. She placed some tinsel to one side on the floor as she dug in the box for something to put on the top of the tree. The wild boar grabbed the sparkly string between his teeth and went running up to Moose to show it off. 'Careful with that,' she said as she began to rise.

'It's okay, he'll be fine,' Ross soothed, from the kitchen. 'He'll lose interest and you'll get it back. If you go after him, he'll decide it's a game.'

Ivy nodded, then set to work hanging some of the sparkly baubles and bunting. There was a large *Ferocactus* sitting on the mantlepiece and on a whim she added a sparkly red bow to the top. By the time Ross brought the drinks over and placed them on the mantlepiece, Ivy was halfway through the box. 'You could probably do with a few more decorations,' she said as she stood aside so he could see her progress.

'I'm sure Bonnibell can help with that.' Ross shoved his hands into his pockets as he perused the room. 'Is that something your da used to do at the garden centre?' he asked, pointing to the glittering succulent, looking amused.

'Not exactly,' Ivy said shyly. 'He brought me a couple of cacti when I was a kid and I take them with me everywhere. I usually decorate them at Christmas – it feels wrong to leave them out.' She flushed. 'They're like part of the family – I even named them Prickles and Needles,' she added, feeling her cheeks burn hotter when he gazed at her with an unreadable expression.

'That's...'

'Weird?' Ivy asked, suddenly wishing she hadn't told him.

'I was going to say charming,' he said softly, fixing her with his whisky-coloured eyes. She watched a myriad of emotions flicker across his face until they settled into something Ivy could only describe as attraction. Ross cleared his throat. 'I've still got the mistletoe. Where should we hang it?' He pointed to the sprig he'd dropped on the sofa when they'd first arrived without moving his gaze from her face.

Ivy's whole body heated as Ross shifted closer.

She'd known this was going to happen – they'd agreed on it – and suddenly Ivy didn't really care whether it was a good idea. She tipped her chin and Ross began to lean in – that's when she heard a loud crash and they both spun around.

'Dammit, Snowball!' Ross yelled as he charged across the room to check on his pet who was now tangled in the tinsel underneath a small oak table lying on its side. The string had hooked itself around the base of the table and Ross unwound it, releasing the wild boar from its grasp.

'Is he okay?' Ivy asked, breathlessly. 'I'm so sorry, this is all my fault.'

'It's not – and he's fine, just a little surprised,' Ross soothed as Snowball leapt up and trotted over to Moose. Ross repositioned the table and then made a distressed sound as he spotted the three picture frames scattered on the floor. Glass was splattered beside one of them, and he carefully gathered it up, looking unsettled.

'Let me find something to clear that up,' Ivy offered, replacing the two intact pictures on the table. When she returned from the utility room with a dustpan and brush, Ross was still staring at the photo in the broken frame. 'Are you okay?' she asked gently, kneeling and quickly dealing with the glass.

'I'm fine.' He put the frame onto the sofa and took the dustpan from Ivy, heading for the bin. When he returned, he picked up the photo again and took it out of the frame. From where Ivy was standing, she could see the picture was of Simon. 'I remember our conversation in the tent,' Ross said, still staring at it. 'It made me think about how it might feel if one day I didn't get the chance to make up with my family. If it was ever too late.'

Ivy waited.

'I suppose we never really know what's going to happen, do we? Like glass. We're all so fragile. Of anyone, I should know that.' He swallowed. 'I'm not sure why I forgot. I think...' He hesitated. 'I mean I know I need to speak to Miriam, but I want to talk to Simon first. We were close once.' He turned and stared at her. 'I need to know why he's decided to walk away from being Laird.' He gazed at the photo he was still clutching. 'I may not have seen my brother for a long time, but I remember it's all he ever wanted. I have to ask him what happened.' He frowned. 'If he's unhappy maybe I can help. But...' He looked anxious.

'What?'

Ross's gaze was suddenly vulnerable. 'I'm terrified. What if Simon doesn't want to know me?'

Ivy let out a long breath. 'He might not,' she admitted. 'But what if he's been waiting for you to get in touch? He might feel the same as you.' She held her breath as Ross considered that.

His face cleared. 'I don't even have his number,' he said, guiltily. 'How awful is that? I walked away and never once considered my brother. I was so sure he felt the same as Miriam and didn't want to know, that I ignored his calls.' He squeezed his eyes shut for an instant before looking at her bleakly. 'I decided a clean break would be best. But I think that's just because it was what I needed.'

'So make it right,' she said softly. 'I've got his number in my mobile if you want to call him now? I can go for a walk with Moose and Snowball and give you some privacy.'

Ross gave her a half smile. 'If I let you outside on your own, you might never come back. You'll be trying to remember the Latin names for all the trees and seeing what plants you can spot in the woods. I'm not sure I want to risk it.' His voice was affectionate. 'I'd like you to stay in the house while I call, if that's okay? That way if things don't go the way I want, I've got a shoulder to cry on. Or at least someone to share a bottle of single malt.'

Ivy nodded and pulled out her phone, suddenly feeling sick. Would Simon reject Ross? If he did, Ivy knew she'd leave Christmas Resort today and tell Miriam her grandson wasn't interested in getting in touch.

Which would also mean any chance of their relationship developing further would be over before it had begun.

'DID YOU SPEAK TO SIMON?' Ivy asked eagerly, her stomach churning as Ross headed down the stairs clutching her mobile.

'Yes,' Ross croaked as he strode to where she was waiting on the sofa.

'And?' Ivy asked, searching Ross's face, suddenly afraid when he handed her back the phone. She hadn't come to Christmas Resort to hurt him – did this mean she was going to have to leave?

Ross smiled suddenly. 'It was great. He sounds just the same.' He slumped onto the sofa and Ivy relaxed too, then he shut his eyes and hissed out air. 'I was half-expecting him to hang up. But...' He opened his eyes and gazed at her. 'He was pleased to hear from me, once he got over the shock of it not being you on the phone. Do you want some whisky?' he asked and stood before Ivy could respond.

'Did he say why he left the castle?' Ivy asked as Ross padded across the kitchen and poured them both a glass. He looked relaxed, the tension in his body gone.

'No.' Ross shook his head. 'He's driving to the resort to meet with me tomorrow. He said it's been too long for our first real conversation not to be face-to-face.' He swallowed. 'I thought I'd ask Bonnibell if we can meet in the lodge. Neutral territory – also, her mince pies might bribe him into a good mood.' He gave her a shy smile as he handed her a glass of whisky and took a sip of his own. 'Dammit.' He pulled a face. 'I promised Grizzle I'd pick up his eBay packages from the post office tomorrow. He's ordered more glasses.'

'That's okay,' Ivy said. 'I can do it.'

'Thank you. I don't want to let him down.' Ross relaxed and sipped some of his drink. 'I guess you can tell I'm nervous. That's a little embarrassing to admit.'

Ivy squeezed his arm. 'I'd be surprised if you weren't. You've been hurt.' She left her hand where it was and sipped from her glass. The amber liquid glided down her throat. 'I hope he'll have answers for you.' She gave him a half-smile. 'I hope they're the right ones – the ones you deserve.'

'What do I deserve?' Ross asked, placing his hand over Ivy's and setting off a wave of goosebumps that flared downwards to her toes.

'I don't know.' Ivy shifted and sipped from her glass, suddenly feeling nervous. She knew where this was leading and knew she wanted it to happen. But she also knew it was going to mean a lot. At least to her. 'To be happy, to have your family back, and...' *To find love.* The words popped into Ivy's mind and she flushed.

'And?' Ross asked, gazing at her. When she didn't respond

he took the glass from her hand and put it on the coffee table along with his.

'I don't know.' Ivy's heart hammered. She looked around the room searching for something to say that wouldn't embarrass her. 'Christmas trees,' she squeaked. 'You deserve those, baubles too, mince pies and...' She was babbling now. 'And, um—'

'Mistletoe?' Ross interrupted, his voice husky. 'Do I deserve that too?'

'Yes,' Ivy whispered, meeting his eyes. 'And kisses,' she added, breathlessly. Because she needed Ross to kiss her now...

20

IVY

'Kisses?' Ross repeated, his eyes darkening.

Ivy gulped as attraction flared through her body. She nodded mutely.

'And what do *you* deserve, Ivy?' Ross asked huskily as he shifted closer to her on the sofa.

Ivy could feel the heat from his body now and let herself lean into him. She could smell balsam wood and pine needles and knew she'd never be able to smell either again without thinking of this man.

'I don't know – I just know I want you.' She stared into his eyes, feeling hers well up. Ross was watching her with the oddest expression and Ivy didn't know what it meant. 'It's not the best idea. But Dad used to say life finds a way.' She gave him a watery smile. 'And that resonates. In summer, whenever I see a pavement with a dandelion growing through the cracks, I always want to celebrate. Because it didn't think about what it deserved, it went against the plan someone else had decided on so it could live.'

'Is that what you want, Ivy?' Ross asked, his voice low. 'To go against the plan.'

'I wish I could,' she choked.

She imagined she could hear Ross's heart now and it was beating like a jackhammer, then she felt his large hands gather up hers. He began to stroke the sensitive skin on the back of them.

The movement soothed her, but then something began to change. Instead of feeling comfort from those calm strokes, the tingles that had been travelling across Ivy's skin grew stronger. Sensation worked its way downwards until need and want twisted at her core. Ivy shifted closer to Ross and eased her hands from his so she could hug him. Now she could hear his heart pounding in her ear, the wild thumps vibrating through her, making everything inside tremble.

It was Ross who pulled away first so he could look down into Ivy's face. His eyes were darker now, and his whisky-coloured irises had almost disappeared into black. She felt the breath catch in her throat as he stared and pressed her fingertips to his chest. Felt the ferocious thump of his heartbeat again, knew the beat was mirrored by hers.

Ivy didn't know who moved first. It might have been Ross, or perhaps she did? All she knew was suddenly they were kissing, her heart racing and her hands roaming across his body as she pressed herself into him, pushing him backwards onto the sofa as the kiss, which had started slow, deepened, pulling her into its depths.

Ivy only realised she'd stripped Ross to his waist when she was dropping his T-shirt on top of the jumper she'd already pulled off. Moose came to snuffle at the clothes, then let out a low whine and trotted towards the kitchen, closely followed by Snowball who'd obviously decided he'd be happier out of the way too.

Ivy ignored them as she pressed her nose to Ross's chest and smelled pine trees. She heard him growl low in his throat and then he tugged off her jumper and T-shirt. Then she was sitting in nothing but canvas trousers and a lacy white bra. She should have felt embarrassed, but she rejoiced in the flames that lit those dark eyes. Neither of them spoke. They didn't have to check that this was what they wanted. They'd already talked too much and this was primal now. Ivy set to work on the buttons and zip of Ross's trousers, while he fumbled with hers. Their arms tangled in their haste to pull them off.

Then Ivy climbed onto her knees on the sofa so she could sit astride Ross's hips. She leaned down so she could kiss him before easing back so she could tug his boxers off, before chucking them over her shoulder. She didn't bother to look at where they'd landed – reluctant to break their gaze. If she did, perhaps this deep connection she could feel would disappear. Or they'd come to their senses. Ross wriggled, then made quick work of his socks before moving Ivy onto her back so he could finish stripping her too.

Ivy moved again, pushing Ross into a sitting position until she was straddling his hips. Then she closed her eyes and let herself feel. Ross's breath was raspy but he didn't speak – there was no need for words. Ivy stilled her mind and sank onto him, felt the firmness of his skin tickle hers. Then she dipped forwards until her breasts brushed his chest and kissed the bottom of his jaw. All the while Ross stroked Ivy's back, exploring the curve of her hips, and the crease at the top of her legs before he traced a path downwards, stopping momentarily at her knees before stroking her calf and ankles. It was as if he were learning every shape and angle, committing them to memory.

Then Ross's hands came up to cup Ivy's breasts before lowering so he could stroke the soft skin of her belly. They moved lower still and she gasped as he continued his slow exploration and moved so she could press her mouth to his neck, peppering tiny kisses until she reached his lips.

Ivy's body was vibrating, every inch of her trembling as her breath shortened into pants as Ross began to rock. Finally, when she was about to scream, he rolled her under him and Ivy looked into his eyes and held his gaze. She reached up and cupped his jaw, felt the prickles from his bristles and stroked them with her fingertips. Trying to memorise every inch.

This time their kisses were warm and gentle like a summer breeze. Ross's hands roamed, feathering Ivy's skin, sensitizing every cell until she could barely stand the sensations.

Then everything changed as the breeze transformed into a storm and their kisses grew hotter and faster. They crashed against each other, suddenly desperate as their fingers explored – until Ivy began to climb. Ross must have read her groans of pleasure because suddenly he was inside her, rocking and stretching until the chaos of sensations got too much and they ripped through her and they both went over the edge.

Ivy lay silent as Ross moved them both until they were spooning on the sofa. The room was dark, aside from the flickers from the fire and the glow of the Christmas lights. He shifted again and suddenly a blanket was thrown over them. Ivy shut her eyes, drifting on sensation, relishing the unfamiliar aches in her body. All the while Ross stroked, his hand gentle as he investigated the angles and planes of her body. Moments later, Ivy fell asleep.

THE FIRE WAS ALMOST out when Ivy woke. Ross was still pressed against her back and she snuggled into him. He pressed a kiss onto the back of her neck and adjusted the arm which was lying across her hip.

'Can't you sleep?' he whispered. 'We can move to my bed if you'd be more comfortable.'

'I'm okay.' Ivy blinked as she took in the Christmas lights which were still twinkling in the darkness. 'Why are you awake?'

'I don't want to miss a moment of this,' Ross said and moved, which made his body brush Ivy's back. She bit her lip to stop herself from groaning. 'And I've been thinking...'

Ivy stiffened. 'What about?'

Ross stroked her hip. 'I still want to speak to Simon, if that's what you're worried about. It's not that...' he said carefully. 'I've been thinking about you.'

Ivy stared at the tree. 'What have you been thinking?' Her stomach churned.

'It's none of my business, but...' Ross hesitated. 'I know what you've told me about your mam, but... Ivy, it's so clear to me that you love working outside. It's more than a vocation – the reason I know that is because I feel the same about being outdoors.' He squeezed her hip. 'Surely if you told her how you felt about it, she'd understand?'

'She wouldn't,' Ivy said tonelessly, touching his hand and drawing it around her because suddenly she needed the warmth. 'I've told you. We've argued about it many times, and she'll never get it. In a lot of ways, I understand.'

'I just...' He paused, mulling his words. 'I don't know how to explain this. But I don't want you to be unhappy. Everything you've done since coming to Christmas Resort has been about helping me find my way back to my family. Because you want me to connect with them. Because you think it's in my best interests.'

Ivy tried not to tense up. She didn't deserve Ross's gratitude. That wasn't why she'd come – at least at first. Now she did want him to be happy, but a small part of her was afraid he was going to get hurt. That perhaps his desire to separate himself from his family had been right all along.

'I'm – look...' Ivy started.

'Trying to make everyone else happy?' Ross suggested.

Ivy pursed her lips. 'The London job is a good opportunity for me...'

'Why?'

'I might love it,' she said, but she knew the tone of her voice signalled she wasn't convinced. She tried to focus on the Christmas tree again. She wasn't ready for reality to seep into the shiny moment they'd created. She wanted to spend a little more time just enjoying being with Ross.

'I know about expectations from watching what Simon went through. At the time, I was always so focused on the fact that no one wanted anything from me. But what I didn't see was how difficult it must be when you don't get to choose what you do for yourself. I've never thought of myself as lucky before, but perhaps I should...' Ross's arm tightened around her. 'I admire that you care so much about your mam, and I really respect you for trying to make her happy. I'm just not sure you should put her feelings before yours.' His sigh was heavy.

'I have to,' Ivy mumbled.

'Aye.' His hug turned into a squeeze. 'Perhaps I just can't understand it because the people I meet aren't usually that selfless.'

'I'm not selfless,' Ivy gasped as guilt flooded through her. 'Please don't say that.'

She felt the blood drain from her face – because Ross's admiration was unwarranted. How would he feel if he knew the reason she'd come to Christmas Resort was to get her coveted job? He wouldn't understand. But suddenly she really wanted him to.

'This isn't just about Mum. It's time I took control of my life. All my worldly possessions could be packed into the boot of my Mini in less than half an hour. That kind of life is fine when you're in younger, but I'm almost thirty – it's time I got myself sorted.' Ivy's mother's words echoed around her mind, like the lyrics to a song you'd heard once and couldn't stop yourself from singing along to. 'What's the definition of madness?'

'Turning up twice a day to an old man's home so he can insult your cooking and set his dog on you?' Ross joked.

Ivy couldn't stop the bark of laughter. 'Well, yes. But one of the motivational quotes on my coaching app told me that the definition of madness is doing the same thing over and over and expecting a different result. That's why I have to change something. I'm not mad, I'm just...' She winced. 'Confused I suppose.'

'Maybe that's because you've been trying to walk someone else's path,' Ross suggested. 'The truth is, someone somewhere is always going to have a piece of advice if you ask for it. I'm not saying your mam's wrong, but I am saying don't live your life because of something someone else says. You're turning yourself inside out trying to make your Mam happy – but are *you* happy, Ivy?'

'I don't know.' Ivy pursed her lips as she considered his question before she shook her head. Her happiness wasn't the issue here. 'I can't have Mum worrying about me for the rest of her life.'

Ross kissed the edge of her neck. 'I'm not trying to tell you what to do, I'm just saying think about it, Ivy.' He eased himself up so he could kiss her cheek too. 'If you want to work with plants, I'm just saying maybe you can find another way – a way you can both be happy?'

'I'll think about it,' Ivy promised as he began to ease her over so she could kiss him back.

She knew she wouldn't. Despite the whispering in her head that Ross might be right.

21

ROSS

Ross heaved in a deep breath as he approached the decking of Christmas Lodge, feeling apprehensive. Now he was here – he wasn't sure if he wanted to go through with meeting his brother. What if Simon didn't really want to see him? What if he'd only come to sever any connection between them once and for all?

Before Ross could change his mind and leave, the front door swung open and he saw Bonnibell beaming at him. His nerves instantly calmed and he relaxed. He realised he had never quite appreciated the soothing power of his friendship with this woman until Ivy had arrived at the resort.

How many other things had she changed about his life since coming? And how would he feel when she left?

'Simon's here,' Bonnibell said in her musical voice and Ross reluctantly pushed all thoughts of Ivy from his mind. The older woman held the door wide open and Moose and Snowball bounded into the hallway ahead of him. 'I put your brother in the kitchen and gave him some hot chocolate and a plate of mince pies.' She winked. 'He's a lot like you lad – a little shorter, but he's got the same appetite.' Her pink cheeks glowed as she let him inside. 'He's jumpy,' she whispered conspiratorially as she guided him through the festive hallway towards the kitchen.

'Maybe he's nervous. I know I am,' Ross admitted, earning himself a shocked glance.

'Aye.' Bonnibell's eyes rounded. 'Well hearing that's a surprise lad, I'd have said nothing phased you.' She indicated that he should go into the kitchen. 'Try not to be,' she advised. 'It's obvious he's just as worried as you. Besides, it's almost Christmas, the perfect time for reconnecting with your ken.'

Simon was sitting at the breakfast bar staring into a mug of hot chocolate. He jerked to his feet the minute Ross and his pets entered the kitchen, looking startled when he spotted Snowball. 'What's that?' he gasped.

'He's my pet. Don't worry, he won't bite,' Ross assured him.

'Ross,' Simon said gruffly, his voice gravelly. He wiped his hands on his trousers – a nervous habit Ross remembered from their childhood, one his da had also had. 'It's grand to see you.'

Ross swallowed a wave of relief. 'Aye, same here.' He forced the words from his throat, overcome, and studied his brother, taking in the changes. They had the same almond-shaped face – inherited from their mother – and Simon's eyes were the same colour as Ross's. His brother had lost weight in the past five years and there were signs of stress in the lines around his forehead and cheeks, which made him look tired and a little troubled.

'You look the same. I could have seen you just a few weeks ago,' Simon said gruffly, stepping around the breakfast bar so he could greet Ross properly.

They gave each other an awkward hug and Ross heard Bonnibell cough from where she was standing by the kitchen door.

'Aye, well I'll leave you two alone to talk, you won't be disturbed,' she promised, her eyes shining as she gazed at them both. 'There are plenty of mince pies and if you fancy something else, check out the gingerbread-shaped tin next to the kettle.' She pointed towards the back of the room. 'There are biscuits in there – I keep them for staff emergencies. They're especially good if you're struggling to find the right words.' Her expression turned serious as she gazed at Ross. 'Good luck,' she said, before closing the door.

Ross stood staring at his brother, his breathing choppy with emotion. For a moment he wished Ivy was here. She'd know the right thing to say to break the ice.

'Thanks for coming.' He tried to channel her – then stared mutely at the stools by the breakfast bar. Bonnibell had already poured him a mug of hot chocolate and Ross could see a plate on the counter piled up with mince pies. Simon had taken a bite out of one of them already, but he hadn't finished.

'I'm nervous,' Simon admitted suddenly. 'Shall we sit?' He strode back to the stool he'd been perched on and eased himself onto it.

Ross took the stool opposite and sat – feeling awkward. 'This is weird,' he finally managed. 'In a good way,' he added when Simon looked dismayed.

'Aye.' His brother's forehead creased. The room fell silent again until he cleared his throat. 'I was glad to hear from you. I thought you'd decided you were done with me.'

Ross looked up, startled. 'I was never done with you,' he said softly. 'After Mam and Da died, I...'

'Blamed yourself.' Simon nodded. He bit another chunk out of his mince pie and slid the large plate towards Ross.

Ross took one and bit into it too.

After a few moments his brother let out an almost soundless purr. 'These are magic. If I lived within a few miles of this place, I'd be the size of a castle.' He took another one and chewed for a moment as the room fell silent again.

Ross followed his lead – he didn't know what to say either.

He only knew for the first time in five years he was sitting in the same room as his brother and it felt... right.

'I never blamed you, Ross,' Simon said finally, taking in a long noisy breath. 'I was grieving and Grandmother, well...' He winced. 'She wanted me to start learning to pick up the reins from Da straight away. There wasn't a lot of time for thinking about what we'd lost.' He shut his eyes. 'For a long time, I couldn't see beyond what I needed to do. I wanted to make them proud. Felt it was my duty.' He shrugged.

'It wasn't until you left the castle for good that I realised in doing so, I'd turned my back on you. I should have recognised you were grieving. I should have known how hard you'd take our parents' deaths.' His voice was tortured.

Ross felt the tightness in his chest ease, surprised. 'This isn't about fault,' he said, his voice low. 'Perhaps neither of us could handle what happened.' He fiddled with his mug, turning it round and round, watching the half-melted marshmallows Bonnibell had placed on the top dissolve, thinking about all the beliefs he'd been holding on to. Wondering if he could let them disappear too. 'You tried to talk to me a hundred times, and you contacted me after I'd left,' he admitted, pursing his lips because the sudden flood of memories went against all the tales he'd told himself. The ones about not being wanted, the ones about being blamed, the ones about being second best.

'Aye, and you didn't call me back,' Simon said. 'But I should have tried harder, I shouldn't have ignored the problem and left it – I just didn't know what to say.'

Ross could hear pain in his voice and felt awful. 'I wouldn't have listened even if you had called. You can't blame yourself, Simon. I honestly didn't think I deserved you,' Ross said quietly. 'And I thought Miriam blamed me, that I wasn't a real part of the family. She only seemed to want you.' He paused. 'It's only recently I've started to wonder if I was just seeing what I thought was there.'

And he'd only wondered because of Ivy. He'd still be living the same lie if she hadn't come along and held up a mirror to the things he'd believed.

'I still could have tried harder,' Simon insisted, straightening his shoulders in a gesture Ross recognised as another of his father's mannerisms. Instead of making him sad, he felt homesick. 'If we want to lay blame, we both have a share and so does Miriam. But that doesn't matter now. What does is we're both finally sitting here,' Simon said, firmly.

Ross nodded and found himself smiling. Simon had always been blunt and honest. Quick to take blame and quicker to forgive. He'd always called a spade a spade and had never tried to pretend it was anything else. Ross had missed his big brother, more than he'd realised.

'Aye, you're right.' Ross let out a long breath. 'So I called you yesterday—'

'On Ivy Heart's mobile,' Simon interrupted, tipping an eyebrow and smirking.

'Aye,' Ross muttered because he wasn't sure how much he wanted to share about that. He was still processing his feelings – and trying to work out how he felt about her leaving. 'She's here because Miriam sent her to find me,' he said. He hadn't given his brother the full story the evening before. It had been enough of a shock to speak to him and he hadn't wanted to overload them both. 'Ivy told me you've decided not to become Laird?'

'Aye.' Simon seemed to shrink. He picked up another mince pie and contemplated it. 'She's right.' He looked unhappy.

'But, why?' Ross asked, leaning forwards. 'It's what you've been prepared for your entire life.' Much like Ivy had been trained by her father for a career working with plants – she'd turned her back on that though. Was there a reason why Simon had decided he couldn't follow through too – was someone forcing him to give it up?

His brother scratched his fingers over his chin. 'It wasn't one thing Ross, it was a thousand,' he said wearily. 'It *is* all I've ever wanted, but I didn't appreciate until recently that it would mean I couldn't have anything else.' His tone was despondent. 'Miriam started telling me who I'd be allowed to marry a couple of weeks ago. Perhaps I should have expected it: I'm only a month away from my thirtieth birthday, after all.' He widened his eyes. 'She wrote me a list of suitable families with daughters she considered to be in the right... circles.' He mashed his lips together as if wrestling with a bad taste.

'Seriously?' Ross checked, hardly able to believe what he was hearing.

Simon nodded, his expression perplexed. 'They had to have the correct looks, intelligence, and be of child-bearing age. *Jeez*, it was like being catapulted into another century.' He shuddered. 'I've always wanted to marry for love. I've been seeing this woman off and on for the last few years.' His eyes darkened. 'We haven't made long-term plans, but I've wondered recently...' He looked unhappy.

'I'm sorry,' Ross replied because he didn't know what else to say. Guilt slinked through him as he realised and accepted what his brother had been going through. The pressure of expectation must have been immense. All the weight he'd carried – with no one to share it.

'I love riding,' Simon continued. 'But Miriam told me I should give that up too. She was concerned in case I got injured – because according to Grandmother, at this point in my life...' Simon gave Ross a loaded look. 'There is no other heir, and I was told I was responsible for delivering one.'

'That's...' Ross gulped.

His brother nodded, clearly still reflecting on the situation. He picked up his mince pie and took another bite. Ross watched as he chewed and swallowed, his face a profusion of pleasure. 'She started to tell me what I could eat at the start of this year – do you know this might be the first time I've overindulged since January?' He blinked, his eyes resentful. Simon had always been even-tempered, but it was obvious even he had his limits.

'Didn't you tell her no?' Ross asked.

Simon pulled a disbelieving face. 'Miriam does what Miriam wants and we're expected to fall into line.' He polished off the mince pie and swiped crumbs off his palms. 'You must remember that?' he asked. 'If I want my own life, the only option I have is to walk away. It might not be what I want, but the pressure of measuring up to her expectations is simply too much.'

He stopped suddenly and his expression turned curious. 'Miriam sent Ivy here to tell you what had happened. Why? Has she hatched some devious plan that involves you trying to convince me to go back to the castle and become Laird? I suppose she remembered we were close once.' For a moment his brother looked disappointed.

'No!' Ross shot back. 'She sent Ivy because she wants me to return to Hawthorn Castle so I can be primed to take over as Laird instead of you,' Ross said, waiting for his brother's reaction.

'She did?' Simon asked, pushing out his lower lip as he eyed another mince pie and obviously though better of it. 'I'm pleased she finally realised you'd be just as deserving of the title as me. What did you decide?'

'I haven't,' Ross said. 'That's why I wanted to talk to you.'

'Do you want my blessing? Because you've got it,' his brother said, hopping down from the stool and collecting the gingerbread-shaped biscuit tin Bonnibell had mentioned. He pulled off the lid and the kitchen filled with the scent of melted chocolate. Simon hummed as he grabbed a snowman-shaped biscuit and bit into it.

'Yet more magic... How about when you go to the castle, I live here?' Simon joked after swallowing. 'Seriously, you'll make a fantastic Laird, Ross: you're dedicated and I can only imagine the work you'd be able to do around the estate. I've never been blessed with green fingers like you.' He sucked air between his teeth. 'I saw the resort grounds on my drive in and I know all about the adventure tours you run, because people talk about them where we live. You're famous around these parts – like Scotland's answer to Bear Grylls.'

'They do?' Ross asked, flushing. 'I mean, I am?'

'Aye. I'm proud of you, little brother. Hawthorn Castle couldn't do better. But–' Simon's eyebrows pinched. 'Think carefully about whether you want to live that kind of life. One where you don't get to decide anything, where every moment of every day isn't your own.'

Ross studied Simon. 'Perhaps we should visit grandmother together – to talk about it?' he suggested. 'We could have a conversation about her expectations, about what she's been pressuring you to do. Maybe there's a solution to this, and you wouldn't have to give your position up?'

'Two heads are better than one?' Simon asked, considering. 'I'm happy to come with you to speak with her, but–' He shook his head. 'Taking these few days out from all the responsibilities has really made me re-evaluate what I want.' He let out a long breath. 'I thought I might miss it, but I've realised I don't want to live every day under that kind of pressure. It's a lot to carry on one set of shoulders. I'm not sure I'm ever going to want to go back. If you want to be Laird, little brother, I'm not going to stand in your way.'

'I'm not sure it's what I want either,' Ross said carefully, looking around. 'I've got a life here. Friends I don't want to leave.' He thought about Grizzle, Bonnibell and Connell, and his mind slid to Ivy too – it was early days, but he already knew he'd miss her when she moved to London. He hesitated. 'But I walked away from our family once and–' He rested his elbows on the table and put his chin in his hands, feeling torn. 'I'm not sure I can do it again.'

'Then we'll go and see our grandmother tomorrow. Bring Ivy,' Simon said, his expression suddenly mischievous. 'Tell her I need her there to brighten up the dull corridors of Hawthorn Castle.'

Ross had to halt the sudden burst of jealousy that rose in his throat. But then Simon began to laugh loudly and Ross felt himself relax, realising his brother had been trying to rile him.

'Aye.' Simon nodded, looking satisfied. 'I did wonder...' He continued to chuckle as he picked up another biscuit and waved it in the air. 'Don't worry little brother, I've nae got designs on your bonnie lass. I've got my own to keep me warm.'

Ross opened his mouth to dismiss Simon's words, but then he closed it again. Because though he might not have seen his brother in years, Simon had clearly been able to see how strong his feelings for Ivy were. Ross just wasn't sure what he was supposed to do about them now...

22

IVY

Ivy locked her Mini and pulled her mobile from the pocket of Ross's coat, clutching Grizzle's parcel in the other hand. She'd visited the post office in Christmas Village earlier to pick up Grizzle's eBay purchases and had decided to visit him now – she was feeling too jittery about Ross's conversation with Simon to wait in Snowman Chalet alone.

Would their meeting go well? What would happen if Simon mentioned Ivy's deal with Miriam? Then again, Ross's brother was unlikely to know about it because Simon and his grand-mother had fallen out. Despite that, anxiety churned in the pit of Ivy's stomach as she checked the pin in her Google map, which Ross had told her would lead to Grizzle's house. It told her to turn right now.

It would just be easier if I told Ross everything, she grumbled to herself. *Only, he might not understand.* Overcome with indecision, she followed the directions and wandered carefully along an icy pathway, stopping to examine a couple of bushy shrubs poking through the blanket of sparkly snow.

Ivy took in deep breath and smelled balsam fir and had to

look over her shoulder to check she couldn't see Ross. Her mobile pinged suddenly and she checked the screen. It was her coaching app. Perhaps this morning she'd get some useful advice? After spending the night with Ross, she was feeling more confused than ever. What did she want, he'd asked. She shook her head because she was so confused.

'Sometimes the wrong turn can take you to the right place.'

'What's the right place?' Ivy groaned, irritated that she never understood what the messages were supposed to mean. Was this a sign that the path she was taking was the wrong one? Ross seemed to think so. But he'd walked away from his family's expectations, an option that wasn't open to her, no matter how much she wanted it to be.

She owed her mother, Ivy reminded herself. Faith had raised her when there'd been no one else, and Ivy wouldn't be responsible for worrying her into another heart episode. She shut the app and her mobile immediately started to ring.

'Ugh.' Ivy had been expecting Miriam to call asking for an update, and didn't particularly want to give her one now. But she had to keep her boss happy – besides, it was the right thing to do.

'Hi,' she said, picking up as she stood staring into the trees.

'What's happening with Ross?' Miriam immediately shot back in her most irritated tone. 'I've been expecting an update for a few days, Ivy. I'm surprised I haven't heard anything from you. Surely you've got something to report? If you haven't, I might have to come to see him myself. You've got work piling up here.'

'You don't need to come here.' Ivy gulped. 'I've spoken to Ross,' she quickly confessed.

'Good,' Miriam snapped. 'So when's my grandson planning to come to the castle? Why hasn't he contacted me yet?'

Ivy pulled a face. She wasn't sure if either of those things would happen, although she knew Ross was softening towards the idea.

'Well?' Miriam pressed, impatient now.

'He's meeting with Simon today,' Ivy blurted, immediately regretting sharing the information as soon as the words left her mouth. Perhaps Simon and Ross wouldn't want their grandmother knowing they'd spoken? Then again, there was no reason to keep it secret, surely? The fact that the brothers were reconnecting was a good thing. She waited while her boss digested the information.

'Well that's good news,' Miriam said finally, her voice oddly satisfied. 'I couldn't have planned that better myself. Well done, Ivy. I'd say you're very close to starting your new career. All you need to do now is to get Ross to agree to return.'

'Oh, well...' Ivy's stomach felt as if a bag of stones had been dropped into it.

'Text me an update as soon as you can,' Miriam demanded before hanging up.

Ivy stood staring at the mobile, feeling uneasy. She couldn't think about Ross now – and she wasn't going to think about the job in London either. She'd just try to enjoy the moments that were left at Christmas Resort while she could.

Ivy clicked back into Google Maps and continued on a few more metres until she heard a shuffling sound in the undergrowth. She spun around, almost jumping out of her snow boots when she spotted a small figure in the far distance. The woman waved and Ivy waited as she approached. When she was a few metres away, she realised it was Mairi Gibson.

'Ach, lass, I'm glad I spotted you,' Mairi said as she drew closer. She was wearing a dark blue coat and a knitted hat, gloves and scarf. Swung over her shoulder was a bulging carrier bag. 'I'm looking for Grizzle McGregor's house.' The older woman stretched her neck, trying to see behind Ivy. 'I've been searching for a wee while – Bonnibell gave me directions but I really don't think they were correct.' Her forehead bunched. 'I never understood why the old man chose to live in the middle of nowhere.' She tried to look behind Ivy again.

'Are you here to visit him?' Ivy asked, eyeing the large bag.

'I've made him a couple of casseroles and a cake – I hear Ross Ballentine's been cooking for him.' She shuddered. 'If that's true, it's a wonder Grizzle's still alive.'

'I'm on my way to see him now,' Ivy said, pointing to the parcels. 'I have to drop these in – would you like me to deliver the food too?' If Mairi spoke to Grizzle, the fact that Ross and not Mairi had been cooking for him might be exposed. The older man might be angry so she'd try to avert them meeting if she could.

'Nae, I've been wanting to see his house for a long time,' Mairi said, tightening her grip on the bag. 'I'll just follow you.' Her expression tensed, as if she'd guessed Ivy might try to persuade her not to go.

In the end, Ivy shrugged, checked the map again and pointed right. 'It's this way, but he's not always welcoming to visitors,' she warned.

'Ach, that's no surprise. I've known Grizzle McGregor for most of my life and he's been contrary the whole time. Nothing he says is going to scare me off – not this time,' she said firmly.

'Okay,' Ivy said as she directed them around a large tree, still following the map, and spotted Grizzle's cabin in the far distance. 'We're getting closer,' she advised as she heard a bark and the patter of paws, then Bowser sprang from behind a cluster of trees.

'Ach, it's the bonnie dog,' Mairi gushed, bending to stroke the pug's head. Bowser leaned into her, and Ivy let out the nervous breath she'd been holding in. 'Let's get you inside,' the older woman said eagerly, overtaking Ivy as they approached Grizzle's cabin.

The door was half-open as they reached the decking and Ivy tentatively knocked – waiting, even as Bowser charged ahead into the sitting room with Mairi following close behind.

'It's just me, Ivy Heart,' Ivy called out. 'Um, and you've got another visitor,' she added as she entered the room too. She was pleased to see the Christmas decorations that she and Ross had hung the day before were switched on and the fire had been lit too, making the space warm and cosy.

Grizzle rose from his seat by the fire. 'Ivy,' he said, sounding delighted. Then he squinted and his face fell as Mairi approached. 'What are *you* doing here?' he challenged, taking a small step back.

'I brought you some food,' Mairi said, her voice matter-of-fact. 'Where should I put it?'

'Ach lass, don't pretend you don't know that already,' Grizzle snapped. 'And I don't want any more of your meals.'

Mairi shook her head, her eyes flashing. 'This is the first time I've cooked for you. We've barely spoken in forty years,' she said, dryly. Then she turned full circle until she spotted the fridge in the opposite corner of the room and went to unload her bag. 'There's not much in here,' she muttered, gazing at the empty shelves. 'No wonder you're so skinny.'

'I picked up your packages from the post office.' Ivy quickly changed the subject, stepping closer to Grizzle who was wearing his thick black glasses again. He was squinting at Mairi and wearing the oddest expression.

'Where's the lad?' he finally asked, still trying to see beyond Ivy.

'Meeting with his brother at Christmas Lodge,' Ivy admitted, offering Grizzle the two parcels.

'Ach.' Grizzle sucked air between his teeth. 'Well, it's about time they made up.'

In the corner of the room Mairi made a snorting sound.

'Thank you for collecting these, lass,' Grizzle said, as if he hadn't heard. He opened one of the parcels and pulled out a pair of sunglasses before putting them on. 'Well they're about as useful as a waterproof teabag,' he complained, tugging them off and throwing them on the table before opening the other package. The glasses inside had royal blue frames that had been decorated with a variety of sparkles and hearts. Grizzle pulled them on, looked around, and beamed. 'They're perfect, lass. I knew I'd get it right in the end.'

His smile dropped as Mairi stepped closer and he took a good look at her for the first time.

'I brought you a Dundee cake I baked this morning,' she said briskly, heading towards the kitchen.

He cleared his throat. 'I'm not hungry.' He watched as she suddenly stopped in her tracks as she took in the mantlepiece.

'I can't believe you kept this.' She reached out to pick up one of the frames Ivy had noticed when she'd first visited Grizzle. 'This is us, when we took that day trip to Inverness,' Mairi said. 'I think that was a week before you broke up with me.' Her face grew sad. 'We look so happy; I never understood...'

The older man sniffed. 'I'm not sure I remember that,' he said breezily, although Ivy guessed he was lying. There was none of the usual irritation in Grizzle's voice, instead he sounded sad too. 'Besides, you married someone else, lass, less than a year after.'

'Well you didn't want me,' Mairi snapped back.

'Shall I put the kettle on and make some tea to go with that cake?' Ivy asked, quickly. She tracked across to the kitchen, wondering what Ross would make of Mairi's visit – or the strange way his friend was behaving.

'You should really get your eyes tested,' Mairi said, pointing to the blue sparkly glasses as she walked past while carrying the cake, her eyes scouring the furniture and knick-knacks as she drank in the surroundings. 'I work in the optician's part-time.'

'Aye,' Grizzle said, dryly. 'I know, lass. Why do you think I haven't been?'

Ivy raised an eyebrow, listening intently. Now things were beginning to make more sense. Although what had happened between the couple was still a mystery.

'I could book you an appointment,' Mairi offered, ignoring the older man's comment as she placed the cake on the sideboard in the kitchen and began to rummage through the drawers.

'These will do me fine. I've sorted it myself,' Grizzle said, patting the glasses as he looked around as if he were seeing his house for the first time.

'Da used to say you were too independent,' Mairi said, continuing her search, and Ivy noticed the older man frown. 'Where do you keep your knives?' she asked.

'I'm surprised you don't know that already,' Grizzle answered, wrinkling his nose at her. 'You've been sneaking into my house for enough months, leaving food, moving things.'

'I've no idea what you're talking about, old man,' Mairi shot back, shaking her head as she continued to look. 'Found one!' She suddenly waved a cake slice in the air. 'Now I need to find plates.' She knelt so she could open a cupboard door.

'I'll find them,' Ivy offered as she finished making the tea, and got out three side plates, forks and a large plate for the cake. 'I'll take them through to the sitting room—'

'I'll take them,' Mairi snapped before her forehead creased. 'I'm sorry lass,' she said, scratching her head. 'That was rude. Someone told me last year that I should try to be nicer to people – but I'm not sure I've practised enough.'

'You were never particularly amiable – it was part of your charm. Don't change now,' Grizzle snorted as he made his way over to his chair, sinking into it and rocking backwards. 'There's no need to cut that cake for me. I'll not be eating any,' he said, sourly.

'You'll try a piece,' Mairi challenged. 'I've nae come all this way for you to refuse – and I'll not be leaving until you do.' Her expression was mulish.

'Give me a slice then, woman,' Grizzle ordered as Ivy set a mug of tea beside him and Mairi handed him the plate. 'After I've forced some down, you should return from whence you came.' He waved a palm.

'Might do,' Mairi said, sounding happier as she dropped into the chair beside him and nibbled her cake. Ivy wandered into the kitchen so she could check on Grizzle's plants. She watched the back and forth between the couple as they continued to bicker and found herself smiling. There was history there – chemistry too, judging from the bright look in their eyes. She wondered if either of them would ever admit it. It was good to see the older man enjoying fresh company. Ivy would've loved to know what had happened between them. She ate a piece of the Dundee cake, raising an eyebrow as she chewed – it was mouth-watering.

Grizzle must have agreed because he let out a sudden whoop. 'Ach lass, what did you do?' he gasped, gazing at Mairi, his eyes wide. 'This is delicious,' he said, taking another swift bite. 'Shame I can't say the same about your casseroles and pies.'

Mairi shook her head and finished her slice as she gazed at the picture on the mantle. 'I can't understand why you'd choose not to see me again – but would keep a picture for all these years.' She sounded bemused.

Grizzle flushed and stared down at his plate.

'Unless, as my Mam told me – you made a mistake and were too cowardly to right it.' She turned and skewered Grizzle with her grey gaze. 'It takes a brave person to risk love, and a stupid one to think they'd be happier without it.'

'Rubbish,' Grizzle said, his tone mild.

'Aye.' Mairi nodded, sagely. 'Perhaps those new glasses of

yours will help you to see things properly. I've got things to do back at the resort, so I'll be off...'

'Already?' Grizzle asked, a look of disappointment flickering across his face. Then it vanished and he wagged a finger. 'Bye then. I won't miss you, lass.'

Mairi gave the older man a thoughtful look. 'I've got a new cake recipe – I'll be back tomorrow so I can test it out.'

'I'm not a guinea pig,' Grizzle grumbled, as he polished off the rest of his slice. 'Make sure you leave the rest of the Dundee cake.' He watched Mairi put on her coat.

'Do you need me to show you the way back through the woods?' Ivy asked as Mairi pulled on her gloves, scarf and hat too.

'Nae, lass,' Mairi said loudly, as she opened the door and walked onto the decking. 'I'll be able to remember it from now on.' With that she shut it again.

'Old friend?' Ivy asked as Grizzle sat in silence.

'Not really,' he said, gazing at the picture on the mantlepiece as the room fell silent.

Ivy watched him for a few moments, then she heard a noise outside. 'I wonder if Mairi's lost?'

'Ach, I'll show her where to go,' Grizzle muttered, rising eagerly from the chair just as Ross breezed in carrying a casserole dish.

'How did it go with Simon?' Ivy asked, blushing when he immediately strode over and pressed his lips to hers, making them tingle.

'Aye.' Ross smiled as he pulled away, his eyes sparkling. 'It was good to see him. I told him I'd go and see Miriam with him tomorrow at Hawthorn Castle.'

'About time, lad,' Grizzle said from where he was sitting. 'No good hiding away from your feelings.' Ross caught Ivy's eye and his cheeks went up in flames.

Ross grasped her hand, looking awkward. 'We wondered if you'd like to come. Since Miriam sent you to persuade me to return, we thought, Simon and I thought...' He cleared his throat.

'Of course I'll come,' Ivy said. 'Are you happy about going? I don't want you to feel pressured.' She might have started this whole thing, but it was important Ross did what he wanted.

'I want to go,' Ross said, fixing her with a warm look that melted her insides. 'It's past time – I realised that today. I can't avoid my family forever. I need to face up to my past.'

'Aye,' Grizzle said as he stared at them both, frowning. 'I suppose if you don't it will catch up with you anyway.' His eyes shifted to the door before they rested on the casserole dish Ross was carrying. 'What's that?'

'Another meal from Mairi,' Ross said lightly, turning and walking towards the fridge.

The older man rose and folded his arms. 'I should have known,' he growled, shaking his head. 'All this time...'

'What?' Ross widened his eyes and looked at Ivy.

'Mairi visited this afternoon,' she explained, pulling a face as Ross paled.

'Turns out the lass is an excellent cook,' Grizzle said. 'Seems she's got it into her head that I need looking after though.' His gaze grew heated.

Ross winced. 'I'm sorry for—' His shoulders sagged. He put the dish onto the table and scratched his head. 'I was—'

'Interfering?' Grizzle growled, then he rubbed his temple and his body relaxed. 'Perhaps I can understand why.' His mouth pinched. 'But you all need to stop trying to take care of me. I'm a grown man.'

'Everyone needs somebody,' Ivy said, ignoring the ache in her chest.

'Aye, they do.' Ross reached out and squeezed her hand.

The older man adjusted his glasses as he considered them. 'Aye, perhaps I'm beginning to see that now,' he said.

Ivy drew in a breath as the men nodded at each other. Everybody did need somebody – but would she ever be lucky enough to find out how that felt?

23

IVY

Ivy followed Ross's Land Rover as he drove through the gates of Hawthorn Castle and she wondered how nervous he felt. Would this visit bring back a lot of unhappy memories for him, or would he immediately feel like he belonged?

For a moment she wished she'd travelled in the car beside him for moral support – but had guessed Miriam would insist she stayed on at the castle after the meeting. Especially since she'd fulfilled her task. So she'd packed her bags and reluctantly moved out of Snowman Chalet in case she was right. Ivy had promised Bonnibell she'd visit again soon, but knew when she got the job in London, it was unlikely she'd return for a while. The thought made her gloomy.

Sunlight hit the pointy turrets and white stone walls as Ivy drove closer, illuminating the castle and making everything shimmer. But despite the beauty, her stomach clenched. Trying to soothe her growing anxiety, Ivy focused on the dense clusters of balsam firs that flanked the gorgeous building, wondering how she hadn't noticed them before today. Why was it that suddenly everywhere she looked, she saw delicate shrubs and towering trees, as if it was her – and not Grizzle – who could see properly for the first time in almost a year...

Ivy's stomach turned over as she pulled up beside Ross's car as he parked. He hadn't brought Snowball or Moose today because he'd wanted to focus on his conversation with Miriam, and as she opened her Mini door Ivy realised it felt wrong without them.

'Home sweet home,' Ross murmured, looking unhappy as she joined him.

'Are you alright?' she whispered, pressing her hands into the pockets of the flimsy green coat she'd decided would be more suited to Hawthorn Castle than her beloved pink snowsuit. She shivered a little as the wind began to whip around them.

'I don't know how I feel,' Ross said gruffly, still staring ahead.

'Shall we go inside so we can find out?' she asked, hoping Ross would find what he was looking for there. 'Where's Simon meeting us?'

'I've no idea.' Ross shook his head. 'It never occurred to me to ask.'

Ivy pulled her mobile from her pocket. 'Shall I text him?'

'Aye,' Ross said, just as a yellow Jeep skidded into the car park and stopped beside them.

'You're here already,' Simon said, sounding pleased as he climbed out and tentatively patted Ross on the back before grinning at Ivy. 'I wasn't sure if you'd both make it.' He nudged his brother. 'I'm glad you didn't change your mind.'

'I said I'd come – and Ivy was happy to join us.' Ross sounded nervous.

'Aye.' Simon looked relieved. 'I'm sorry – I have to get used to you being around again. I can hardly believe it.' He glanced at the castle. 'It's been a long time, but the place feels complete with you here.' Simon sucked in a breath. 'Shall we go in?' He started to walk and then stopped suddenly, frowning. 'Does Miriam know we're coming?'

'I messaged her last night and told her Ross was visiting, but I didn't mention you,' Ivy admitted. 'I wasn't sure if you wanted it to be a surprise...'

Delivering Simon to the castle alongside Ross hadn't been part of their deal. And, she'd wanted Miriam to focus on her youngest grandson for a change, to give Ross the attention he deserved. She wondered if the brothers coming together was a mistake.

'That's good.' Simon smiled and opened the massive oak front door, pushing it wide and waiting for them to walk in ahead. The hallway was somewhere between frigid and freezing and the temperature made Ivy shiver more.

Despite the multiple Christmas decorations and lush vegetation that had been hung along the walls and staircase, the atmosphere wasn't welcoming. Ivy wondered how a young grieving boy would have coped living here and her insides churned.

'I expect Miriam will be waiting in her office.' Ivy headed past the staircase, wondering why her stomach was in so many knots. This was what the older woman wanted, and Ross seemed happy to be here – but there was an odd tingling growing at the back of her spine, a sense that something wasn't right.

'Life has a way of delivering the unexpected – try to embrace it.'

Today's motivational quote swam into Ivy's mind as she knocked on Miriam's door and she tried to dismiss it. Then her whole body tensed when the older woman boomed, 'Come in!'

Miriam got up from her chair as they entered and smiled her tiger's smile, her eyes glittering. She'd dressed up in one of her rigid red suits and wore matching lipstick – an ensemble Ivy knew she used to intimidate guests. The outfit immediately put Ivy on alert. Surely if she wanted to welcome her youngest grandson, she'd have gone for something less... aggressive?

Why wasn't Miriam hugging Ross? Instead, she stood behind the desk, her body taut as her eyes swept over Ivy and skimmed over Ross as if she couldn't be bothered to acknowledge him. Ivy saw her lips thin, and then her gaze landed on Simon and she gave him a wide, genuine smile.

'Both of my grandsons are here,' she said, sounding satisfied. 'Ivy Heart, you've more than delivered on your task.'

'Hello, Grandmother,' Ross said, his voice gruff. Ivy could tell from his tone that he was uncomfortable, and Ivy's insides ached.

'It's been a long time.' Miriam nodded, then her gaze slid back to Simon as she sat. Both men stepped forwards and Simon got three chairs from the edges of the room so they could sit too. 'I trust you're well?' Miriam asked, her tone clipped, her attention still focused on Simon.

Ross jerked his chin and swallowed. 'Ivy told me you wanted to see me?'

Miriam reached up to play with the string of pearls around her neck as she finally focused on Ross and nodded. 'I did,' she said. 'Although...' Her gaze slid to Simon again. 'Now you're both here things may have changed.'

'Changed how?' Simon snapped, sounding suspicious.

Miriam's eyes flickered. 'Don't play games, lad. I'm sure that hearing your brother was going to become Laird finally brought you to your senses. That's why you're here, isn't it?'

Beside Ivy, Ross flinched, and she wanted to take his hand so she could reassure him, but Simon was sitting between them. She squirmed in her chair, trying to give Miriam the benefit of the doubt. Miriam had wanted Ross here, hadn't she? That was why she'd sent Ivy to Christmas Resort. But if that were true, why wasn't she welcoming him with open arms? Why did she only seem interested in her oldest grandson?

'What do you mean?' Ross asked, sounding resigned.

'Aye, what do you mean?' Simon echoed.

A lead weight lodged in Ivy's windpipe and she blew out a breath trying to clear it.

Miriam shrugged and her eyes skirted the room again – this time they rested on the frames on the sideboard under the window. Ivy glanced at them too. The photos had been rearranged and there were no pictures of Ross there now. Dread flooded her as she considered the implications of that. Surely Miriam had another picture of Ross? If so, why hadn't she replaced it? Especially since she wanted him to be Laird.

'I guessed if you heard Ross was coming to take over your position it would make you think twice about giving all this up,' Miriam explained gaily, waving a hand to take in the room.

Simon jerked back in his seat. 'That's *not* why I'm here,' he said incredulously. 'I've come to support my brother.' He squeezed Ross's shoulder. 'I didn't give him that when we were kids so I'm finally showing up for him now.' His voice was gruff.

'Ross left because that was what he wanted,' Miriam said, haughtily.

Simon widened his eyes, looking shocked. 'He left because he didn't think he was a part of this family. But he is – and I've wanted him all along,' he added. 'I think he'll make an excellent Laird.'

Miriam sniffed and shook her head. 'This isn't about Ross – it's about *you*, Simon,' she said slowly as if her grandson was stupid. Her attention suddenly travelled to Ivy. 'I asked Ms Heart to track down your brother in the hope the news would get back to you.' She rubbed her hands together. 'I knew you'd come around – being Laird is what you've spent your life preparing for, after all. I knew you'd never be able to give it up. Your bloodline demands it.'

'Ross is from the *same* bloodline,' Simon said tersely as he rose to his feet. 'He's welcome to become Laird. The way I've been living the last few years is too much.' He looked unhappy.

Miriam rose too. 'This isn't about want. It's your duty.' Her eyes skirted back to Ross.

Ivy's heart ached. His fears about his grandmother had been correct – Miriam had never wanted him.

'I'm sorry, Ross. Obviously it's wonderful to see you again,' she said stiffly, fiddling with her pearls. 'Perhaps Ivy can make you some tea while Simon and I catch up privately?'

'Of course.' Ross dipped his chin and rose, his voice calm. Then he patted a hand on Simon's shoulder, as his brother stood too and tried to block Ross's path.

'No, Ross.' Simon shook his head. 'That's not why we came, remember?' He turned to his grandmother, his face dark with fury. 'I'm not turning my back on my brother again. That's not part of the deal and I won't accept it.'

'Forget it. This honestly isn't a surprise,' Ross said tersely. 'I half expected it and it's really okay.'

'Ross!' Simon looked shocked.

'I'm leaving. I appreciate what you're trying to do,' he said to his brother. 'But I should have known this was always going to be about you. Miriam never forgave me for our parents.'

'Wait with Ivy, I won't be long,' Simon demanded before turning back to his grandmother, his eyes flashing.

Ross moved slowly around his brother, his body stiff, and Ivy felt something inside her break. She'd done this – forced him to return to the castle. Regaled him with tales of a grandmother who wanted him back. She'd fed him lies – lies she guessed he'd never forgive her for. But Ivy had believed everything her boss had told her. She'd been convinced Miriam had wanted and needed Ross back in her life. But she'd been wrong.

Ross headed for the door, and Ivy went to follow. She had to talk with him, had to tell him she hadn't expected this. That her heart was as broken as his. She had to explain that she cared for him – that he deserved nothing less.

'You can come back to my office after my meeting with Simon, Ms Heart. I've got some work for you to do,' Miriam said as Ivy got to the door. 'Obviously you've more than earned the recommendation I offered in return for bringing my youngest grandson to the castle.' Ivy's blood froze. 'I'll email my friend after this meeting,' Miriam continued, looking happy. 'And I'll expect he'll contact you before the end of the day. I'm confident now that you've got what it takes to be a big success – I'm sure your mother will be delighted.'

'Please, no,' Ivy whispered, turning to look at Ross.

He was still holding onto the door handle. His body frozen.

'It's not what you think,' Ivy spluttered.

'Isn't it?' Ross stared back at her, his expression blank. 'I can't imagine what else it could be.' Then he shook his head and opened the door.

'Ross, you have to listen,' Ivy implored.

'I really don't,' Ross said as he turned his back on her and walked at speed into the hall.

Ivy watched him go, feeling wretched – wondering how she'd ever be able to fix this.

24

ROSS

'I always was the spare,' Ross muttered as he headed past Ivy's desk into the main hallway, ignoring her shouts. His insides felt like they were withering to dust but he refused to acknowledge those feelings. All he knew was he had to get home to Christmas Resort so he could lick his wounds and reset. To withdraw to a place where he'd be able to forget this last week. 'But I was still enough of an eejit to fall for it.' He stormed along the hallway, berating himself. He'd been stupid enough to fall for Ivy too.

Ross ignored the multiple paintings of his ancestors as he got closer to the front of the castle, trying to catch his breath. He'd *known* this would happen – had predicted from the very first moment he'd heard Miriam's PA had booked an appointment to see him at the resort that engaging with his grandmother again would end badly. Sure, he hadn't known exactly what she had wanted, but he'd known deep in his bones that he didn't matter. That Miriam only cared about Simon. But he'd let Ivy seduce him into believing something else. Worse, he hadn't seen that she'd been using him too.

'Eejit,' he snapped, sick with hurt and self-disgust.

He reached the portcullis and heard Ivy yell his name again. Heard the sound of her silly red boots sliding on the tiled floor. He contemplated opening the door and sprinting to his Land Rover so he could leave before she caught up. But he'd spent too many years hiding from his problems. So instead, he stopped and turned, shoving his hands into his pockets as he watched Ivy approach, his expression deliberately cold.

'It's not how it sounds,' Ivy said, her voice hoarse. 'I mean, it is, but it wasn't supposed to end like this.'

She looked so upset Ross had to stop himself from immediately forgiving her. Every cell in his body wanted to tell her everything was okay. That he'd forget what had just happened.

But he couldn't. She'd lied to him, deceived him – and all for a job. He'd never felt so betrayed. But he should have seen it coming. He'd always been second best; he should have been used to it by now.

'I'm listening,' Ross said, coldly. Not because he wanted to hear what Ivy had to say, but because he was sure once she began to explain, she'd realise there really was no justification for what she'd done. To draw him here on false pretences? Had Simon known too? Just the thought made the breath catch in his throat.

'It wasn't about the job,' Ivy implored before muttering an oath. 'Okay, that's not true. We both know that. At first it was.' She swallowed, her expression shattered.

Ivy took a step towards him and Ross forced himself to hold his ground because he didn't want her to know how much she affected him.

'But then I met you and you told me what had happened with your parents. I saw how much your family meant to you – so I wanted to help you put things right. I wanted you to reconnect. Everything I told you was true. I believed Miriam wanted you here. I had no idea this was all a ploy to trick Simon into coming back instead.' Ivy's eyes welled when he didn't say a word. 'Everything you told me about your grandmother was true...' she whispered.

Ross sucked in air as he looked around the hallway for one last time. At the wide staircase he remembered his parents walking down, at the floors that were always buffed to a shine, at the chandelier above them that threw colours across the walls when the sun set. There were so many memories wound into the fabric of this place. A few were even happy, but most he'd rather forget. Especially today.

It was no wonder he'd shut himself away in Christmas Resort, no wonder he'd turned his back on Hawthorn Castle and his family.

'Well, I thank you for your efforts,' Ross said stiffly, steeling himself from caving in when Ivy's eyes filled. 'It sounds like you've been rewarded adequately for your services to the family cause. Simon's back where he belongs, and you've got the future you and your mam have been craving. Well done.' He looked at her coldly.

'I know how this looks. But I only wanted you to be happy,' Ivy implored, twisting her hands in knots.

He could see hurt on her face, hurt at his rejection – but the anger he felt burned away any sympathy he might also have.

'I know how it feels to miss your family,' she said, her voice thick. 'I didn't want that for you.'

'I appreciate that,' Ross said dispassionately. 'But I'm afraid you didn't quite get the desired result. You should have left me alone. I was content.' He heard the rough rasp in his voice that proved he was lying and hoped Ivy hadn't heard it too.

'I know what I did was wrong,' she said, nodding. 'If I'd realised Miriam was just trying to manipulate you, that this was only ever about Simon...' She swallowed, her eyes shining with more tears. 'I would have said no. I wish I had.'

She took a step closer and Ross held his ground, determined not to show her how close he was to breaking down.

'I'm second choice,' he said flatly. 'I accepted that a long time ago – and I should probably thank you for reminding me.'

'You're not second choice for me.' A tear escaped and slid down Ivy's cheek. 'I care about you,' she choked.

'I don't think I can bring myself to believe that, Ivy,' Ross said, his voice emotionless. He scratched a hand through his hair, feeling desolate. 'You sold me out for the price of a job.' He saw the shock of his words hit as if she'd been punched. 'I knew I didn't measure up as a grandson or Laird, but I've never come second to a rung on a career ladder before. Perhaps I should thank you – for reminding me to never let my guard down, for showing me exactly how low someone is prepared to stoop to get what they want.'

Ivy gasped, gaping at him as more tears spilled from her eyes. 'That's not what happened. And I don't even want the job.' Her voice wobbled.

Ross wondered if those were the first honest words she'd spoken since they'd met.

'I really don't know if I'm going to take it.' The minute the words left Ivy's mouth she looked surprised.

'You won't let your mother down,' Ross said, dismissing her words. 'Especially considering it'll be a sad waste of all that time and effort you invested.' He narrowed his eyes. 'You were so good at it too: I believed every word you said.' Ivy flinched and he frowned as a thought occurred to him. 'Was the story about your da true, or did you make it up because you wanted me to fall for you?' He swallowed because it had worked, and he knew it would be a long time before he could think about letting anyone get close to him again. Perhaps he never would. Maybe he would end up like Grizzle, living alone in the woods with his pets. Right now the thought appealed.

'It wasn't like that,' Ivy whispered, her face paling, and she went to rest a hand on the banister of the large staircase as if she were struggling to stand on her own. 'And, yes, everything I told you about my family was the truth. I didn't lie, Ross.'

'Aside from when you omitted to tell me that this whole thing' – he waved a hand between them, feeling a fresh wave of bitterness – 'was about a job.'

Ivy's face fell and Ross's stomach pitched.

'I know it was wrong of me not to mention it,' she said, rushing to get the words out. 'I guessed you'd get the wrong idea and I didn't want you to think I was using you.'

'Yet you did use me, Ivy,' Ross said, leaning back against the door. Drawing comfort from the fact that he was only a few moments away from walking through it. That as soon as he did, he'd be leaving Ivy, his grandmother and Simon in his past once and for all.

She shook her head. 'I don't know how many times I can say that I didn't know what Miriam was planning.' She straightened and wrapped her arms around herself. 'I honestly believed your grandmother wanted you here. Ross, you have to believe me,' she pleaded, her cheeks reddening. 'She never told me what she was planning—'

'You even let me call Simon on *your* mobile. Because you'd been planning for me to talk to him first the whole time,' Ross continued blandly, as if she hadn't spoken. 'I went along with it.' There had been so many clues that Ivy had been manipulating him. Things that were suddenly so clear.

'It wasn't like that,' Ivy said, her voice a whisper. 'You must know I'm not like that.'

'It was exactly like that,' Ross said flatly. 'I hope you're happy in your new life,' he added, moving away from the door because he couldn't bear to hear her lies anymore. 'At least your mam will finally stop worrying and you'll get the career she always wanted you to have. Just—'

Ross wanted to fight the words, wanted to hurt Ivy even more, but as he sharpened his claws and tried to come up with the right things to say to eviscerate her, he couldn't go through with it. 'Just—' His shoulders sagged. 'Think about what *you* want, Ivy,' he said as tears streamed down her face. 'Don't live your life trying to make someone else happy – because I promise you it won't be enough.'

'I—' Ivy sobbed as he turned and reached for the door handle.

'Take it from someone who knows,' he added softly. Then Ross marched from the castle without looking back, ignoring Ivy as she called for him to return.

It was only when he was in his car and halfway down the driveway that he realised there were tears on his cheeks too.

25

IVY

Ivy watched Ross's car shoot down the driveway, feeling every single part of her ache. She didn't know what to do, didn't know how to feel – she only knew she'd just devastated Ross, conspired with his grandmother to trick him into getting Simon to return. And, in turn, she'd confirmed everything he'd always believed. That he wasn't enough, that no one really wanted him. That he'd always come second to something... Worse, he was right, because she had befriended him and persuaded him to return to the castle – and it had all been for a job. At least at first.

'Dammit,' she cursed as Ross's car disappeared out of sight and she shut the castle door just as she heard footsteps sprinting down the corridor.

'Where's Ross?' Simon shouted as he joined Ivy in the hall-way, frantically searching for his brother.

'He's gone,' Ivy said flatly, pressing a hand to her heart, which felt like it had been shredded.

'Where?' Simon asked, his eyes widening. 'I told him to wait, I told him I had to speak to Miriam.'

'About you coming back to be Laird?' Ivy asked, unable to

keep the despair from her voice. Because Ross had been right, neither Simon nor Miriam had ever really wanted him. How could she have been so stupid? How could she have believed in them?

'Of course not!' Simon looked shocked. 'I had to talk to our grandmother because we need to find a way for this whole thing...' He wriggled his hands, taking in their surroundings. 'To work with Ross. I have to speak with him now,' he said, agitated. 'Miriam does too.' He looked angry. 'She has some serious apologising to do.'

'I don't think he's going to listen to any of us.' Ivy's voice wobbled. He hadn't listened to her. He'd left – but she couldn't blame him.

Ross was right, this whole thing had never been about him. It had always been about *her* finding the right path. Ivy swiped away a tear. She knew she'd lost him. This was a man who'd separated himself from his family for five years after they'd hurt him, so there was no way he'd ever forgive her... But if she couldn't fix things between them, there was at least one thing she could do to make things right.

'I need to go,' she said, opening the door.

'Are you going to speak to Ross?' Simon asked hopefully.

'No,' Ivy murmured as she stepped onto the driveway. 'I don't think he'll listen to anything I have to say again – but I do have to talk to my mother.'

'Why?' Simon asked, looking confused.

'Because Ross was right. I'm done living someone else's life and I'm going to turn down the job in London. It's the least I owe him.' Then she marched out of the door, leaving Simon gaping after her.

Ivy SAT on the sofa in the small cold cottage at Hawthorn Castle, staring at her mobile. She'd texted her mother half an hour ago, saying they had to talk.

Ivy had no idea when Faith would be free, but was determined to speak to her before she lost her nerve. So she was just going to wait until her mother called.

Ivy almost jumped off the sofa when her mobile pinged. But when she checked the screen, it was just her coaching app. Ivy flicked to it, frowning as she read.

'Your time is limited, so don't waste it living someone else's life.' – Steve Jobs

If she'd needed another reminder that she'd totally messed things up, this message had come at the perfect time.

I think I'm finally starting to realise that I've been living my life wrong for the last year, she said to herself, feeling foolish.

She glanced around the stark room with the high grey-brick walls, cold dark floor and brown rug – even the sofa was uncomfortable – and it was difficult not to compare it with the cabin Bonnibell had given her in Christmas Resort. Ivy had loved the festive decorations, warm fire and the stunning views of the woods. But the thing she'd loved most was being so close to nature again. Walking in the woods with Ross, smelling the trees, just being outdoors – it had made her realise that it was where she was supposed to be. The only place she'd truly be happy.

Her mobile pinged with a message from her mother saying she'd be able to call in ten minutes. Ivy got up and paced, trying to work out exactly what she was going to say. Her stomach was churning but she knew she was doing the right thing. She only wished it hadn't taken losing Ross to figure out what she truly wanted, or at least have the courage to grab it.

Ivy felt sick when her mobile finally rang. She picked up and heaved in a breath. 'Mum.'

'Ivy, Miriam's just contacted me to let me know you've been accepted onto the training programme,' she gushed.

'Have I?' Ivy asked flatly, because it was the first she'd heard. Not that it mattered now.

'I'm so delighted for you,' Faith continued. 'It's such a relief to know you're going to be settled and safe and that I can stop worrying about your future.'

Ivy winced. 'About that,' Ivy said slowly. She stroked her suddenly sweaty hands on her clothes and took in a long breath. 'Mum, I'm sorry but I'm not going to take the job.' As she said it Ivy felt a rush of relief which told her she was doing the right thing.

The mobile fell silent. 'Why not?' her mother asked, finally. 'Is it because you've had a better offer from somewhere else?'

'I'm not taking the job because it's not what I want,' Ivy said. 'I'm sorry, Mum, but I wasn't born to work in an office, I think we both know that.' She hesitated, then forced herself to continue. 'You know how much I enjoy working with plants—'

'That again...' Her mother huffed. 'We've talked about this,' she said, her voice rising.

Ivy could tell her mother was getting upset. Had to stop herself from immediately backing down. Fear shot through her, but she knew she had to push through.

'Please don't get upset,' Ivy begged. Tears pricked her eyes again and she sank back into the sofa. It had been such an emotional day already, and she felt drained, but she owed it to herself and Ross to finish the conversation.

'Of course I'm upset, Ivy,' her mother said sharply. 'We've talked about this. You can potter in a garden anytime you want in your own time, but if you want to be secure, you need something you can count on. A career you know can support you.'

'I'm not Dad,' Ivy said as she stood and went to stare out of a small arched window at the edge of the sitting room. It was still snowing and the castle grounds were blanketed in white. In the distance Ivy could see a small copse of balsam fir and her mind wandered to Ross. Where was he now? What was he going to do? Her heart ached, but thinking about him gave her the courage to continue.

'I know you're worried about me making what you think of as a proper living, but I *can* make this work. Thousands of people do. Being outside, working with plants – Mum, it's where I'm happiest.'

'Ivy, your dad was a... wonderful man,' her mother said sadly. 'And I know you're just like him, which is why I worry so much.' She paused. 'But you wear such rose-coloured spectacles when it comes to him. He loved plants, yes, but he never took anything else seriously, which is why the business failed. You remember we lost everything when he died?'

'I remember,' Ivy said, and the weight of the words made her shoulders sink. 'I also remember he was never happier than when he was knee-deep in earth.'

'I know.' Her mother sounded dreamy. 'That look on his face when something he'd planted flowered – it was the same one he gave you when you were born.' She fell silent. 'It's a shame he didn't feel the same way about looking after the accounts...'

'Mum. I'm not a hundred per cent dad, remember,' Ivy said gently. 'A big part of me is you. The part that can actively manage a spreadsheet in Excel, even though I'll admit I don't enjoy it much.' She pulled a face. 'And I'd rather eat a mud pie than balance the books – but that doesn't mean I'm going to actively avoid it. I've no idea where I'm going to end up, but that's okay.'

She thought about Christmas Resort before shaking her head. 'All I do know is wherever it is, I'll be working outside, probably knee-deep in plants. Because I know it's the only way

I'm ever going to be truly happy. Life can be short; we both know that. I don't want to waste what time I have.'

'Oh, Ivy,' her mother said.

'I want you to trust me to make my own choices, to live my own life...'

'This was never about trust, Ivy,' her mother said. 'I just want you to be safe.' The line fell silent again. 'When I had the heart attack...'

'Oh Mum, you don't—'

'*When* I had the heart attack,' her mother continued, her voice firm, 'the thing that worried me most wasn't that I almost died.' She stopped for a beat, as if gathering herself. 'The thing that terrified me was what would happen to you. I never wanted you to follow in your father's footsteps and you were always determined to do just that. I was worried before, but suddenly me not being around became so much more real. All I could think about was how important it was that you were safe. I suppose that's why I've been pressuring you so much to get this job. Why I insisted you worked with Miriam.'

'But I'm fine, Mum,' Ivy soothed.

'I never want you to feel the way I did when your dad died. I was grieving – but when we lost everything, life felt so out of control...' She let out a long, noisy sigh.

'But you coped,' Ivy said. 'More than that – you thrived. Are you okay?' Ivy asked, suddenly worried when her mother didn't respond. 'It's not your heart, is it?'

'I'm fine, darling,' Faith promised. 'I'm just digesting what you've said. I know you worry about my health,' she added. 'I love you for it, but you don't need to. We know the problem. I'm on medication and I'm fine. It was just the stress of the job and I wasn't looking after myself properly. Now I am.'

'It wasn't the stress of the job, it was because you were arguing with me,' Ivy blurted as guilt flooded her.

'Of course it wasn't!' Her mother sounded horrified.

'But we were fighting about my job,' Ivy said.

'We had a disagreement. If you want to see me have a real argument, you should come and spend the day at the hospital sometime.'

'I'd love to,' Ivy shot back, realising it was true.

'Okay.' Faith hesitated. 'When?'

Ivy pursed her lips as she looked around. There was nothing for her here – Ross hated her; Miriam was going to be furious when she turned down the job. She was owed some holiday – she hadn't taken any since starting the maternity leave cover. It would be short notice, but perhaps a few days with her mother, talking things out, would help her aching heart?

'Now?' she suggested. 'I could drive down later today?' Ivy held her breath as her mother considered.

'I'd love that, as long as Miriam doesn't mind,' her mother said.

Ivy grimaced. 'I'll make sure it's okay.'

Faith paused. 'I'll be working, but I can see if I can swing some time off.'

'Maybe we can talk a bit more about Dad?' Ivy asked, hopefully. 'I know you don't like to...'

Her mother fell silent for a beat. 'I try not to because it makes me sad.' She hesitated. 'But, I'll admit, every now and then, especially when I walk to work, or smell a bouquet beside one of my patient's beds in the hospital, I can't help thinking about him. Then I wonder what he'd be doing if he was still alive...'

'I know.' Ivy shut her eyes and she could see him. 'He'd be in a greenhouse with his hands in a plant pot, covered in earth,' she said, wondering if she'd have been standing beside him – guessing she would have.

'And he'd be beaming from ear to ear,' her mother murmured. Then she sighed heavily. 'Are you sure you don't want the job in London, Ivy? It's an opportunity you may not get again.'

'I'm sorry, Mum, but it's taken me a long time to realise what I need – and the last few months have shown me I've been travelling down the wrong path. I've never been more miserable,' she admitted. 'Even that app you subscribed me to knows I'm doing the wrong thing.' She paused. 'Today it told me I shouldn't try to live someone else's life.'

Her mother hesitated and Ivy waited for her to try to talk her out of it again. She could almost hear the worry vibrating down the line, but knew she had to hold her ground.

'Okay, darling,' her mother said eventually. 'All I ever really wanted was for you to be safe and happy. I'm going to worry, I wouldn't be me if I didn't, but I'll try to back off and let you do your own thing. Just – after your visit, you have to promise to update me on what you're doing – and for goodness' sake, keep a firm eye on your accounts!'

'I promise I will.' Ivy chuckled. 'I'll call you when I leave,' she said as she hung up the phone, feeling relief slide through her. Why hadn't she done this before?

Then her smile dropped as Ivy remembered the look on Ross's face when he'd been standing in the castle hallway. He'd helped her to realise what she needed, to escape from a path that someone else was forcing her down. While she'd tried to push him back into a world where he didn't belong. She longed to see him again, to put things right. But how could she?

Ivy shook her head. Ross Ballentine was perfectly happy living at Christmas Resort. She was going to do what she should have done from the start – which was leave him alone.

26

ROSS

Ross ignored Moose and Snowball as they began to whine on the approach to Grizzle's cabin, guessing they sensed his unhappiness. It had been a hard couple of days as he'd adjusted to what had happened with his family – and he still hadn't come to terms with it yet.

He slowed as he drew closer to the ramshackle building. He'd visited his old friend a few times since he'd been to Hawthorn Castle, and hadn't been up to talking. But today he was determined to get himself back on track. Being home should have grounded him after his encounter with Miriam and Simon – after learning Ivy had been lying to him – but he was finding it difficult. He stopped so he could breathe in the crisp air, inhaling the smell of pine needles which usually made him feel centred. But his heart ached and he wished things could go back to the way they were, that he could wipe the last two weeks from his memories.

'Grizzle,' he said as he knocked and entered the older man's home, with Moose and Snowball tentatively following behind.

Bowser immediately shot to his feet and began to bark, until

Mairi, who was sitting beside the fire with the older man, patted the pug on the head and he quieted.

'Do you want a Scottish cookie?' she enquired, rising to her feet.

'Aye, they're good. Make sure you have some apple butter with it,' Grizzle insisted, waving at his empty plate. 'You could take a few lessons from the cook.'

'I'm available anytime.' Mairi gave Ross a penetrating look. 'You look like you've lost weight, lad,' she said, sounding concerned.

'He's just been eating his own food.' The older man chuckled to himself.

'Nae.' Mairi stepped closer to Ross as she headed for the kitchen. 'Put your glasses back on, you old dafty, and take a proper look. He's pale too.' She looked worried.

Grizzle huffed but did as he was told and rose to his feet so he could study Ross.

'I'm fine,' Ross insisted, embarrassed. 'I came to see if you needed anything. But I can see you don't, so I'll be off.' He was happy his friend had company – but couldn't help feeling a little lost. His whole life felt like it had just been through a washing machine cycle and everything he used to take comfort from had been rinsed away.

'You take a seat and eat,' Mairi demanded as she pointed to the chair she'd just vacated. 'I need to get back home, anyway.' She checked her watch. 'I've got a casserole in the oven that needs taking out soon.'

'Does the casserole have dumplings in it?' Grizzle asked, his eyes brightening.

'Aye.' Mairi nodded as the hint of a smile played across her lips. 'And I'll be bringing some over for you, old man.' She eyed him critically. 'There's finally more meat on those bones,' she joked. 'But you could do with a lot more.'

'When will you be back?' Grizzle asked, idly, trying not to look at her.

'I'm not sure,' Mairi said brusquely.

'Suit yourself,' Grizzle said, turning away. 'Can't promise I'll be in when you visit, but you know how to get in.'

'Old fool,' Mairi huffed, and Ross took a seat as a plate was shoved into his hands. 'Make sure you eat it all,' she instructed as she headed for the door to put on her coat.

After she'd left, the room fell silent, apart from a couple of low growls from Bowser as Moose and Snowball slumped carefully in front of the fire. Ross ate the two cookies, even though his appetite was non-existent, barely registering he'd finished them until he was staring at an empty plate.

'I know you don't want to talk about what happened,' Grizzle said finally. 'And God knows I don't either.' He huffed. 'But hiding yourself away from people and not sharing isn't the answer to anything, lad.'

'Are you talking about you and Mairi?' Ross asked, curious.

Grizzle shook his head. 'This has nothing to do with the old hen,' he complained. 'She was only here because she keeps turning up at my house and insisting on feeding me.'

'And you keep letting her in,' Ross pointed out, smiling for the first time in forty-eight hours.

The hermit winced.

'I'm not criticising,' Ross said gently. 'I'm happy for you.' His love life might be a disaster but that didn't mean he wished the same for everyone else.

'Ach well.' Grizzle looked embarrassed. 'I figured if I locked the door, she'd just find some other way to sneak in. Besides, her food's a lot better than yours.'

'She cares about you,' Ross said, staring down at his plate. It reminded him of his life – empty and a bit tragic.

'The lass – Ivy – cares for you too.' Grizzle waved a hand. 'Any eejit can see that.'

'I don't want to talk about it,' Ross insisted.

'You should,' the older man shot back.

Ross turned towards him and raised an eyebrow. 'Which is why you've been chatting to me about Mairi ever since I arrived,' he said sarcastically.

'Aye, well.' Grizzle's shoulders heaved and he took off his glasses and began to rub them on his jumper. 'That was just me being a numpty.'

Ross was going to ask why, but sensed Grizzle wouldn't confide if he interrupted. So, instead, he leaned back in his chair and waited, listening to the crackle of the fire until Grizzle cleared his throat. 'There's not much to tell,' he said eventually. 'I was an eejit.'

Ross continued to contemplate the fire.

'Ach, if you're gonna keep nagging at me lad, I'll have to tell you or I'm guessing you won't ever shut up. I'm going to tell it fast and you'd better not interrupt,' Grizzle said eventually, the words tumbling from his mouth. He finished cleaning his glasses and perched them back on the tip of his nose. 'When I was a lad, we dated for three months and towards the end we took this trip to Inverness.' He pulled a face. 'I remember sitting on the bus and this shaft of light from the sun just passed across Mairi, illuminating her like... I dinnae know, an angel or something.' Wings of pink spread across his cheeks. 'There was this lad sitting opposite us and he smiled at her.' He scratched a hand across his chin. 'And I was *so* jealous.' His voice dipped. 'And I realised I loved her then, and it terrified me.'

'Why?' Ross asked.

Grizzle gulped. 'Because love is a risk,' he said simply. 'Even watching that lad smile at her hurt.'

'So you broke things off and moved to the middle of nowhere so you could be safe?' Ross asked, incredulous.

'Aye.' Grizzle nodded. 'And she married someone else.' He blinked. 'That hurt too.'

'You're right. You are an eejit,' Ross murmured.

Grizzle chuckled. 'Aye, well. Then don't end up like me. Whatever happened with your lass, put it right. Don't run because you're too terrified of being hurt.'

'I *am* hurt.' Ross rubbed a palm against his chest, trying to soothe the dull ache. 'Ivy lied to me, so it's not the same.'

'Maybe not exactly. But from what I can see' – Grizzle tapped a finger on his glasses – 'and I can see a lot more than I could... You've been running away for the last five years. Hiding from everyone because it's easier than getting hurt. Are you sure your fight with Ivy wasn't just the same – you searching for an easy escape?'

'Of course not,' Ross said as the words penetrated. She'd lied to him, conspired with Miriam and Simon, hadn't she? He remembered her tears as she'd tried to talk to him in the hallway at the castle before he'd driven away. She'd told him things hadn't been exactly as he believed. He'd ignored Connell and Bonnibell too when they'd told him Simon had called the resort multiple times trying to get in touch.

Was it because he was afraid? Was his old friend right? Ross sucked in a breath – he wasn't sure about anything anymore.

Ross was still thinking about Ivy and Simon when he entered his house a couple of hours later. He tugged off his snow boots and coat, then paused. He perused the pictures on the wall of the hallway, stopping at the one of him standing beside Simon in the castle grounds. He reached up, intending to take the picture down. Then dropped his arm to his side, as Grizzle's words swam in his mind. Had he turned his back on his brother? Was it because he was afraid? And was he doing the same to Ivy too?

Shaking his head, Ross wandered into the kitchen so he could pour himself a glass of whisky. He paused as he uncapped the bottle and started to tip out a shot, suddenly recalling Ivy telling him it was Miriam's favourite brand. He sniffed the liquid and put the bottle down without pouring. Tomorrow he'd go into Christmas Village and buy a different make. For today, he was done thinking about Ivy and his family. It was time to move on.

He wandered to the fireplace so he could light a fire, trying to ignore the silence as it stretched. It suddenly seemed so quiet – too quiet. He went to switch on some Christmas music but it didn't help.

Ross had just got a fire burning when he heard the doorbell and for a second his heart jumped as he imagined Ivy had followed him here. He almost leapt to his feet. Then he pushed away all the doubts Grizzle had put in his head as he remembered the job in London Miriam had got her and that Ivy had probably never had any genuine feelings for him.

So when Ross opened the door and saw his brother and grandmother standing on the other side, he wasn't sure how to react. He stood gaping until Simon raised an eyebrow and held up a bag.

'I stopped in Christmas Village to buy mince pies. I doubt they'll compete with the ones your friend Bonnibell makes, but I hoped we might be able to bond over sugar while we're here.' Beside Simon, his grandmother scowled. 'Can we come in?' his brother asked.

Ross hesitated, then cleared his throat. 'Aye.' He stood back so they could join him, batting off Moose and Snowball as his pets came to welcome their guests.

Simon stroked them both before he shoved the bag into Ross's hands and began to remove his boots and coat, stopping momentarily to take in the pictures on the wall, looking emotional.

'How did you find me?' Ross asked as they made their way into the main sitting room.

'After a lot of badgering, Connell told me,' Simon admitted.

Ross watched his grandmother take in the room. What was she thinking? Why had she come?

'Why are you here?' Ross asked after a few moments and folded his arms. 'I thought you'd got what you wanted.' He didn't add that it was at his expense, or that the rejection had wounded him.

Simon shook his head. 'I asked you to wait at the castle for me,' he said, before his eyes slid to Miriam. 'I suppose I understand why you didn't wait, why you might not trust me yet.'

Ross could see pain slide across his brother's face and didn't understand.

'But you should have,' Simon finished. 'Because that meeting was exactly what I said it was. A chance for all of us to talk, a way to work out what we're going to do from this moment forwards. I'm not going to return to the castle without you, Ross. I lost my brother once and I'm not going to do it again.' His eyes shifted to their grandmother. 'I think we all understand that now.'

Miriam looked unhappy. 'Can I have a glass of whisky?' she said stiffly.

'Aye, that's a good idea,' Simon said, wandering into the kitchen and nodding at the bottle of whisky Ross had left out. He opened three cupboard doors before drawing out two glasses, then he placed them beside the one Ross had left out and poured them each a shot. 'Plates?' he asked, and Ross nodded and opened another cupboard and got them out. He watched his brother lay out the mince pies, before taking one for himself.

'So...' Ross said as a glass of whisky was shoved at him. He watched Simon take a sip of the amber liquid before nodding.

'Good brand,' Simon said, his eyes twinkling. Then he turned to Miriam as she swallowed the contents of her glass in one.

'Fine, your point has been received and understood,' she said, slamming her glass on the counter. 'Simon...' She hesitated. 'Has pointed out that I may not have been very welcoming when you visited the castle and that I was wrong.'

'You mean when you told us all the only reason you wanted me to visit, was to entice him back? That you never thought I was good enough to be Laird and it was all a trick to get him to return?' Ross asked dryly. He tried to freeze the hurt burning in his chest. He knew he'd get over it. He had before. 'And that you sent Ivy Heart to convince me to come by offering her the job she wanted in London?' The stab of pain that jabbed at his solar plexus would be more difficult to forget. But Ross knew he'd get over that too. Eventually.

'Aye.' His grandmother rubbed a hand over her brow. 'You have to understand all I've ever wanted was to preserve the Ballentine traditions,' she said.

'And I'm not part of those?' Ross asked. He knew the time for dancing around what had happened in the past was gone. That this conversation would hurt, but it was better than avoiding it. Even Grizzle had told him as much.

'I never said that.' Miriam's shoulders sagged.

'But we both behaved as if Ross didn't matter,' Simon interjected. 'Whatever we meant, we left him to wallow in his grief alone until he decided to leave.'

Miriam's back straightened. 'I did what I had to do. My son died.' She frowned. 'And it was my responsibility to ensure everything continued as seamlessly as it should. I won't apologise for being single-minded.' She looked over at Ross, and her expression softened a little. 'It doesn't mean I didn't care about you, it's just—'

'I didn't matter,' Ross said flatly.

Miriam considered his words and then jerked her chin. 'I wasn't raised to think about feelings or to consider what children needed,' she said, her tone cool. 'It was always about doing the right thing, keeping the family going. There's never been room for sentimentality or people's hearts. Not even my own.' She swallowed.

'Did you blame me for our parents' deaths?' Ross asked, picking up the bottle of whisky and pouring a fresh shot into each of their empty glasses. They were still standing in the kitchen and suddenly he felt too weary to remain on his feet. 'Shall we sit?' he asked and walked to the sofa, trying not to think about the last time he'd been there with Ivy. He sat and waited for Miriam to respond.

'In some ways—' The older woman shrugged and sat too, then she began to fiddle with her pearl necklace. 'I may have done, at least at first. It's difficult, losing a child, and a little easier if you can find someone to hold responsible.' Her expression darkened. 'I knew it wasn't your fault, of course.' Her voice was gruff. 'But I grieved, and there was never enough time to process and move on. There was always too much else to worry about.' She drank more of the whisky, staring into the fire. 'I had a job to do and nothing else mattered. Perhaps that's what I used to get me through.'

She glanced up, took in Simon and Ross, who were both gazing at her.

'I think I got used to living like that. It's all I knew how to do,' she said.

'I wasn't perfect either,' Simon admitted. 'That's why I want things to be different.'

Ross stared into his glass as something inside him eased. There was a lot to think about, but at least he had a few answers now. The fact that no one really blamed him for his parents' deaths had lifted a weight he'd barely acknowledged he was still carrying. 'So what now?' he asked.

Miriam took in a long breath. 'Your brother's suggested something.' Her mouth pinched.

'A compromise,' Simon said, going to grab the plate of mince pies and offering them to Miriam and Ross. When they both refused, he took one and bit into it.

'Simon...' Miriam warned.

He swallowed. 'I eat what I like now, remember?' His brother smiled as he deliberately swallowed the rest in one go. 'I don't want all the responsibilities of being Laird on my shoulders.' He turned to Ross. 'I love Hawthorn Castle and I want to be a part of our family – but shouldering it all is both an honour and a curse.' His eyes shifted back to Miriam. 'The responsibility, the pressure you've applied for so many years, is suffocating.'

'Aye.' Ross nodded. 'But what's the solution?' He couldn't imagine he'd ever be part of it. And yet just having his brother sitting on his sofa made him feel better. Made him feel wanted. But he was sure that was as far as it would ever go.

'I have a plan,' Simon said. 'One I'd have shared days ago if you hadn't run off.' He leaned forwards. 'I'd like to share the responsibilities with you.'

He paused, giving Ross time to understand. But he couldn't quite process what Simon wanted.

'I don't follow,' Ross said, glancing at his grandmother, who was frowning.

'We could run the castle and grounds together. Make all the decisions. Equal partners, just like we were when we were kids. It's like what we were saying when we talked at Christmas Lodge, two heads are—'

'Better than one,' Ross finished. He frowned as he considered. 'But there can only be one Laird,' he said.

'And it should be Simon,' his grandmother interjected. 'Not that I'm saying you wouldn't make a good one...' She looked awkward. 'But he's the oldest, so it's only right.'

'Aye. Etiquette.' His brother frowned. 'I can be the figurehead, the media face of the family, unless you want to do it?'

'Absolutely not.' Ross shook his head.

'Fine.' Simon didn't look surprised. 'But... I don't want to do the rest alone. I want you to be part of the future of our family too.'

'You'll be giving up a lot – autonomy.' Ross's voice was croaky with emotion as he processed what this meant.

'I've never had any, so I won't miss it,' Simon snorted as he grabbed another mince pie. 'As far as I'm concerned, I'll be gaining more. A partner. Someone to share the stress with. If I'm honest, little brother – you'll be doing me a favour.'

Ross frowned. He wasn't sure what he wanted anymore, but being accepted back into the family fold appealed. He glanced at the two picture frames on the small oak table, at the photograph of Simon that he'd removed from the broken frame. He hadn't been able to put those away either. 'It might work, I suppose,' he said finally.

'And it would mean you could still work and live at Christmas Resort if you wanted,' Simon said gently. 'Perhaps you could get someone to help you to look after the grounds and run your adventures on the days you're working with me.'

'An assistant?' Ross said. Connell had been nagging him about getting one. For a while he'd even wondered if Ivy would be a perfect fit – she clearly had a flair for the outdoors. But she'd be on her way to London soon, leaving for her big new job. He swallowed. 'I...'

'Think about it,' Simon said as he finished his mince pie and picked up another, ignoring the irritated groan from his grandmother. 'It means we both get the best of both worlds – I'll be able to eat as many of these as I like.' He grinned. 'And you'll be back in our lives.'

Ross glanced over at Miriam. 'And what do you think?' he asked, his voice husky, expecting the worst.

His grandmother dropped her hands from her pearls and placed them in her lap. 'I want to preserve the family and castle. It's all I've ever wanted,' she said stiffly.

'And you'll put up with me being around so that can happen?' Ross asked, his heart in his throat.

'It's not a case of putting up with you.' Miriam slumped in her seat, looking older suddenly. 'I...' She swallowed and Ross could swear her eyes filled. Then she glanced away and when she looked back all sign of tears had disappeared. 'I may be an old fool, but perhaps even I can see the benefit of having two of my grandsons working together.' Her mouth twisted and Ross knew she was finding the words difficult to say. 'Especially if it means they're happier and my family is whole again.' She swallowed the rest of her whisky in one and straightened her shoulders – and the moment passed. 'It's up to you though, Ross,' she said hoarsely.

Ross knew this was the most emotion Miriam would show – but he also knew it was genuine.

'So will you do it?' Simon asked eagerly.

Ross considered the question. 'Aye,' he said, wishing suddenly that Ivy was here to share the news with. Then he frowned, because she wasn't part of his life anymore. She had a new one in London, a career she was determined to chase. Even though she knew it wouldn't make her happy.

His brother let out a small whoop. 'You've made me happier than I've been in a long time.' He patted Ross's back. 'I know Ivy will be relieved.'

At the mention of her name Ross shook his head. 'Why, because it'll secure the job Grandmother promised her?' he asked bitterly.

'But she's not going to London,' Simon said.

'Nae, she's not,' Miriam said, sounding annoyed.

'What?' Ross asked.

'I thought you knew?' Simon looked confused. 'She told me she's not taking the job. Last time I saw her she was about to tell her mother that.'

'So what's she doing instead?' Ross asked, searching his brother's face.

Simon shrugged.

'She's taken a holiday.' Miriam's disapproval was clear from her tone. 'She'll be back in a couple of days. When my PA returns from her maternity leave, Ivy will be free to do whatever she pleases – whatever that is.'

Ross sat back on the sofa. Ivy had given up the job she'd lied to him to get. What did that mean? He felt a stir in his chest and knew it was hope. Knew he had to talk to her.

'I need to see her,' he said, gazing at his brother.

Miriam cleared her throat. 'I think I can arrange that,' she said. 'I suppose it's the least I can do. Besides...' A twinkle flared in her eyes before disappearing. 'If you're going to be living at the castle from now on, I'd prefer you had a smile on your face...'

27

IVY

Ivy's stomach sank to her toes as she drove her Mini up the long snow-covered driveway and saw Hawthorn Castle in the distance. She'd been away for six days in all, staying with her mother – and while their time together had been special and cathartic, Ivy had been dreading coming back. This morning Miriam had messaged first thing, demanding a meeting at nine a.m. sharp, so Ivy was already dressed and ready in her green coat and red boots, determined to get it over with.

The older woman had been irritated when Ivy had asked to take the time off to see her mother, but had still let her go. Either because she'd felt guilty about what had happened with Ross, or because Ivy had been in floods of tears and Miriam hadn't wanted to deal with all those inconvenient emotions. So Ivy had been allowed to take the break, on the understanding that she'd return in plenty of time to oversee the arrangements for the party on Christmas Eve.

Ivy guessed the event would be used to announce that Simon was about to take on the responsibilities of Laird. She swallowed the flood of guilt, wondering what Ross would be doing now. Would he be hurting? Did he still blame her for what had happened? She definitely blamed herself.

Ivy drew the car to a stop and left her suitcase on the back seat. She'd unpack her clothes and Prickles and Needles later because she only had five minutes to get to Miriam's office, or she'd be late. She took a quick moment to open her coaching app to see if it would offer any useful nuggets of advice before she entered the lioness's den. The app was the only thing her mother had insisted Ivy continue with, hoping the messages would remind her to keep her life on a positive trajectory – although Ivy still had no clue where she was going to end up.

'This is a good day to make the right choice.'

Ivy read. 'What choice?' she huffed as she quickly made her way to the portcullis, ignoring the snow as it soaked through her boots.

She pushed open the door, swallowing as she entered and a barrage of memories mobbed her. Memories of Ross accusing her of lying to him, of the look on his face just before he'd stormed down the driveway. She'd hurt him and knew she'd never be able to forgive herself.

'Only ten days to go,' Ivy mumbled. After the party on Christmas Eve, Miriam would probably let her leave. Her mother had already offered her a place to stay while she worked out her next steps. The main thing was once she was gone, she wouldn't be in the Scottish Highlands anymore, being constantly reminded of Ross.

Ivy's heart hammered wildly as she made her way down the brightly lit corridor towards Miriam's office, ignoring the festive decorations, which seemed so much more sparkly now, and keeping her attention firmly fixed on her destination.

Ivy's desk was empty and Miriam's door was shut. Ivy put her handbag onto her chair and shut her eyes, breathing in the sweet scent of her African violet, trying to calm her jittery pulse. *You can do this.* She repeated the mantra a couple of times before tapping on the door.

'Come in.'

The voice that called from inside the office was muffled and Ivy wondered if Miriam had caught a cold. She pushed the door and entered, then immediately stopped when she saw Ross sitting behind his grandmother's desk.

Ivy blinked a couple of times to check she wasn't dreaming. When Ross smiled, she knew something must be very wrong. She blinked again, then almost tripped over Moose and Snowball as they came bounding towards her – sniffing and purring, nuzzling against her legs.

'Hang on, what is this?' she exclaimed.

'Careful, boys!' Ross ordered as he stood and walked slowly around the desk, then leaned back onto it, folding his arms and drinking her in.

'Why are you here?' Ivy croaked as she glanced around. 'Did something happen to Miriam? Where's Simon?' What had happened while she'd been gone?

Ross shrugged, looking relaxed. 'Somewhere in the castle I expect.'

'I have a meeting with your grandmother,' Ivy squeaked, as her stomach churned. Why was Ross still smiling at her? Was this a trick? Despite her distress, her body responded to him, tingling and heating from the inside out. 'I'm... I don't understand.'

'Miriam booked this meeting for me, so we could talk,' Ross said simply.

'Look.' Ivy's stomach turned over and she took a step forwards. 'I feel awful about what happened. I honestly had no idea what your grandmother was planning.' Tears pricked at the edges of her eyes and Ivy wondered if she'd ever be able to think of Ross without wanting to cry.

'You turned the job down.' Ross eased himself away from the desk so he could take a step.

'What?' Ivy's voice scraped the edges of her throat.

'You turned down the job – Simon told me.' He raised an eyebrow, looking amused. 'Grandmother was really annoyed.'

'I know.' Ivy gulped. 'But it wasn't what I wanted. You showed me that.'

Ross nodded and took a larger stride. Moose and Snowball were now sitting on their haunches between them, their heads shifting back and forth.

'Ross, I'm so sorry.' Ivy wrung her hands as she studied him. He looked good, far better than her. Ivy knew she'd lost weight over the last week, knew her skin looked pasty and pale. But until this moment, she hadn't cared.

Ross held up a palm. 'You can stop apologising. Because it's me who should be saying sorry, Ivy,' he said softly.

'You?' Ivy jerked back. 'Why?'

'Because I didn't listen to you, I wouldn't let you explain and I made you sleep on an argument; I refused to make up.' He sighed. 'I should have realised you'd never put a job before someone's happiness. Not unless it was yours.' He looked pained. 'I know Miriam well enough to understand she can be ruthless when she wants something.' He shrugged. 'But over the last week, I've come to realise, despite that, she does have a heart – it's just not always easy to see.'

Ivy frowned, trying to process what Ross was telling her. 'So you've made up with your grandmother?' she checked, sure she must have misunderstood.

Ross pulled a face. 'Let's just say we're working on a new relationship.'

'And Simon?' She stepped forwards, her body responding as if she were a flower being drawn towards the sun.

He smiled. 'We're good.'

'So...' Ivy spread her palms, confused. 'What's going to happen? Why are you here?'

'Simon and I are working together at Hawthorn Castle now,' Ross explained. 'He's going to be the figurehead – the Laird – but aside from that, we're sharing responsibilities equally. It means I get to stay working part-time at Christmas Resort.' He gave her a shy smile. 'Although, I have to admit, I'm going to be a bit stretched.'

Ivy watched silently as he shifted closer and ordered Moose and Snowball to move out of his way. When Ross took her hand, Ivy could only gape as he wrapped both of his around hers.

'I don't understand,' she whispered.

'I missed you, Ivy.' Ross gently squeezed her fingers. 'I wanted to call, I even borrowed Simon's mobile – but I didn't know if you'd want to talk to me.'

Ivy released the breath she hadn't realised she'd been holding. 'Why did you want to talk to me?' she asked, hoping she'd already guessed. 'I tricked you. I mean, I didn't know it at the time, but...' She hissed out her frustration because she didn't know what to say. Instead, she took a step forwards until her red boots were toe to toe with Ross's shoes. Then she gazed into his whisky-coloured eyes.

'I wanted to talk to you because I realised I care for you. A lot,' Ross confessed. 'That perhaps I didn't listen to what you were saying because I wasn't ready to put myself out there yet.' His forehead creased. 'I think I was scared that you'd hurt me. Maybe I've just spent the last few years expecting to be rejected. As my brother and Grizzle have told me at least fifty times in the last week – I'm a numpty, an eejit and at least a dozen other types of idiot.' He smiled down at her. 'Do you think you'll ever be able to forgive me?'

Ivy nodded mutely as the tears she'd been holding in spilled down her cheeks.

Ross frowned and cupped her face in his palms, swiping them away. 'I'm sorry.' He winced and his smile dropped. 'I'm so sorry, Ivy.'

'No.' She quickly put her hands over his. 'These are happy tears. I missed you, Ross. I'm so sorry for my part in getting you to come here, for what happened. And you were right, I need to follow in my dad's footsteps; it's the only way I'm going to be happy. And I want to find a way of doing it so I can be close to you. If you want that?'

'Of course I do.' Ross grinned again and pressed his forehead to hers. 'And I just happen to know about a vacancy you might be interested in too.' He tentatively pressed his lips to hers.

Ivy wrapped her arms around his neck and stretched onto her tiptoes so she could kiss him back. Their kiss deepened and she giggled when Ross suddenly picked her up and spun her around. Moose started barking and Snowball began to run in circles around the room.

'What are you talking about?' Ivy laughed as he finally put her back on her feet, hugging her close as he continued to press slow kisses onto her cheeks.

'I need someone to look after the grounds at Christmas Resort,' he whispered between kisses. 'I'm still going to run the adventures, but I'll need to free up time to help Simon here. Are you interested?'

Ivy pulled back, her eyes shining. 'In the job, or you?' she asked, her voice rough.

Ross kissed her again, dipping her backwards and making her stomach swoop. Then he eased her up and reluctantly let her go. 'I'll take whatever you're prepared to offer me, Ivy,' he said seriously. 'I've been stupid and I hope you can forgive me in time. My whole life has changed for the better since you arrived at Christmas Resort. The only thing that would make it perfect is having you by my side.'

'This is a good day to make the right choice,' Ivy whispered as she kissed his mouth.

'What does that mean?' Ross asked, looking confused.

'It means I choose *you*,' Ivy said. 'It means yes, I'll take the job and stay.' Then she went up onto her tiptoes and kissed him again.

THE CHRISTMAS PARTY was in full swing when Ivy and Ross approached the main ballroom at Hawthorn Castle. Ivy stopped just outside of the entrance and adjusted her sparkly red dress before checking the buttons of Ross's shirt were all done up – then she grinned up at him. She'd been going through some last-minute checks with the caterer half an hour before, when Ross had tugged her into his office so he could kiss her senseless. It had taken all of Ivy's willpower to make him stop.

'Are you ready?' she asked, huskily.

'Aye.' Ross beamed down at her. 'But when this is done, I'm looking forward to picking up where we left off.' He winked.

Ivy took in a shaky breath and pushed the door open. Then she stopped and took her time admiring the glorious spectacle as her stomach overflowed with a combination of butterflies and excitement. The room was filled with an abundance of decorations that shone, glittered and sparkled – and were interspersed with swathes of holly, poinsettia, fir trees and mistletoe. All of which had been chosen by Ivy. Ross took her hand and led her further into the room, just as the string orchestra began to play 'Jingle Bell Rock' and a couple of the guests started to wiggle and sing along.

'Grizzle's here,' Ross said quickly, guiding Ivy through the crowd so they could greet him first.

He was wearing a green and black kilt – and standing beside Mairi. As he spotted them, he tugged at the collar of his shirt, looking uncomfortable. They drew closer and Ivy realised he was wearing a pair of glasses she hadn't seen.

'A new purchase from eBay?' she guessed, as she gave him a peck on the cheek.

'Nae.' The older man let out a long-suffering groan. 'Mairi insisted I had my eyes tested at the opticians and I got these.' He shook his head as he nodded at his partner, who was dressed in a bright pink suit. 'Not that there was anything wrong with the ones I had,' he grumbled. 'They were working perfectly well.'

'Yet you look so much more handsome in this pair,' Mairi said. 'They suit you better than blue sparkles and hearts.' She leaned in to give him a kiss.

'Aye, well.' He cleared his throat as his face went up in pink flames. One of the caterers wandered past and Grizzle grabbed an hors d'œuvre before wincing and washing it down with whisky. 'Next time you should get Mairi to make the food,' he advised.

'If I did that, how would I keep up with feeding you?' Mairi joked, and selected one of the delicate morsels too.

As she did, Ivy noticed she was wearing a stunning ruby ring.

'Is that new too – it's beautiful?' she gasped.

Mairi flushed pink in response and flapped her hand so Ivy could see the jewellery. The large red stone – which was set inside a cluster of diamonds – caught the light from the chandelier and sparkled. 'Aye, now the old man has his new glasses, he's started working on his treasures again,' she said.

Grizzle cleared his throat. 'I found the ring in my spare room.' His forehead crinkled. 'It must have been there for years. I cleaned it up and—' He looked embarrassed.

'He gifted it to me.' Mairi grinned.

'Only because she wouldn't stop nagging me about it,' he said huskily, before leaning over to give her another light peck.

'Don't forget, I've got plenty of treasures if you're ever looking for something special,' he whispered loudly, winking at Ross.

Ross chuckled and squeezed Ivy's hand. 'I'll probably speak to you about that sometime soon,' he said gruffly as everything inside her expanded and filled. It was early days in their relationship, but it had bloomed since Ivy had returned to Hawthorn Castle.

'Speaking of nagging...' Grizzle changed the subject and pointed across the ballroom to where Bonnibell and Connell were chatting with Edina, Kenzy and Logan. Kenzy spotted them and waved.

'Shall we join them?' Ivy asked, collecting herself.

They were about to weave their way across the room when Miriam spotted them.

'Ross!' she demanded. She was wearing a black and white dress and her favourite pearls. Her hair was done up in a tight bun and she wore her customary bright red lipstick. Miriam still reminded Ivy of Cruella de Vil – but now her outfit was where the similarity ended. Since Ross had returned to the castle, she had softened so much, and her relationship with both of her grandsons had bloomed.

'Shall we formally introduce you and Simon to our guests?' Miriam asked, holding out a hand.

Ross took it and winked at Ivy. 'Make sure you stay close,' he whispered as he allowed himself to be guided towards his brother who was waiting beside the large roaring fire at the top of the ballroom. 'You're just as much a part of this as me.'

'I'm exactly where I want to be,' Ivy said, grinning as she followed, her heart filled with love and excitement. Because she knew, whatever happened from this moment forwards, she was finally on her perfect path.

A LETTER FROM DONNA

Dear reader,

I want to say a big thank you for choosing to read *Winter Wishes in the Scottish Highlands*. If you enjoyed it and want to keep up to date with all my latest releases, just sign up at the following link. Your email address will never be shared and you can unsubscribe at any time.

www.bookouture.com/donna-ashcroft

Winter Wishes in the Scottish Highlands transported us back to gorgeous Christmas Village and the wonderfully festive Christmas Resort. I hope you enjoyed meeting the new characters as well as some familiar faces from previous books.

Winter Wishes in the Scottish Highlands was about finding the right path in life. For Ross Ballentine, who'd decided to walk away from his family because he didn't think he was wanted, the right path was about ostracising himself. For Ivy Heart, who wanted to follow in her father's footsteps, it was about leaving that path so she could make her mother happy. By meeting each other and finally facing up to their decisions, they both learned what paths they needed to follow to be happy. I hope you enjoyed joining Ross and Ivy on their wildlife spotting adventures, camping in the snow, sleigh rides, mistletoe kisses and wintery walks in the woods – and seeing how they dealt with the emotional journeys that brought them together and ultimately changed their lives.

If you did enjoy the book, it would be wonderful if you could please leave a short review. Not only do I want to know what you thought, it might encourage a new reader to pick up my book for the first time.

I really love hearing from my readers – you can get in touch with me on social media or via my beautiful website.

Thanks,

Donna Ashcroft

www.donna-writes.co.uk

facebook.com/DonnaAshcroftAuthor

x.com/Donnashc

instagram.com/donnaashcroftauthor

tiktok.com/@donnaashcroftauthor

ACKNOWLEDGMENTS

I found this book difficult to write for various reasons. In fact, there were a few times when I never thought I'd finish. Even though my mantra is supposed to be 'trust the process', in the end, to find the story I had to put it down for a month so I could take a break from my self-doubt. Then when I picked it up again, everything fell into place (so I guess I really should trust that mantra, after all).

One of the wonderful things I got to hold onto while I was quite honestly terrified that I might never finish a book again, were the lovely messages I received from people. Readers, bloggers, strangers and friends (please, never underestimate the power of a supportive text, email or social media comment!) So firstly, I want to say thank you to everyone for those (you know who you are).

Next, I want to say a few special thank yous, some you may have seen before. To Alison Phillips, who this book is dedicated to: thank you for all of the lovely things you've ever said about my books – they honestly mean the world to me. Thank you also to Jules Wake (cheerleader, writing buddy, fab friend), to Sarah Bennett, Bella Osborne, Anita Chapman, Elizabeth Finn, Jackie Campbell, Julie Anderson, Trish Osborne, Caroline Kelly, Sue Moseley, Amanda Baker, Mel and Rob Harrison, Claire Hornbuckle, Danel Munday, Linzi Stainton, Emma York, Meena Kumari, Grace Power, Fiona Jenkins, Ian Wilfred, Cindy Wilson, Cindy L Spear, Cindy Siler, Mags Evans, Anne Winckworth, Katy Walker, Tina Mullauer, and all the Love and Chocolate members. Not to mention, Chris, Erren and Charlie Cardoza.

As always, thanks to the fabulous team at Bookouture, including Natasha Harding, Lizzie Brien, Ruth Jones, Lauren Morrissette, Melanie Price, Noelle Holten, Kim Nash, Jess Readett, Lauren Finger, Hannah Snetsinger, Natasha Hodgson, Rachel Rowlands, Peta Nightingale, Richard King and Saidah Graham. Thanks also to the other Bookouture authors for your support.

Thanks to all the amazing bloggers who turn up every time I have a cover reveal, need a review, or publication day support. I can't mention everyone (and apologies if I haven't mentioned you), but I will shout-out those who were part of the blog tour for my last book: Stardust Book Reviews, Vegan Book Blogger, Page Turners, Open Book Post, Sam's Fireside, Liana Reads, Splashes into Books, StaceyWH_17, Bookworm 86 and @short-bookthyme. A HUGE thank you.

Thanks as always to my family: Dad, Mum, John, Peter, Christelle, Lucie, Mathis, Joseph, Lynda, Louis, Auntie Rita, Tina, Ruth, Auntie Gillian, Tanya, James, Rosie, Ava, Philip, Sonia, Stephanie and Muriel.

Finally, to the readers who have been there with me throughout my journey – thank you. Xx

PUBLISHING TEAM

Turning a manuscript into a book requires the efforts of many people. The publishing team at Bookouture would like to acknowledge everyone who contributed to this publication.

Commercial
Lauren Morrissette
Hannah Richmond
Imogen Allport

Cover design
Debbie Clement

Data and analysis
Mark Alder
Mohamed Bussuri

Editorial
Natasha Harding
Lizzie Brien

Copyeditor
Natasha Hodgson

Proofreader
Rachel Rowlands